DEATH *of a* SHOWMAN

DEATH *of a* SHOWMAN

Mariah Fredericks

MINOTAUR BOOKS
NEW YORK

First published in the United States by Minotaur Books,
an imprint of St. Martin's Publishing Group

DEATH OF A SHOWMAN. Copyright © 2021 by Mariah Fredericks.
All rights reserved. Printed in the United States of America.
For information, address St. Martin's Publishing Group,
120 Broadway, New York, NY 10271.

www.minotaurbooks.com

Library of Congress Cataloging-in-Publication Data

Names: Fredericks, Mariah, author.
Title: Death of a showman / Mariah Fredericks.
Description: First edition. | New York : Minotaur Books, 2021. |
    Series: A Jane Prescott novel; 4
Identifiers: LCCN 2020047623 | ISBN 9781250210906 (hardcover) |
    ISBN 9781250210913 (ebook)
Classification: LCC PS3606.R435 D42913 2021 | DDC 813/.6—dc23
LC record available at https://lccn.loc.gov/2020047623

Our books may be purchased in bulk for promotional, educational,
or business use. Please contact your local bookseller or the Macmillan Corporate
and Premium Sales Department at 1-800-221-7945, extension 5442, or by
email at MacmillanSpecialMarkets@macmillan.com.

First Edition: 2021

10 9 8 7 6 5 4 3 2 1

For all the performers, musicians, playwrights, directors, stage managers, choreographers, costume and set designers, prop people, carpenters, stagehands, wardrobe staff, lighting technicians, painters, ushers, box office staff—everyone who acts, jokes, sings, dances, or self-immolates onstage and all those who support them.

It will be so nice to have you back where you belong.

I'm a Yankee Doodle Dandy,

A Yankee Doodle, do or die;

A real live nephew of my Uncle Sam

Born on the Fourth of July.

—George M. Cohan

DEATH *of a*
SHOWMAN

Last night, my grandson and his wife took me to the theater. "I know you've seen a lot of shows," he said. "But I don't think you've ever seen anything like this." My firstborn grandchild, he likes to be first in everything, using words like "best" and "most" and "biggest" without a trace of irony.

The show's creators have been very secretive as to what the show actually is, beyond its title and a pair of glowing yellow eyes above the marquee. Leo feels this is an excellent way to get people wildly curious when you don't have much to show them. He was annoyed by the news that they had renovated the theater to accommodate the new show, reportedly tearing out several rows of seats, painting the walls black, and even punching a hole through the ceiling. I reminded him that the Winter Garden had started life as a horse exchange and this was hardly its first renovation.

"Cats." He shook out the newspaper. "What's next? Aardvarks?"

"Amy likes cats."

"Amy is six years old. What's everyone else's excuse?"

Amy *was* my excuse. My great-granddaughter is a shy child who has not quite found her place among her contemporaries and so prefers four legs to two. As the oldest and youngest in the family, we are both sometimes puzzled by the world in which we find ourselves. Perhaps because I am too old to register as fully human, she often seeks me out at gatherings. It was my hand she held as we went into the theater and she kept hold of it as we sat down, both intrigued and alarmed by a young woman in a leotard and whiskers who pranced down the aisle and made a great show of licking her arm.

As promised, there were cats. Many cats. There was leaping and pouncing and singing. There was not, so far as I could tell, a story. Someone once told me that all good stories are about love, and I waited for the beasts to form attachments. But they just jumped around hissing and announcing themselves. The idea seemed to be that they wanted to go somewhere, some finer place, and if they performed well enough, they would be chosen. All in all, it was a lot of animals writhing in a junkyard.

"It does have the one good song," I told Leo over lunch. "And it's quite the spectacular. At the end, two cats go floating off on an enormous tire."

"So, that's why they punched a hole in the ceiling. Well, at least there were no accidents and nobody got killed."

"No."

We went on with our lunch. But I knew we were both thinking of his first Broadway show. When someone had been killed.

And not at all by accident.

1

Louise Tyler was in a rage.

The provocation was Dr. Brown's Cel-Ray Tonic—or rather the absence of it. On our voyage back from Europe, Louise had sent several ship-to-shore telegrams with instructions to the new cook to have the beverage at hand when we returned. We had been home only fifteen minutes when we discovered the tonic was not in the house. Neither was the cook.

I could not recall ever seeing Louise Tyler in a rage. Nor, from his expression, could her husband, William, who watched helplessly as she tore around the house, calling down vengeance on the cook, on all cooks, and all telegrams, and all empty iceboxes. This led to a general damnation of sea travel and weddings that required them, culminating in a derisive dismissal of Europe itself. Except for the London Zoo and its penguins. They had been charming. The rest of the continent could go hang.

When the mistress is out of sorts, the maid must find remedies.

I said, "Mrs. Tyler, why don't you let me run you a bath? Then later, I can go to the market . . ."

"Why don't you go now, Jane?" urged William. "Take the car, it'll be faster."

Having just picked us up from the Chelsea Piers, Horst the chauffeur had not even finished bringing in the trunks when William told him to take me to Gristedes in the family's newest acquisition: a Rolls-Royce called the Silver Ghost. William had encountered the car in London and fallen madly in love.

"It's been a long journey," I reassured William. "Mrs. Tyler will feel better now that she's home."

At least I hoped she would. We had been traveling since September 1913 and it was now June 1914. For nine of those months, Louise's composure had been heroic. But over the last few weeks, she had finally . . . well, cracked. The trip abroad had been fraught from the start. Weddings are always difficult, a sister's wedding particularly so, and the wedding of the lovely and unscrupulous Charlotte Benchley—no blood had been shed, and for that we could all be grateful. Petite, blond, and exceedingly wealthy, Charlotte had charmed the old world into submission. The acid tongue was used sparingly, the fluttered lashes employed steadily. As an American, she was permitted to be outrageous at times; she could ask if it were true that the Meissen went missing in any great house visited by Queen Mary, if the duke of Beaumont was really so fond of telegraph boys, and why on earth would anyone fight over Alsace and Lorraine, the food was so terrible. Under the count's tutelage, she had become an excellent shot, a talent she claimed in the name of Wild Bill Hickok and Jesse James. No one believed it, but they enjoyed her willingness to play into the American myth where infants chewed on raw bison meat and played with guns instead of rattles. I did not get to know the count well, but William indicated there might not be that much to know.

As was so often the case, Charlotte's success was Louise's burden. Under the aegis of the captivating countess-to-be, the Tylers were whisked from one European capital to the next in an endless series of balls, operas, teas, and shooting parties. The protocols in each country were varied and byzantine; a virtual nightmare for anyone who had both a terror of committing faux pas and a fatalistic certainty that she would. Louise passed her hours in a state of deadly tedium laced with deep anxiety. Still, she soldiered on, climbing in and out of several outfits a day and as many packing cases in a month. In addition, Charlotte having lived without the responsibility of her mother for over a year refused to take up that duty again, and so the job of managing Mrs. Benchley on the continent without diplomatic incident fell to William and Louise—and myself. I was very fond of the family matriarch, but after several months in her constant company, even I flinched at the sound of her voice, piercing and simple like a child's whistle.

By the time we reached Vienna, where the wedding was to be held, Louise's nerves were frayed to the point of breaking. One evening, she had collapsed on the bed—I winced as she crushed a gorgeous dress of sunset-red silk chiffon—to announce, "I'm sick to death of aristocrats. Count, duke, prince, I don't care if I meet another in my lifetime. They speak five languages and haven't a single interesting thing to say in any of them. I never knew how American I was until I came to Europe."

I had reassured her that we would soon be home and life would seem much brighter. Peeling jewels and gloves from her wrists, Louise had sighed. "I hope so." Unfortunately, the voyage had not been smooth and low spirits were not improved by seasickness.

Still, now we were back in New York. I had missed the city more than I could have imagined, its arrogant skyscrapers that turned avenues into shaded canyons, the mad bustle of its streets with trolleys, horses, cars, and pedestrians rushing in all directions. I missed the smells, the multilingual invective, and the sense that everyone was here to go somewhere and do something.

And I missed its people. William had instructed the staff remaining at home to forward all mail, but as the letters had to follow us around the continent, things were delayed. Or lost. I had nothing from my oldest friend, Anna, and a single letter from my uncle, reporting a leak in the roof and Berthe's twisted ankle. Only one person had promised to write and kept that promise. Were it not for Michael Behan, I would have had no idea what was happening in America during our absence. His first letter arrived in London two weeks after we did.

> *Dear Miss Prescott,*
> *Having bid farewell to you and the sulfurous purga-*
> *tory that is New York in August, a young man's*
> *fancy turns lightly to baseball. Christy Mathewson's*
> *arm is stout, his aim true. The streets are redolent*
> *with the stench of horse droppings and politics. The*
> *first milch goat show was held in Rochester. No*
> *doubt you are sorry to have missed it.*
>
> > *Yours,*
> > *MB*

> *Dear Mr. Behan,*
> *There is no baseball in London, but horse droppings*
> *are in fashion here as well. I would gladly report on*
> *the question of Home Rule or the new wax figures of*

Balkan monarchs at Madame Tussauds. But all I've
seen are backstairs and bad tempers.

Sincerely,
Jane Prescott

Dear Miss Prescott,
The new income tax law became law today. Times
predicts, "Some confusion is certain." Everyone
seems to think something should be done about
Mexico, no one seems to know what. Have you met
Czar? He seems an idiot.

Dear Mr. Behan,
Have not met Czar. We are in Paris now and I
have learned to swear at porters in three different
languages. Travel is enlarging.

His next letter was less cheerful.

Dear Miss Prescott,
It is after midnight in the newsroom. Maybe it's the
rain, maybe I'm tired. But yours truly is in a foul
mood. I have no great fondness for the old country,
but things have gone awry in our new one. Take
recent events in Ludlow, Colorado. Rockefeller may
preach "workaday religion," but his vision of do unto
and so forth doesn't seem to stretch to his employees,
many of whom are on strike. Rather than do some-
thing sensible like pay them, he turned a bunch of
thugs loose on them with the predictable result that
a lot of people are dead. Including two women and
eleven children who were burned to death. The city's

pure and earnest are naturally vying for the title of most outraged. But I wonder if they don't have a point this time. Who the hell turns ex-convicts and mercenaries on women and children?

 Sorry to be grim. Will go kick Harry Knowles to feel better.

Briefly, I wondered if this was why I had not heard from Anna. If the murder of striking women and children upset the normally apolitical Michael Behan, it would inspire a lethal rage in my anarchist friend. In fact, I preferred not to think how Anna might respond. I wrote back to Mr. Behan that he should kick gently; it was not Mr. Knowles's fault. And that I hoped my letter found him feeling more cheerful. As it happened, it did.

Dear Miss Prescott,
The city continues its decline in your absence. The Bergen Avenue gang caused a riot in the Bronx, the Gophers are shooting it up on the West Side, and a diplomat's wife has been arrested for shoplifting.
 In happier news, I announce the coming of an heir. The infant Behan should make his appearance sometime in September.

It took me a moment to understand that Mr. Behan had, in his own cheeky way, informed me that the long hoped for Behan baby was on its way; by fall, he would be a father. How wonderful, I thought, taking up a pen. How absolutely . . . wonderful.

Dear Mr. Behan,
All Europe rejoices to hear of the coming of the Infant Behan. Bells have rung at Westminster,

*prayers of thanksgiving said at Notre Dame, and the
Kaiser's army stands ready to sound the cannons on
arrival. I congratulate you. And feel compelled to
remind you that babies come in all manner of sizes
and shapes—including female.*

After that, while Behan kept up his usual stream of city news
and gossip, the Infant Behan—or Tib and occasionally Lump for
short—was clearly at the forefront of his thoughts. And happiness.
His last letter arrived just before we left.

*Wilson's losing what's left of his hair over Mexico.
Becker's trial continues in all its squalor. The hippo
at the Central Park Zoo has had a baby, 55 lbs.
Mother and child are well. So you see, dear old New
York is much the same. Except not quite. Maybe it's
the light, maybe the breeze off the Hudson's not as
fresh, or the city's brewers have lost their touch. But
something's missing. And I hope it soon returns.*

As I came out of Gristedes, I saw a young couple, walking arm
in arm. He said something and she laughed, as much in pleasure
that he cared to amuse her as at the joke. And suddenly I thought
of Leo Hirschfeld.

I was proud of how I managed the issue of Mr. Hirschfeld. Yes,
I had enjoyed his company more than I should have last summer,
given that I made a vow not to see him again. But as he pointed
out, I had never told *him* I wasn't going to see him again and did
I really want to spend the whole summer having no fun? Maybe
it didn't speak well of my character, but it turned out I didn't. I
only had one day off a week. How much trouble could I get into
on one day off?

The answer was, in the company of Leo Hirschfeld, enough to feel guilty when I remembered Clara, a studious girl with strong views on education whom his mother often invited to supper. So before leaving for Europe, I gave Leo a well-practiced speech in which I reminded him of Clara's qualities and expectations (I was vague on the particulars of both, but felt certain they existed) and said it was best if we parted for good. Leo said I was being pompous.

We had been walking back from the movie theater where he played piano, reaching the point where I turned for the Tyler house and he for the train. He said, "For the hundred and thirty-fourth time, I'm not marrying Clara. I'm not marrying anyone."

Anyone. Yes, it was not only Clara; there were after all seven days in the week, and I only took up one. Wishing him the best of luck with his music, I started walking. He ran after me, caught hold of my arm. He looked unexpectedly serious and for a moment, declaration was in the air.

"I don't want to say the things everybody says," he told me.

Disappointed, I reclaimed my arm. "No, that would be very dull."

Now as I rode back to the Tylers', I felt certain that I had done the right thing. One misspent summer might be excused, two would be . . . I couldn't decide between the words "stupid" and "immoral," so I decided on "pointless." Above all, I had avoided my worst nightmare, in which Leo looked deeply into my eyes, and said he was sorry, but he was marrying Clara next month. And I was devastated because somehow, on my one day off, I had fallen in love with him. In another imagining, Leo said he had found a better fox-trotter than me, so our Fridays were over. I was no less devastated. No, I thought, fox-trot or matrimony, it was a very good thing I had avoided that.

Cel-Ray in hand, I entered the house through the kitchen door and heard neither wailing nor pleading. Then I heard Louise say, "Perhaps we shouldn't tell her."

And William, "No, better she hears it from us."

Sorrowful, I thought. Kind. This was not the cook, nor the parlormaid. This was someone they knew well, this person with bad news coming to her. I was suddenly aware of my heartbeat, hard and hurtful in my chest. We had been out of the country for months, only sporadically reachable. Anything might have happened. No, not anything. Something awful. Something . . . death. Without thinking, I pushed open the swinging door between kitchen and dining room. Louise and William looked up, startled. Between them, they held a newspaper.

"Has something happened?" I asked. Reluctantly, Louise showed me.

FOLLIES STAR NEDDA FISKE JOINS WARBURTON AND HIRSCHFELD'S *TWO LOVES HAVE I*
CAST TO INCLUDE SONGWRITER'S
CHORUS GIRL BRIDE

My first response was to exhale in relief; the word "death" was nowhere on the page. This was the arts section, full of jaunty headlines about hits and flops. "Bride," there was a happy word. "Star." "Songwriter." Slowly, I took in the first paragraph.

> Comic actress Nedda Fiske joins the cast of Sidney Warburton's ragtime extravaganza featuring songs by "But on Fridays" composer Leo Hirschfeld. The show, set for an August 4 opening, boasts a glittering cast, headlined by dance sensations Claude and Blanche

Arden, as well as the composer's wife, chorus girl Violet Tempest. The pair married six months ago after meeting on the show *Everybody Does It.*

The composer's . . . wife. Leo had gotten married. The man who said he would never marry. And he had not married intelligent, sensible Clara of whom his mother approved, but a woman of such abundant charms she had been dubbed Jelly on Pins, Salome on Stairs, and the Weary Man's Hope. From the article, I gathered that Violet Tempest's chief talent was walking down stairs wearing very little and in a manner that—according to the *Times*—"made grown men weep."

Her views on education were probably quite rudimentary.

2

The household was made aware: I had been disappointed and was to be treated with kindness. In vain, I assured the Tylers I was fine. Yes, it had been a surprise. But my heart was not chipped nor cracked in the slightest. William and Louise nodded sympathetically. Of course I was fine—and I wasn't to think about it a moment longer. Never mind that I didn't think about it at all except when someone else raised the subject.

Then Louise surprised everyone by announcing that rather than traveling on to her mother-in-law's summer home in Oyster Bay as planned, she preferred to stay in the city. William was expected to return to work at her father's firm and Louise declared that she, too, wished to stay put.

"I feel I've only just got home. The thought of rushing off somewhere else gives me a headache." She gazed at me in the mirror. "You don't mind, do you, Jane?"

"Of course not, Mrs. Tyler."

"Only you did see a great deal of Mr. Hirschfeld last summer. I thought you might want to get away."

I was more concerned as to where to store the resort clothes made in Paris—and how Louise would keep herself occupied in a city that was deserted for the summer. Even her fellow members of the Dumb Friends committee for animal welfare were out of town. True—she was no longer weeping from seasickness or tearing around the house in a rage over beverages. But to me, she seemed more weary than content. With William at the office, she spent long aimless hours gazing out the window. Occasionally, she resolved to address household matters—fresh curtains or moving the piano to the other side of the room. But all such projects floundered after brief effort and were forgotten. The senior Mrs. Tyler, not used to her plans being countermanded, called daily to demand Louise's presence on Long Island. At one point, I suggested a visit to Louise's mother, now visiting family in Scarsdale—only to receive a look that said had Louise Tyler been the sort of woman who slapped servants, my cheek would sting.

The best part of Louise's day was breakfast, as husband and wife began their day together. Dining room and kitchen were separated by a short pantry hallway, which meant the staff ate in discreet silence, maintaining the pretense that we didn't hear everything William and Louise said. When they first started married life, there hadn't been much to hear beyond "Good morning, dear," and "Did you sleep well?" But after two years, there was a nice uxorial hum of conversation along with the tinkle of silverware on china and companionable flap of newspaper.

One morning, William's raised voice cut through the quiet. "Dear God, we met him."

"Met whom, dearest?"

"The . . . duke, no, archduke." He read aloud, "'Heir to Austria's

Throne Slain with His Wife by a Bosnian Youth.' You remember, we were presented to him at Welbeck."

"Yes," said Louise with sudden enthusiasm. "His wife didn't often travel with him because his family thought her unsuitable. They have children," she added sadly.

"He was shot at Welbeck, too. A loader fell down and the gun went off. Imagine surviving that, just to get killed in . . . Sarayevo. Gevo? Yevo. I think."

There was a silence. Then Louise asked, "Is it bad? Will something happen?"

"I don't know," said William. "Oh, look—there's going to be an aeroplane race for July Fourth, right here in the city."

"How exciting," said Louise.

* * *

"An annual carnival of noise, smoke, and bloodshed," was the ungenerous assessment given by some to the celebration of our nation's independence. This year, the mayor had banned all fireworks and declared the city would have a "safe and sane" July Fourth. Instead of unnerving pops, cracks, and booms, City Hall would be illuminated with electric lights. There would be baseball games, public concerts. Eight aeroplanes and flying boats would race from Governors Island to Spuyten Duyvil. Having spent the last several months in rarefied company, the younger Tylers were keen to "be among the people." The newly hired cook, Mrs. Avery, would be persuaded to pack a picnic lunch. The staff would be given the day off. But when William and Louise learned that I intended to spend July Fourth on my own, they insisted I come picnicking with them. No, I would not be intruding! Of course they wished to spend their holiday with me. Anyone, they said, eyes solemn, would want to spend time with me.

Happy to be behind the wheel of his beloved new vehicle,

William was eager to see the start of the race, and so we chose Battery Park as our picnic spot. The Tylers' enthusiasm for the masses was tested by the enormous crowds gathered at the tip of the island. Finally, we managed to find a postage stamp of grass on which to set the blanket. (Columbus-like, William stood astride the few meager feet and announced he claimed this land in the name of Tyler. Adding "And Prescott!" after a beat.)

Still, the sky was blue, the crowds merry, and the *pom pom* of the tuba lively enough that we managed to enjoy a good meal of ham sandwiches, tomato salad, and walnut cake before the crowds began to shift toward the river for the start of the race. I packed away the dishes and folded the blanket, returning them to the car before joining William and Louise in the throng.

A man was watching Governors Island through binoculars, barking updates through a megaphone. It was about to start, ladies and gentlemen, any moment, it would happen, keep a lookout! The crowd swayed this way and that as people craned necks and jockeyed for view. Pressed and jostled from all sides, Louise grew anxious. William put his arm around her, and she said, "I'm so silly, I don't know why I feel nervous." She tried a smile, but it faded the moment he looked away.

I was about to offer my own reassurance when I heard the thrum and pop of engines starting. The rattling buzz grew louder and all of a sudden, two monoplanes sped into view, with a great cheer from below that seemed to lift them even higher. As the planes swooped around the Statue of Liberty, I heard a gasp and turned to see that Louise had gone white. Her jaw was rigid, her breath erratic, and she was trembling violently. "It's madness," she whispered. "Complete madness."

Alarmed, I met William's eye and without speaking, we began to make our way out of the crush. When we were free of the crowd, Louise apologized. She had ruined everything. She didn't know why, what had come over her. She had simply felt . . . terrified.

"It doesn't matter," said William. "We've seen the best part. I say we go home."

On the ride back, William said he hoped it wouldn't distress Louise too much, but he might not want to work for her father for forever. Louise pronounced herself delighted and we had a humorous conversation about the many careers he might pursue, from circus performer to senator. Then Louise announced a desire for ice cream, and William declared that she should have it. She announced a desire for a dog. He declared that she could have that, too, only he should be called Alfonso, because someone should be. Which left me dwelling on what other new arrivals to the family there might be one day and the profound hope that they not be named Alfonso.

"Cards!" shouted William as he pulled the Ghost to a halt outside the house. "I want ice cream and dogs and a magnificent tournament of—"

Louise gasped. Puzzled over the break in mood, I looked where she was looking, and saw Leo Hirschfeld standing at the front door. A weight I had not known I carried suddenly lifted. A mistake, it had been a mistake . . .

Removing herself from the car, Louise said, "Mr. Hirschfeld. You must be here to see Jane."

Leo gave me the briefest glance before taking off his hat. "Actually, Mrs. Tyler, I'm here to see you."

★ ★ ★

As my presence had been rejected, I took myself upstairs to my room. There was, I reminded myself, a great deal of work to do. Really, I should never have gone picnicking, it had been tremendously presumptuous, a waste of time, and if I was miserable now, it was no more than I deserved.

Why? Why had I felt so happy on seeing him? Because I was foolish, that was why. I had been a fool and now it was time to stop being a fool and get on with work. The hem of Louise's favorite day dress, yellow with black piping, had come loose. Taking up the dress, needle, and thread, I set myself to the task as if the day had just begun, banishing all other events from memory.

There was a knock at the door. Louise offering sympathy, I thought with dread. "Please don't worry on my account, Mrs. Tyler . . ."

The door opened. I heard Leo say, "Hello."

A quick glance affirmed he was no longer a singing waiter in apron and shirtsleeves. He wore a seersucker suit with a light gray stripe and a paisley tie. His dark springy hair was neatly trimmed, his oxfords polished. The straw boater turning like a wheel in his hands was fresh, with a snappy black band. He had done well in the time I was away. Become a successful songwriter as he had predicted. Was about to have his own show, as he had also predicted. Other things had not turned out as predicted.

I offered my congratulations. He looked puzzled. Then said, "Oh, that."

For a moment, we watched each other. Sticking the needle through the cloth I said in a rush, "It's just so odd because I thought you were going to marry Clara."

"I told you I wasn't going to marry Clara."

"You told me you weren't going to marry anyone."

"I . . ." He was stuck. ". . . forgot."

Yes, that sounded likely. For all his ability to predict the future, Leo had a habit of getting lost in the present, especially when it was female. It was why, I reminded myself, I had ended our friendship before leaving for Europe.

"Poor Clara," I said lightly. "Was she upset?"

"Very. So upset she married her philosophy professor the month before." Holding up a hand to forestall sympathy, he said, "Violet and I were acquainted well before then."

Violet. That's right, she had a name. She had Leo and she had a name. Leo's name in fact.

He said, "Well, I hope you can forgive me."

"Surely, that isn't why you came all the way here on July Fourth, to ask my forgiveness."

"No. I was wondering if you wanted to see the show."

Starring the stunning Mrs. Hirschfeld. The words "not on your life" were on my lips, but he added, "I've invited Mrs. Tyler to tomorrow's rehearsal. She'd like to come, but she won't do it unless she knows you're not mad at me."

At first I was baffled by Louise's interest. Then I recalled one summer afternoon when Leo had entertained a luncheon gathering on the Tyler piano. He had been charming, the ladies charmed. Louise especially. Now that I thought of it, Leo had always made a point of keeping her abreast of his plans to one day have a show of his own. But Broadway shows cost money. Perhaps his visit today should not have been a surprise. Perhaps even his interest in me . . .

"And I want to know you're not mad at me."

"I'm not mad at you." I presented the statement as you would a receipt. "And beyond her attire, how Mrs. Tyler spends her afternoon is none of my concern."

Wretched silence followed. I sewed. Leo's clasped hands bobbed between his knees. Then he stood up and said, "Please come? I want you to see . . . it's what we talked about and it won't feel . . ."

The discussion having turned to feelings, Leo lapsed into awkward silence. Then he added, "Besides, it has your song in it. It's the best thing in the whole show."

Leo had always insisted he wrote "But on Fridays" for me. For a moment, I saw the boy I had splashed on the beach, who had then chased me down the sand, who argued over the last piece of coconut candy before surrendering it with a sigh in exchange for one kiss, two kisses, oh, let's not count. The boy who had devised schemes and dreams as he ambled along the shore, the Atlantic Ocean framing the scope of his ambition: he would do this tomorrow, then that next week, and then *I* should, then *we* would . . .

"If Mrs. Tyler wants me to accompany her, then of course, I'll go." Struggling for manners, I added, "It will be a pleasure to meet Mrs. Hirschfeld."

At that, he grinned. "If you say so."

★ ★ ★

The next morning I awoke to discover that despite the absence of fireworks, the Fourth had not been entirely safe and sane. A bomb had gone off, destroying a building and killing four people. The bomb, the papers explained, had been meant for Rockefeller. Revenge for the deaths of two women and eleven children at Ludlow. But the bomb had exploded before it could be delivered, killing the would-be assassins. The Industrial Workers of the World was said to be responsible.

When I left for Europe, Anna had been working for the IWW.

Heart pounding, I looked for the address. It was uptown, nowhere near the Gorman Refuge run by my uncle, nowhere near . . . anyone I knew. I scanned the names of the dead: Berg, Caron, Chavez, Hanson. Three men. One woman.

One woman. Not Anna.

The chief assassins might be dead, but the police thought

other plotters were still at large. They were particularly interested in finding a Michael Murphy, but he was presumed on the run. Had Anna ever mentioned the names Berg or Caron? Hanson or Murphy? I couldn't remember. I had talked to her so little before leaving. When had I last seen her? Not since . . . summer. No— had I seen her in the summer? My days off had been spent mostly with Leo. It had, I realized with a pang of guilt, been some time.

Before leaving for the theater, I made a hurried telephone call to Anna's uncle's restaurant. In the past, that had always been the best way to reach her. When her uncle answered, I said I was Anna's friend, yes, the girl from the neighborhood. Did he know, by any chance, where she was staying? I had been away and had not heard from her.

No, said her uncle, he didn't know where Anna was living. But she was working hard. No, he wasn't sure where. Implied in that statement was that he was also working hard, and after asking him to give my love to his wife and her sister, I let him go. Then I sat with the knowledge that my oldest and dearest friend was angry with me.

3

My uncle, having fallen out with one church, was not inclined to set foot in another ever again. Sunday services at the refuge were held in the parlor, a side table serving as the altar. My first employer, Mrs. Armslow, was wealthy enough that God came to her, in the form of a pink-cheeked bishop. And so it was not until I saw St. Paul's in London that I found myself in a space created to encounter the divine. For an hour, I had wandered in a state of awe, jaw loose, eyes wide. Everything about the cathedral drew your gaze up and made you feel a speck, nothing more significant than the dust motes that floated for a brief time in the sun. I stood transfixed beneath the dome, newly certain that God existed, because here was His abode in all its majesty. When I came out blinking into the daylight, I felt I had had a mystical experience. Although it could have been dizziness from tilting my head for so long.

I recalled that memory as I walked into the Sidney Theater with Louise that afternoon. As with church, there were outer circles you traversed as you got closer to the chamber of worship: the box office, the lobby, then through gilt doors and into the theater itself. Here, too, the gaze was drawn up to the altar. Here, too, that sense of vastness and mysterious purpose. But unlike church, how the miracles were achieved was not a mystery. You heard it in the plink of a piano, the hammering and shouts of the stagehands, sudden bursts of song, and just as sudden bursts of complaint.

Only seven years old, the Sidney Theater was equipped with the most modern advances—hydraulics, a lighting board, and set workshops on the lower floors with an elevator to carry the results up to the stage—as well as the most lavish of interior design. Its creator had said he wanted the audience to feel as if they were in someone's home, and so they might, if that someone were a Vanderbilt. Glossy oak paneling shone as red brown as a setter's coat, alongside Tiffany stained glass and murals of the more titillating Greek myths. The seats were covered in red velvet; swaths of velvet hung at the balconies and doorways, bolstering the impression that this was a temple where the miraculous would be revealed to the worthy and chosen few.

Leo explained to Louise that as some things were not yet decided—"like the ending"—we would be seeing just a few of the big numbers. As we sat in a middle row, I noticed another gentleman sitting in one of the balconies. He was diminutive, with high, graying hair and protuberant eyes. A silver-topped cane rested against his chair, and he watched the stage with a proprietary gaze. If the theater was a church, he clearly considered himself God. This, I realized, must be Sidney Warburton, the man who had raised Leo from singing waiter to score composer.

The lights dimmed and a plump young woman called everyone to places. Louise whispered, "What is the show about, Mr. Hirschfeld?"

"What all good stories are about, Mrs. Tyler. Love."

A slim, dark-haired man stepped into the center of the stage. From his air of command—or was it preening?—this would be Claude Arden, half of the celebrated dance team, with a voice that could "melt maids' hearts from Brooklyn to Bugtussle."

"Meet our hero," said Leo. "A man in love. Deeply, sincerely in love."

Blanche Arden whirled in from the wings, a vision of blond hair and white chiffon. Hand to his heart, Claude inclined toward her. She extended a long, graceful arm and they glided rapturously around the stage. Claude returned to center. Blanche stepped back.

Louise made to applaud, but Leo held up his finger. A second actress burst onto the stage like a pinwheel firework. This had to be Nedda Fiske, the ragtime dancer with a face of rubber who had mugged and pratfalled her way to stardom. Physically, the former Ziegfeld star was small, not above five feet. But every facial feature, from her endless mouth to perennially rolling eyes, was so vivid as to be visible at the back row. No chiffon for her, she wore a plain dark dress, not unlike my own. She circled Claude with long, loping strides, before sticking out her hand as if to seal a bargain. Galvanized, Claude slapped his hand into hers and the pair set off in a raucous cakewalk.

"Only he has a problem," said Leo. "He loves two women. One, a society lady far above him, the other, a poor factory girl with a heart of gold."

"That is a problem," said Louise, glancing at me. "How will he solve it?"

"Just wait and see, Mrs. Tyler."

The lovers left the stage and Louise gave a cry of delight as a small brown-and-white dog trotted out, followed by a portly disaster of a man. As he staggered after the dog, bellowing "Pea-nut!" I thought he was either actually drunk or a supremely good actor.

Part man, part basset hound, he had a heavy, reddened face that sagged from bloodshot eyes to jowl. He had an odd hitch in his walk, and to watch him sway and lurch about the stage was to see a sailor dance on the deck of a ship that had wrecked long ago. You felt horribly sorry for him—and yet you couldn't stop laughing and just when it seemed our little audience would collapse, Nedda Fiske stepped on to sing, "I Want a New Man Who's Nothing Like My Old Man."

As more numbers followed, even I couldn't deny that Leo Hirschfeld had done it. The songs ran the gamut from clever, infectious rags to swooningly beautiful melodies. As a matter of philosophical inquiry, I wondered if a lady like Blanche Arden's socialite had occupied Leo's Tuesdays or if Nedda Fiske's plucky factory girl bore any resemblance to Clara. And there was another mystery: where was Mrs. Hirschfeld?

Then a set piece of a staircase was rolled onstage and Violet Tempest appeared at the top in the shortest, tightest maid's uniform I had ever seen.

"Oh, dear," murmured Louise, sinking slightly in her seat.

She knew how to descend, I gave her that. Every step was negotiated with a tremulous uncertainty that allowed for the artful display of delicate ankle, adorable knee, and quivering bosom. In a song called "One Smart Gal," Claude Arden sang of "Your insights on Voltaire / Appreciation of Molière," while Violet leaned over the railing, "unaware" that she was exposing a lot of herself in the process. It was a splendid backside, one could not fault it, even in the lengthy time one had to examine it. The voluptuous, dim-witted servant, I thought. How very true to life.

Last came a five-part rendition of "But on Fridays," which I might have found exquisite had I not been contemplating the many and varied ways to dismember a songwriter. When it was all over, I brought my hands together—once. But Leo was too busy being praised by Louise to notice. The show was just . . . *my*, and the songs were *oh*, and the Ardens *such*, and Nedda Fiske . . . *well!*

When she had caught her breath, she said, "But it's your songs, Mr. Hirschfeld. You must be so proud. And Mrs. Hirschfeld is quite . . ."

Louise blushed, unable to utter the adjective "risqué," much less the ones I might have chosen: vulgar, tasteless, insulting.

"The stairs are Miss Tempest's métier; her fans will love it." The little silver-haired man had joined us from the balcony. He leaned on his cane and crossed his feet, revealing a rather startling pair of yellow spats. Then he showed his teeth. "Introduce me, Leo."

Leo paused just long enough for discomfort, then said, "May I present the great Sidney Warburton, owner of the theater."

"And the producer of the show," said Mr. Warburton.

Extending her hand, Louise was startled to find it kissed. "It's a wonderful show, Mr. Warburton. I'm sure it'll be an enormous success."

"How would you like to be part of that success, Mrs. Tyler?" Leo wondered.

★ ★ ★

That evening, there was a spirited discussion between husband and wife. The subject: family finances, spending thereof. The first party, hereafter to be known as William, posited that a theatrical venture was a poor investment. The second party, hereafter known as Louise, disagreed. William asked on what grounds did she disagree? On the grounds, said Louise, that it was a very, very good show. Also, the Ardens were in it. Also, Nedda Fiske. William said he had never heard of the Ardens nor Nedda Fiske, so their participation could not be offered in evidence. Louise said he hadn't even seen the thing so his opinion on the matter was entirely irrelevant. After a long pause, William answered that his opinion on their finances was very much relevant. This led Louise to observe that it might be their finances, but it was her money. There followed a pause. Which grew into silence. And was punctuated with a slammed door.

Later that night, William came to the cellar where I was putting Louise's delicates up to dry. It was a surprising visit for the gentleman of the house, yet I was not surprised. I had known William since I was thirteen years old; even then, he had a habit of wandering to the servants' side of the house. The Tylers were one of New York's oldest families, yet William had never been entirely at ease in the affluent world to which he had been born. Enthusiastic about his fellow man, instinctively kind, he trampled social barriers as a hound puppy might trample a flower bed. I think he even disliked my calling him Mr. Tyler. Wearing a navy silk robe and slippers, he apologized for disturbing me. I said that was not possible. Then we went upstairs to the kitchen and I poured him a glass of milk.

He took a long swallow, then said, "My mother called this morning. She's upset that Louise hasn't come to Oyster Bay. Now Louise says she has to stay in the city to attend rehearsals. Apparently, Mr. Hirschfeld is keen to hear her opinions."

Yes, Leo had been extravagant in his praise for Louise's insights. "She did enjoy it," I said.

William's glum nod indicated he knew how little Louise had enjoyed since their return. "That's why I said she could go. But I insisted you go with her."

The word "insisted" meant Louise did not welcome my presence. "Mr. Tyler . . ."

William hurried to add, "I can't let her spend her days in some music hall without a chaperone, Mother would have a fit. Or . . .

an even greater fit. If that's possible. Louise says she's only promised the show a little money, but she can be . . ."

"Naïve," was the word he wanted. I thought to say, Yes, and
perhaps she doesn't want to be any longer. Still, he was calling on
our old alliance and I found it hard to refuse.

"I mean, you *know* Mr. Hirschfeld," he said.

"Yes, I know Mr. Hirschfeld."

"Would you, then? Just so there's no trouble?"

And so it was that I witnessed the creation of *Two Loves Have I*.
Unfortunately, in my charge of preventing trouble, I failed quite
spectacularly.

4

Having spent my career working for the extremely wealthy, I thought myself well acquainted with people who confused luxury with necessity. To deny the perennially indulged so much as a strawberry out of season could be seen as an affront bordering on assault. My first employer, Mrs. Armslow, had a cousin, a Mrs. Montrose, for whom a single misplaced hand towel was a sign the social order had collapsed. Unless the culprit was screamed at, threatened with dismissal and possibly arrest, anarchy would follow.

But Mrs. Montrose was a lamb compared to the denizens of the Sidney Theater. Unlike that delicate lady, they did labor and they were talented. But it seemed those talents could only thrive if certain needs were met, the primary need being the worshipful subservience of everyone around them. The worst of all was the little silver-haired producer, Sidney Warburton.

The name Sidney Warburton is not now much remembered; even his own theater bears a different title. But at the time, he had every intention of joining the ranks of Diaghilev and D'Oyly Carte. Small, impeccably dressed, never without his yellow spats or silver-topped cane, he certainly looked the part of an impresario. There were many apocryphal stories about how he started in show business: cheating the fleas in his childhood circus, revenge for a Punch and Judy show where he had been mistaken for one of the puppets. The mere facts were, he had started in vaudeville, managing acts on the circuit. He had prospered and bought his own theater, going up against the powerful syndicate that controlled the theater world until 1910. His shows had grown more elaborate and sophisticated. Ziegfeld had his *Follies*, Warburton his *Spectaculars*.

But his partnership with Leo signaled that he was ready to leave the variety show and launch into a new kind of theater: the musical. And not just a musical, but a ragtime musical. To the papers, he said Leo Hirschfeld was the future. To Leo, he said he was a no-talent nobody who'd struck lucky and would do what he was told. To the papers, Leo proclaimed Warburton a giant, a legend, and mentor. The same day, he would wonder why Warburton didn't go back to bearded ladies and goldfish swallowers and let him handle the actual show.

The two men fought about the beginning of the show, the end of the show, and everything in between. The action could not progress above a minute without one of them calling a halt and reworking some bit of business agreed to the minute before. Warburton liked the graceful dance that opened the show, Leo found it hopelessly old-fashioned. It was a ragtime show, he argued, it should jolt, shock, make people move. Staging was changed, songs were shifted, cuts suggested, and additions requested. I didn't see how they managed to remember anything, but all the changes were recorded by Mr. Warburton's assistant, Harriet Biederman, a young woman with auburn hair and a light Austrian accent who kept the entire history of the show in her notebook and seemed to be the only rational person in the building.

I was more concerned with the tensions between a different pair: namely, myself and Louise. As I had predicted, she did not welcome my chaperonage. She was silent on our rides to and from the theater; our exchanges at home were stilted and perfunctory. She knew it wasn't my choice, but still, she felt spied on. I could think of no way to apologize without criticizing her husband, and so we were stuck. During rehearsals, I sat three rows behind Louise and tried to be inconspicuous while she chatted gaily with the actors eager to make the acquaintance of their new patroness. Leo, I ignored. But then he ignored me.

At the end of the week, as Louise sat enraptured by Mr. Arden's recitation of his footwear requirements, I heard a woman shout, "Utterly revolting, and I will not do it."

Keeping one step ahead of her, Warburton said: "Claude and Blanche want you on costumes, Adele, that means costumes. Everyone's costumes."

"This isn't costumes, it's bottom wiping. I am *not* a nursemaid and I am *not* a laundress," she said in an accent somewhere between Boston and Windsor.

At this, Louise looked up. "Do you need assistance, Mrs. St. John? Perhaps my maid could help, she's tremendously capable." Glancing at me, she added, "It would be nice for her to have something to occupy her time."

Meeting her gaze, I asked, Was she sure? Truly, she didn't need me for anything? No, said Louise, she was quite certain: she did not need me.

So dismissed, I presented myself to Mrs. St. John, who led me upstairs to a small, cramped corridor that led to several dressing rooms. Knocking on the third door, she got a high-pitched bark in response. Mrs. St. John gave the knob a vicious twist and the door swung wide to reveal the actor who played Nedda Fiske's father snoring in a chair. There was the sharp tang of accident in the air. I looked at the dog; it yapped a firm denial.

"Congratulations," she said. "You are now in charge of Mr. Roland Harney."

Being "in charge" of Roland Harney was a very different prospect than managing Louise Tyler. His wardrobe was far more limited, but far more filthy. I learned quickly: hold all garments at arm's length. In addition to keeping the comic hygienic, I was also charged with keeping him off the gin. I began with an earnest appeal; surely an artist of his gifts would want to show respect to his fellow actors by rehearsing sober?

I held up his flask. "Why don't I hold on to this and return it at the end of the day?"

To my surprise, he gazed mournfully at the flask, then said, "I suppose that's best. Thank you, my dear. Thank you."

I felt extremely smug—managing actors was no difficulty, you just had to be firm with them—until the next day when I found a gin bottle hidden under seat twenty-four in row H.

And so I spent my days wandering the Sidney Theater, collecting bottles, soiled clothes, and Peanut when he ran off in search of rodent life. The inside of a theater was strangely public; yet there were many hidden spots where untoward things might happen. I heard a great deal that supported the senior Mrs. Tyler's suspicion that the theater was a place of greed and lax morals. For instance, Nedda Fiske was not married, but a gentleman often kept her company at the theater. One day outside her dressing room, I chanced to hear, "I need it, Nedda!"

"And I'm telling you, I don't have it!"

The gentleman called her a liar in abusive terms. Nedda returned the compliment in language even more colorful. There was a short scream, a crash, and the tinkling sound of breakage. Hurrying to the door, I knocked and called, "Miss Fiske?"

The door opened just enough for me to see the actress, her face grim set as she said, "We're fine, Jane. Thank you." Then she shut the door in my face.

I asked Mr. Harney if he knew Miss Fiske's companion. Blowing out his cheeks, he said, "Floyd Lombardo. She keeps him in jewels and silks and what he doesn't gamble away, he spends on other women. Poor Nedda's besotted with him. Ziegfeld barred him from the theater when he started bullying stagehands into lending him money. Nedda refused to work without him and signed with Sidney. Steer clear of him, my dear, if you don't want your bottom pinched or your pocket picked."

Mr. Harney proved correct. I was often in the wings ready with ice for Mr. Harney or to catch Peanut as he came offstage. From this vantage point, I saw that the moment Miss Fiske's back was turned, Floyd Lombardo's covetous gaze slid elsewhere. Blanche Arden was too big a star to tolerate such familiarity, so he settled for the celebrated shape of Violet Tempest. In this, he was no different from 99 percent of the men on the show, including and especially Leo.

I did not want to dislike Violet Tempest—Violet Hirschfeld, rather. I told myself it was petty to bear ill will toward the woman Leo had married. But if I didn't dislike Violet Hirschfeld, I can't say I enjoyed being around her. Comparisons were pointless and irresistible. No matter how hard I tried, the inevitable question of Leo's choice presented itself. Why her? Why her and not . . . ? The answer was depressingly obvious. Oh, we were alike in some ways. I was a woman, she was a woman, but there the similarities ended. On her, all parts that distinguished male from female were buoyantly, generously . . . present. She was Eve, *après pomme*. And

where'er she went, Leo's moony gaze followed. Rehearsals sometimes came to a halt because husband and wife had suddenly disappeared. This did not endear Violet to the rest of the cast, who
felt the show could do without her even if Leo couldn't. Her talents were limited and, as the composer's wife and a former chorus
girl, she was resented.

Leo had given her a lovely song called "Why Not Me?" One
afternoon, Warburton announced that it should be sung by
Mr. Arden.

"She doesn't have the voice to put it across," said Warburton.
"Arden will make it a hit. Look what he did with 'But on Fridays.'"

"Yeah, I saw exactly what he did," said Leo. "And how much
you and he made off it."

Waiting in the wings, I glanced at Mr. Harney. He passed a
finger along his lips.

Then Warburton offered, "Maybe Violet can sing the song if
we cut 'One Smart Gal.' That song makes the fellow look like a
drooling chimp. Know what I mean?"

Leo did know what he meant, as evidenced by the fact that his
hands became fists.

Warburton was fond of belittling nicknames. Louise was the
debutante, Harney the has-been. Mrs. St. John was Horse Face,
Nedda Fiske was Big Mouth (she called Warburton the Dwarf).
Violet was referred to in anatomical terms, and I cannot repeat
what he called Mr. Lombardo. The Ardens were generally ex-
empt, but I once heard Warburton refer to "the Duchess" and
when Miss Biederman tentatively inquired if he meant Blanche,
he said, "Claude, Blanche—either one."

No one received more abuse than Miss Biederman herself.
His malice toward her was casual, a matter of habit; he almost
never addressed her without screaming. Most of the time, she
seemed distressingly used to it. But not always.

Once as I passed Warburton's office, I heard the predictable bellows of "idiot," "imbecile," and "useless." Soon after, a red-eyed Harriet Biederman exited. Shutting the door behind her, she dabbed at her eyes. Small and pleasantly rounded, she gave the brief impression of being a child. Then she gathered her notebook and pen to her bosom, shook her auburn curls, and took a deep breath.

"If I were you," I told her, "I'd take that gentleman's fancy silver cane and stick it right up his backside."

She gasped. Then smiled.

"Come," I said. "Let's tidy up."

In the ladies' room, as Miss Biederman washed her face, I burst forth with a litany of complaints. The Ardens were unbearably arrogant, Nedda Fiske delusional, Floyd Lombardo a menace. And dear God, the compulsively amorous Mr. and Mrs. Hirschfeld . . .

Harriet met my gaze in the mirror. I had the sense I had revealed rather too much. Quickly, I changed subjects. "And I don't see how you can work for that insufferable bully."

"He is a great man with many pressures on him," she said. "My father was like him. He also shouted and said cruel things. But he was an artist and when he played the violin, you heard only the beauty of the music."

I thought to say that there were many great men in the world— and great women—who did not use creation as an excuse to be cruel. I settled for the observation that the "artists" seemed like a pack of overindulged brats to me.

"They are childish because what they do is terrifying. Think of their courage, to stand there alone, to take what is in here." She put a small fist to her lower midsection. "And show it to the world."

She was so earnest, I found it impossible to argue. "Well, Mr. Warburton is lucky to have you."

"He will lose me in September," she said sadly. "I am getting married, and my fiancé wants me to work in his butcher shop. But I love the theater. When the lights go down and the curtains open, I get . . ." She rubbed her arms to suggest chills. "But perhaps it is for the best. One day, I might take your advice—and that would be the end of a very fine silver cane!"

Whether it was fine silver canes or a tube of Leichner's greasepaint, tempers were such that someone was going to do someone an injury. Leo and Warburton's shouting matches grew more heated. There were daily arguments about spending. One day, as I made my way through the cramped corridors, I heard Leo say, "Money was no object on your last disaster. What's the problem? Your investor getting cold feet? Or maybe they've had enough of the lies."

Mrs. St. John stepped in a leaving of Peanut's and subjected me and Mr. Harney to a tirade that included words I would not have suspected she knew. Violet was caught gossiping on the only private phone in the theater, which happened to be in Warburton's office. This sent the producer into a rage—which grew even uglier when the story of Peanut's accident and Adele St. John's ruined shoe appeared in the newspapers, along with speculation that Warburton's new show was in trouble.

"You can't talk to the newspapers, Vi," Leo explained wearily.

"I didn't, it was just my friends."

"Well, then you can't talk to your friends."

"But I don't have anything else to do."

The dispute that caused the most friction was the question at the heart of the show: which lady should the gentleman choose? Warburton, a longtime collaborator with the Ardens, said Claude should choose Blanche—because who would not choose Blanche? Leo insisted Nedda was the more modern choice; as a working girl, she was someone the audience would cheer for.

As he often did these days, Leo turned to Louise. "Do you have an opinion, Mrs. Tyler?"

Blushing, Louise said it was an impossible choice.

One saw Mr. Warburton's point. Next to Vernon and Irene Castle, the Ardens were the most famous dance team in the country. In town after town, people turned out to see Blanche tease, escape, then finally surrender to her obsessive paramour. Their actual love story was well known: Claude had been a popular singer of romantic ballads. On a tour of upstate New York, he had spied in the front row "the loveliest of creatures, a girl of moonlight and stars. I knew at once that I would be dancing with her for the rest of my life." That night, he had appeared at Blanche's window and sung of his love. She had run off with him on the spot.

The public might expect Blanche to be Claude's choice, but personally, I rooted for Nedda Fiske. When she strode onstage, she captured the spotlight not just for herself, but for all of us not born to wealth. Maybe we didn't have money—or other obvious attractions—but we had humor and talent and heart. One of her hallmarks as a performer was to ape the elegant, well-born lady she was so clearly not. Offstage, she sometimes drawled to an imaginary butler, "Wentworth, the caviar eggs are the wrong shape. Tell the fish: rounder. My ermine needs fluffing, my diamonds buffing, and my backside could use a good smooch!"

As in the show, the ladies were rivals. But the affections of the gentleman were no way in doubt. Nedda Fiske took this as a challenge. In one rehearsal, she writhed so energetically against a miserable Claude that Warburton bellowed at her to stop, insisting, "This isn't some cheap burlesque theater!" Nedda launched into an exaggerated belly dance. Standing in the wings with Mr. Harney's cold towel, I heard Leo laugh.

"I will not be mocked in this way!" shouted Claude.

Nedda rolled her eyes. "Oh, cut the histrionics."

Claude glared at her and then Violet, who had wandered in in her maid's outfit. Snarling, "So many things I'd like to cut," he stalked into the wings just as Mr. Harney ambled on to rehearse "A New Man" with Miss Fiske.

As Mr. Arden approached, I drew into the shadows. In the past, the singer had pointedly ignored me. Now, rather than storm off to his dressing room, he sank, winded, onto a chair. Head down, shirt dark with sweat, legs akimbo, he was the picture of exhaustion. The black hair was thinning—and dyed—and when he raised his head, his neck and eyes showed signs of age. Blanche, I realized, was at least a decade younger.

I offered the ice-laden towel. He took it without a word and buried his face. Then after a moment, he asked, "Tell me—would you fall in love with this man? You're a young girl."

Wanting to be kind, I said, "Yes, he's . . . wonderfully romantic."

Crow's-feet deepened as he peered at me. "You don't think he's a bit of a cad? I mean, he loves this one, he loves that one, he wants to fall in bed with the maid. I can't help thinking the audience will despise him. 'Make up your mind already!' If he's flitting back and forth, don't you just want to hit him with a chair?"

Looking to the piano where Violet was turning Leo's pages, I said, ". . . Possibly."

Just then we heard Blanche trill as she came into the theater, calling, "Mr. Hirschfeld—Oh, I'm terribly sorry to interrupt, Miss Fiske, but Mr. Hirschfeld, I wonder if I could talk to you about that second act song . . ."

At the sound of his wife's voice, Claude pulled back the curtain to gaze at her. "One girl," he said softly. "He loves one girl and all he wants to do is win her heart."

"I'm sure you've won it, Mr. Arden."

He smiled sadly, patted my arm. "One girl—tell your boss that's what you'd pay to see."

I had been sincere in my reassurances to Mr. Arden concerning his wife's devotion. But I began to wonder. Mrs. Arden had told the press how excited she was to be working with a bold young songwriter, and she expressed her enthusiasm in private as well. She pronounced herself fascinated with Leo's hair, touching it often. Amused by his fights with Warburton; so much passion! Enchanted by his syncopation; so . . . seductive.

Two days after my talk with her husband, I watched Blanche as she twirled onstage alone in Mrs. St. John's latest creation. Leo approached from the opposite wings and she danced prettily up to him. As they stood facing each other in the narrow space, she said, "What do you think of the dress? Does it show too much?"

With a slight smile, Leo said, "You know just what to show, Mrs. Arden. You don't need my advice."

Hand above her knee, she drew the fabric up. "But would it be better so . . ."

The silk slid higher; she bent her leg to nudge his. ". . . or so?"

Leo swallowed. "So," he managed. "Very, very much so."

The next day, I was returning cleaned clothes to the dressing rooms when I saw that the door to the Ardens' room was closed. But no matter how hard one tries, a servant cannot always avoid trespass on moments of intimacy. Not when they are conducted as operatically as this particular conjugal episode. The voice was soprano; the birdlike dancer exhorting her husband on as if he were a horse at the track. I made my way back down the rickety stairs. Reaching the stage level, I heard Claude Arden, running through his *mee, may, ma, mo, moo*'s. Violet lolled in the front row, yawning.

Leo was nowhere to be seen.

★ ★ ★

That evening on the drive home, I recalled the splendors of Mrs. Tyler's rose garden on Long Island in the vain hopes that

Louise would pronounce herself in need of a change of scene. She merely plucked at the fingers of her gloves and looked pensive.

Then she said, "I'm sorry, Jane. I know it's difficult seeing Mr. Hirschfeld. I told Mr. Tyler he was putting you in a terrible position, but he wouldn't listen. He's worried his mother will find out he let me go unescorted to a . . . den of iniquity. It's very silly, but there it is."

"It isn't difficult to see Mr. Hirschfeld." At least not on the rare occasions when he wasn't exercising himself. "But they're some-what . . . irregular people."

"But aren't they wonderful?" breathed Louise, thrilled to have the chance to discuss her passion. "The dancing, the costumes, little Peanut. And the songs! Just to spend the day listening to those wonderful songs. Maybe they aren't such regular people, but I . . . can't say I mind that."

This last was said with uncertainty, she expected correction. But it was wonderful to see her so animated. Bidding a private farewell to the hope of sea air and rose-scented gardens, I said life in the theater was certainly not dull.

"I do wish Mr. Warburton would stop shouting at people," said Louise, as if wanting to concede a point to me.

As we approached the house, Louise gathered her coat about her. I moved to help her and noticed that the diamond-and-opal brooch I had placed on the breast that morning was gone.

"Mrs. Tyler, your brooch."

We searched the seat and the floor of the car. "Maybe it fell off at the theater," I suggested. Although the clasp had been secure, I had made sure when I fastened it. "I'll search the cloakroom tomorrow."

"Please don't mention this to Mr. Tyler."

"Of course not."

I strongly suspected I would not find it in the cloakroom. Or anywhere in the theater. Floyd Lombardo had a very handsome straw hat that he kept in the cloakroom. And as he went in and out of the theater several times a day, he was often there. Alone.

As expected, the brooch was nowhere to be found. Louise refused to tell Leo or Warburton, saying she had many other brooches and she didn't want to cause difficulties. This reticence was natural to her, and I suspected she didn't want to give Warburton an excuse to bar her from the theater. I, however, was less reticent.

I had noticed that Mr. Lombardo often had his appointments during scenes when all the actors were onstage. During one such scene, I saw him rise from his seat and make his way toward the lobby where the cloakroom was. I followed—and found him making a leisurely inventory of Claude Arden's coat pocket.

"I believe your hat is in the cubby, Mr. Lombardo."

With the smoothness of one often caught in compromising situations, he removed his hand and stepped around the counter. Nedda Fiske kept him well. His dark hair was slick as an otter's, his cleft chin beautifully shaved, his left hand expensively jeweled. On the right hand, however, he wore a cast.

"And you are?" he said.

I gave my name, adding, "I work for Mrs. William Tyler."

He raised an impressed eyebrow. "You know I've wondered, how does Mrs. Tyler come to be at Sidney Warburton's squalid little theater?"

"She is a supporter of his protégé, Mr. Hirschfeld."

"'Protégé,' is that what we're calling him?"

I didn't understand the joke and I didn't like it. "Returning to the subject of Mrs. Tyler. Her brooch went missing the other day. I don't suppose you've seen it."

"Oh, Miss Prescott, that sounds like an accusation."

"It's a request."

"Miss Fiske is not partial to opals."

"How did you know they were opals?"

The second's hesitation in answering was an admission of guilt and Mr. Lombardo knew it. I turned. He grabbed hold of my arm. I smelled lime, tobacco, and desperation.

"We could have a nice arrangement, you and I. Mrs. St. John foisted the laundry off on you, didn't she? You pass some things my way, I'll make sure you get a cut. Fortune favors the bold."

"I'd hate to scream, Mr. Lombardo, let me go."

"Oh, I'd hate to scream, too, Miss Prescott. No one really trusts servants, do they? Paid so little, treated so badly, you almost can't blame them if they get light-fingered . . ."

The hand that took hold of my backside was not a show of carnal interest. Lust was not absent, but primarily, he was motivated by a desire to take, to cheat, to get what he could while no one was looking. Unfortunately for him, someone was looking.

"Beat it, Lombardo," said Violet Hirschfeld.

The hand was removed. For a moment, Floyd Lombardo assessed Violet Hirschfeld; did she have influence? Would she be believed? Then tipping his straw hat, he said, "Adieu, Salome," and left the theater.

When he had made his departure, she said, "You all right?"

"Fine. Thank you."

"A lady as smart as Nedda, you'd think she'd have better taste, right? But some women, no matter how bad their man treats them, they can't give him up."

How well, I wondered, did Leo treat her? I thought to ask Violet about Lombardo's protégé snipe, but decided that would show an unnecessary interest in her husband. Instead I asked how Floyd had injured his hand.

"Says he broke it playing polo." She rolled her eyes. "I sure didn't know Owney Davis liked the ponies. Not for polo, anyway."

Owney Davis was a gangster who had been so successful at the racetrack, it was said he had single-handedly shut down Belmont for two years by fixing races. He had attained a peculiar glamour that gave him entrée into venues that would have ejected any other steamfitter's son from Brooklyn. He was rumored to be generous in his lending—and ruthless in collection. No wonder Lombardo was desperate. I recalled the fight I had overheard between him and Miss Fiske. He had said he needed money. She said she didn't have it to give. The truth? Or had she noticed his wandering eye and wanted to remind him who held the upper hand?

Glancing back at the coats, I said, "I caught him rifling through Mr. Arden's pockets. Should I tell Mr. Warburton?"

She winced. "I don't know. Nedda won't see sense about Lombardo and Sidney thinks the show needs her. Maybe better to just keep an eye on Mrs. Tyler's things."

It was sound advice and I followed it. But other things began to go missing. Blanche lost a pair of earrings. A bracelet disappeared from Violet's dressing room. Harriet became frantic when she could not find her pen. All these items were labeled "misplaced." But when Mrs. St. John opened her wallet to find twenty dollars gone, she acidly inquired if Nedda had lost anything—or perhaps gained. Nedda went red, but she pronounced herself as broke as Stanley Ketchel's front teeth.

The next day I found Mr. Harney lingering outside the closed door to Warburton's office, Peanut in the crook of his arm like a stuffed toy. Mr. Arden's celebrated voice could be clearly heard. "This is not the show we signed on for, Sidney. Stand up to her; tell her you won't put up with it."

I had to strain to hear Warburton mumble something about "contracts."

"You have to get rid of him, Sidney." Blanche Arden was more soft-spoken but no less insistent than her partner. "We can't work like this. If she feels she needs him . . ."

"Then she can go straight into the gutter with him," shouted Claude. "At a certain point, Sidney, it's her or us."

I thought I caught Leo's voice, low and surprisingly earnest. The Ardens lowered their tones to match his, which made it difficult to hear. Mr. Harney and I frowned at each other; discretion could be so frustrating.

Then Leo declared, "Well, if she goes, I go."

This was dramatic. Mr. Harney pulled a face.

Also dramatic was the sound of a cane being slammed onto a surface and Warburton's bellow, "Who owns this theater? You talk about gutters—where would any of you be without me? You? You'd be singing that same sad song to old women in Boise. You'd be offering your rear end at every stage door in town, and you . . ." For a moment, the producer strangled on his rage. When he found breath, he screamed, "You don't tell me what I have to do. None of you! I put the lights on you. I take them away—you're nothing."

In extremely colorful terms, he invited them to leave his office. At which point, Mr. Harney and I departed as well.

For a day, it was strangely silent; everyone strained to be agreeable. Nedda carried on, seemingly unaware of the animosity. Not so Floyd Lombardo, who sat with the triumphant smile of a nasty little boy hiding behind a giant of a mother.

That afternoon, I came into the theater to find it empty except for Louise and Mr. Lombardo, who had curled into the aisle seat next to her in the second row. In a quavering voice, Louise said, "I'm afraid I couldn't, Mr. Lombardo."

I hurried to her, saying, "Mrs. Tyler, you have an appointment with your dressmaker at four."

She affected to look at her watch. "Oh, dear, and it's after three. Mr. Lombardo, would you excuse me?"

She waited for him to stand so that she could pass. He stayed put. "I really would like to talk to you about this investment opportunity. Fortune favors the bold, Mrs. Tyler." He gave me what was meant to be a smile. "I said just that to Miss Prescott in the cloakroom the other day."

I was trying to judge the exact nature of the threat when I heard an explosion of foul language and saw Sidney Warburton charge through a curtained entry, Harriet Biederman behind him. The enraged producer hauled Lombardo out of the seat, spraying him with spit and curses, before demanding, "Where's my cane?"

"How should I know?" I heard a tremor in the affected drawl.

Warburton gave him a hard shove. "Don't lie to me! Where is it?"

The shouting drew the Ardens and Mrs. St. John, then Violet and Leo, doing up the odd button, and finally, Nedda, who warily assessed the situation.

Warburton took a deep breath. "Nedda, he's got to go." The Ardens exchanged glances.

"Calm down, Sidney, I'll talk to him . . ."

"No talking! I want him out, gone!" Then as Nedda began to object, he bellowed, "Stop defending him, for God's sake. Just the other day, he was pawing that one in the lobby."

He gestured to me and Louise gasped. Nedda looked to Lombardo, eyes cold. "Is that true, Floyd? Those hands been wandering?"

For a man who habituated theaters, Lombardo was a poor actor. "Nedda, you can't think . . ."

Louise said, "I'm sorry, Miss Fiske, but I must agree with Mr. Warburton."

There was a long, painful pause. Clasping her hands in the rigid manner of a hostess on edge, Nedda said, "Don't be sorry, Mrs. Tyler. Out he goes, with the trash as they say." She snapped her fingers. "Wentworth, remove this person. I'm off to bathe my emeralds."

Floyd Lombardo was escorted from the building.

5

Nedda Fiske put on a brave face—and kept it on for all of two days. By day three, she was anxious, forgetting lines, lacking in sparkle. Floyd had not returned to their apartment and she didn't know where he was. "He hasn't been home in days," she told anyone who would listen. "He's never been gone this long." As Mr. Harney observed, "Her life is a shambles with him. Her work a shambles without him."

By the end of the week, Nedda broke. She begged Warburton to allow Floyd back to the theater. She knew, absolutely knew, that if he felt certain of his welcome, he would return to her. He would behave, she promised. She would make him behave. Only he must be allowed back. He had to come back. She needed him back.

Warburton refused.

Nedda Fiske retaliated. She was late, moped through her numbers; at times, she failed to show up for rehearsals at all. As Mr. Arden observed, it didn't make much difference, her performance was so lackluster. Everywhere, there was conspiracy. Behind closed doors, the Ardens plotted. Leo and Warburton argued. Violet and Louise tried to cajole Miss Fiske into better humor. Mrs. St. John designed. Mr. Harney drank. And I took Peanut for his walks and tried to decide if I wanted Leo's show to fail or not.

With opening night less than a month away, the emotional collapse of one of its stars was cause for concern. To raise morale, Mr. Warburton decided to take everyone out to Rector's, the lobster palace where "Broadway and Fifth Avenue met." Its creator, Charles Rector, had spent a quarter of a million dollars on the culinary fun house. Mirrored walls multiplied the images of its celebrated customers a hundredfold. Built at the end of the gay '90s, this "court of triviality" was a haven for the brash, gaudy new wealth: the financiers, gamblers, cattle barons, and performers of every kind. Chorus girls who had nabbed the richest stage-door Johnnies insisted on Rector's. Its most famous customer was Diamond Jim Brady, who was said to consume three dozen oysters, a dozen hard-shell crabs, six lobsters, and an entire dessert tray at a sitting—all washed down with orange juice. The restaurant's colors were money: gold and dark green. The 175 tables were covered in Irish linen, the silverware emblazoned with the Rector griffin. The saucier had been stolen from Delmonico's, and the chef kept a note from Queen Victoria, praising his terrapin à la Maryland, in his hat. The food was as gaudy as its clientele: African peaches, Lynnhaven oysters, mousselines, nectarines, duck, and of course lobster. Four private dining rooms enabled enough bad behavior to keep tongues wagging and the restaurant's name on everyone's lips. A fourteen-story hotel built on top of the dining concern had increased its reputation as a bawdy house. New investors had added a dance floor, which some thought tacky. But it was still beloved. The excitement began as you entered as Rector's boasted the city's very first revolving doors. Guests liked to spin until they were dizzy, making a game of who could stay in the longest before being flung into the bright warmth of the interior or the darkness outside.

Always after rehearsals, I had rushed from the theater to the Tylers' waiting car, anxious to get Louise home. So I hadn't really taken in Times Square at nighttime. Over the past few years, electric signs had begun to appear, selling everything from cereal to shoes to chewing gum. Leaving the Sidney, I entered a wonderland where the night sky was ablaze with tens of thousands of light bulbs, each blinking in sequence to create the illusion of movement. Mundane life at street level faded as I stared, gape-mouthed, at an electric bucking bronco and an incandescent kitten twenty feet high playing with a ball of yarn. A polo player swung his mallet, and a girl's skirt was blown tantalizingly upward. As if inspired by the dramatics played out on stages far below them, these bright, glowing figures held the eye and mind captive. I spun idly as I walked, not wanting to miss a single blink of light and fantasy. Harriet Biederman, I could tell, was much amused.

Located on Forty-Eighth Street, Rector's was close to the Tenderloin. So close that the kind of men Jack London had dubbed the "Haut Beaux," and others called tramps, wandered outside the restaurant. Most of the vagrants kept their distance, slumped against buildings, calling to passersby, hand outstretched. But as we approached the famous revolving door, a large man rambled into view. His gray hair was greasy and matted, his clothes filthy, and his mind unhinged by drink or madness or both. By chance or drunken design, he stumbled between us and the entrance. I instinctively drew close to Louise and Claude Arden moved to stand in front of Blanche as the man careened among us, an urban Lear hurling curses at the stars above and below. "Leeches," was one of the less obscene insults. "Bloodsuckers" another. A cheaply carved wooden leg contributed to his lack of balance. He lurched, seemed about to take his leave, when all of a sudden, he turned and hurled himself at Mr. Warburton, resplendent in yellow spats and top hat, screaming "You! Look at you . . ."

Choking, he threw the bottle to the pavement, where it shattered, eliciting a scream from Violet. That galvanized our party into action and we surged toward the doors. As we gave our coats, Louise gave me a dollar and begged me to give it to the tramp. Back through the revolving doors I went, but the poor man was long gone.

We were seated in the pink-and-gold Ballroom de Luxe, where people danced beneath colored lights. As we came in, the band struck up "Lady Lion Tamer," to acknowledge Leo's arrival. Given the size of our party, two round tables were set close together; Leo was at one end, Mr. Warburton on the other. I took some interest in where everyone sat; which side would they choose? The Ardens sat close to Mr. Warburton, as did Harriet Biederman. Louise and I sat on Leo's side, along with Nedda Fiske, who had come under protest. Mrs. St. John sat firmly in the middle, as did Mr. Harney, who carried Peanut under his coat. She ordered an Alexander. Mr. Harney said he'd just have the gin, hold the cream and chocolate. Also a water bowl for Peanut. Violet spotted friends and went off to say hello.

Leo insisted Louise take the seat directly next to him. Louise pulled me down beside her. Nedda Fiske took the chair on the other side of Leo. When she returned to the table, Violet found the seats near her husband occupied and only the seat opposite me left to her. If Leo noticed the hurt look she gave him, he showed no sign of it, being far too busy regaling Louise with the mishaps involving a baby elephant whose stage fright took a messy turn on Warburton's last show. Sitting, Violet grabbed ahold of the waiter and ordered a bottle of champagne, one glass.

Our arrival caused quite a stir, with fans and well-wishers approaching the Ardens, Miss Fiske, and Leo, who was looking handsome and vital in white tie. He was, I noticed with irritation, also wearing yellow spats, perhaps as a peace offering to his producer. I looked to Mrs. St. John to lead the conversation, but she was intent on persuading Harriet on the necessity of something called lamé and the idiocy of Mr. Warburton in refusing to cover the expense. Nedda was the target of gentle interrogation by Leo, who was aided by Louise. This left me and Violet as companions. The friendliness of the other day was gone. Mrs. Hirschfeld only had eyes for Leo's intent conversation with Nedda Fiske—and when it arrived, the champagne. Violet drank one glass speedily, then a second. I saw Mrs. St. John was free of her exchange with Harriet and hoped she might say something to the neglected chorus girl. Instead, she turned to Mr. Harney and asked if he preferred to work with Jack Russells or beagles. The snub was not subtle and Violet started on her third glass.

Claude Arden, I'm sorry to say, was pressing Mr. Warburton on the matter of "Why Not Me?" saying, "It should be my song, you know it should." Blanche Arden was gazing down at our end of the table. She let a single finger drift down the length of her throat, her lips parted, eyes all languor and invitation. Never insensitive to such overtures, Leo glanced up and I thought I saw a brief frown of warning.

Just then, a violently beautiful young man approached Louise. His skin was olive, his hair dark. His mouth was curiously small, almost feminine. But the eyes, under a high, romantic forehead, were magnetic. He was, he claimed, desolate to interrupt. Also, to presume. But he had to ask: would the lady do him the great honor of dancing with him? He unfurled his arm in an elegant, well-practiced gesture. From his accent, he was Italian and not long in this country.

I could see from Leo's expression that he knew the young man was a taxi dancer who had deduced that Louise was a woman of wealth. I also saw from her expression that Louise was completely unaware of this fact. I told the young man in Italian that the signorina was a signora and that her husband was large and ill-tempered.

He sighed. "The greatest jewels are always belonging to another man."

Violet laughed into her champagne glass. Louise, mistaking the young man's sorrow as genuine, said, "Oh, but perhaps you'd like to dance with Jane . . ."

I was so shocked that while my mouth said no, my voice lagged behind. This gave Leo enough time to say, "Absolutely!" and deposit money into the man's pocket.

The arm unfurled in my direction. I was aware of Louise's desire to distract me from heartache. Also Leo's enjoyment of a joke at my expense. But above all, I felt my own disinterest in spending another second next to the sullen Miss Tempest—Mrs. Hirschfeld, rather—and her champagne burps. I rose and took the young man's hand.

Casting his eye on Warburton's table, he wondered if "the divine Mr. and Mrs. Arden" would consent to share the dance floor. Then he pulled me into a desultory fox-trot.

I was not in the mood for desultory. Humiliation and sitting too long had given me a ferocious determination to show off— which I did in a flurry of steps, rolling my shoulders and tossing my head rather provocatively. The young man grudgingly admitted that I was not terrible and asked if I knew the tango. Gaze averted from Leo, I said that I did.

"Good," he said. "You help me make show to Warburton."

"You're an actor," I said as he yanked me to him.

"Yes. I am Rodolfo."

"I am Jane."

As we danced, he pointed out the many famous people in the crowd. There was Mr. Cohan, there Billie Burke. None of the Barrymores were in tonight, but John Drew had sat at that table just the other evening. That man had made a fortune in Colorado— no one quite knew how. That woman was on her fourth husband and none of the previous three were still among the living. There was an assemblyman who lived for his two poodles, a Russian addicted to morphine, and a baseball player who had almost certainly been paid to drop a fly ball in the last series. Two tables over, the man who had paid him, Owney Davis.

I turned to get a look at the gangster, but Rodolfo pulled me sharply back into the dance. As he did, there was an outburst of clapping: the Ardens had decided to put on a show after all. Some couples returned to their tables, but others raced onto the dance floor, eager to share it with the celebrated pair. Rodolfo maneuvered me closer, hoping to attract the Ardens' attention. But they were inclined toward each other in ecstatic embrace. Her lips to her husband's ear, Blanche hissed, "You can't possibly be upset. It's for the good of the family business . . ."

As we swung back toward the tables, I saw that the Ardens' departure meant a change in the seating. Louise was safely chatting with Mrs. St. John; Mr. Harney was fast asleep. Peanut was making the rounds and being fed enough steak and lobster to collapse Diamond Jim. Nedda was nowhere to be seen. This had freed Leo to take Claude Arden's vacant seat next to Mr. Warburton. Violet had moved with him, bringing her friend, the champagne bottle. Someone else was missing, but before I could think who, Rodolfo swung me in the other direction.

When we turned back a few moments later, I saw that the conversation between Leo and Warburton had once again turned combative. Warburton's jaw was thrust out, his arms were crossed, his head down; his entire aspect was that of a man resisting under siege. Leo sat forward, his finger striking the table again and again, his other hand spread and balanced on fingertips. He had his point and he was making it. But Warburton wasn't buying.

"Why don't we dance closer to Warburton's table?" I suggested.

"If you look ecstatic," Rodolfo whispered in my ear. "I give you a dollar."

Unfortunately, by the time we tangoed our way through the crush, Warburton was focused on a lovely brunette who was professing breathy admiration for everything he had done since the dawn of time. He was so moved, he had taken her hand. Cards and compliments were exchanged. Knowing he could not compete for the producer's attentions, Rodolfo started maneuvering us toward the Ardens.

We were at the far end of the dance floor when I heard a thud, shocked cries, and the clatter of silverware. Looking back, I saw Leo was on his feet, his chair turned over. I glanced at the Ardens, but they kept their eyes averted from the fracas—ostentatiously, I thought. Leo flung his napkin at Warburton. Then followed it with a glass, a tumbler that could have done real harm if Leo's pitching arm had been equal to his piano playing. It flew past Warburton's head to crash against the wall. Warburton seemed strangely exhilarated by the outburst, gazing at Leo as if the moment he'd been waiting for had finally come to pass.

Leo stormed out of the dining room. Startled out of her alcohol-laced nonchalance, Violet twisted uncertainly in her seat. Then leaping up, she followed her husband.

As the song came to an end, a round of applause went up for the Ardens. I smiled a thank-you at Rodolfo and was about to head back to the table when a drunken young man in evening dress whirled me into the next song. He was laughing his head off and I suspected he had asked me on a dare. I waited until he shouted something to another man, then blocked his foot with mine, causing him to trip and sprawl. Calling "I'm so sorry!" I hurried back to the table. But I stopped short as I saw Roland Harney staggering toward the swinging doors, a hand to his mouth. I switched direction, asking, "May I help you, Mr. Harney?" He waved me off.

Warburton's seat was now also empty. The Ardens were gone, Leo and Violet had disappeared, as had Nedda Fiske. And someone else, but as I looked at the deserted tables, I couldn't think who. I was about to ask what on earth the two men had fought about when Mrs. St. John beckoned me back over. Gesturing to the dance floor, she drawled, "Well, what was *that* like?"

"He's an actor," I said. "Or wants to be. Mrs. Tyler, I wonder if we shouldn't be going."

"Certainly pretty enough," said Blanche Arden as she rejoined us. "Where's the life of the party?"

She nodded to Nedda's empty chair. Louise said defensively, "She went to telephone home to see if Mr. Lombardo has returned."

"Mrs. Tyler, I really do think—"

A champagne cork—in the miasma of merriment, that was my first thought. Loud, explosive . . . no, far louder than a cork. Like the assaultive, nerve-jangling pop of firecrackers, supposedly so festive, but really quite unnerving because they sounded like gunshots. It put me in mind of the hell of those long shooting parties in Europe, the relentless crack of weaponry, the odd jolliness of the return, the carcasses piled high on the wagon.

"What was that?" said Louise.

We opened our mouths to supply reassurance. Car backfiring, slammed door. The band started playing again—yes, there had been a pause. But now, all was well. I felt my shoulders relax. Louise smiled and shook her head: so silly. Blanche asked Mrs. St. John if she'd been able to persuade Harriet about the lamé. Harriet, I realized, that's who was missing.

"Did Miss Biederman leave?" I asked.

"She did," said Louise. "She mentioned her fiancé. She seemed upset."

"He came by the theater once, such a brute." Blanche shuddered. "We'd gone late, and he was furious. I told her, 'Better to be screamed at by Sidney in English than that man in German.'"

I was about to express concern when I heard shouts coming from the end of the room, saw people hurrying at new speeds. A drunken bellow, "Shot! He's been shot . . . !" A strange ripple of laughter, it had to be a joke. Then the rumble of the truth rolling from waiter to waiter, overheard at tables, circling, leaping from group to group.

Louise touched the arm of a woman at the next table. "What are they saying?"

"They're saying someone's been shot."

Mrs. St. John made a noise of aristocratic disdain. "I'm sure it's just . . ."

But then Violet Tempest burst through the doors shrieking, "He's dead! Oh my God, he's dead!" And everyone began screaming.

6

Sidney Warburton had met his end on the toilet—that was the first ugly fact of the matter. Except for his killer, he had been alone at the time of the shooting. Amid the raucous frivolity of the diners and the clatter of the kitchen, the shot had not been immediately understood. It was minutes later when the next gentleman stepped into the lounge that the body was discovered. It was not hard to think that had this been a Sidney Warburton production, his death would have been staged in a more dignified way. Leo identified the body. Then asked if the producer's pants might be pulled up and the chain pulled down.

Those of us in Sidney Warburton's party had been gathered up and detained in one of the private dining rooms. We sat around a large, bare table. Someone brought us water. We were not told how long we might be there or what we were waiting for.

"Was it suicide?" asked a tearful Violet Hirschfeld.

"He was shot in the chest, ninny," said Blanche Arden.

"A person could shoot himself in the chest," argued Violet. "That's where the heart is."

A weary wave from Blanche indicated she would forgo the obvious joke about producers and lack of hearts. Leo gently informed his wife that the head was the traditional target.

"It's where the brains are," said Blanche. "Although there are exceptions." I marveled that she would expend the energy to be quite so spiteful to Violet. A leading lady's contempt for a chorus girl or something more personal?

"Perhaps now is not the time for insults," said Louise.

Denied their preferred form of communication, the group fell silent. An unconscious Mr. Harney had been deposited in a corner. Peanut lay between his feet. Nedda Fiske sat slumped in a chair, chin on her hand like a sullen student kept after school. Claude Arden on the other hand was agitated, sitting with elbows on the table, eyes on the door as he awaited the arrival of the police.

"This is intolerable," he said more than once. "Intolerable." His wife advised him to be quiet. He shot her an ugly look.

Adele St. John said, "Where on earth are the police?"

On cue, the door opened and an enormous man appeared. The more tactful "large" or unkind "fat" failed to do him justice. He was proudly, pointedly massive, belly straining at his tan overcoat with bombast as if he had added six inches to his girth since breakfast and wished to show it off. The sleeves were so tight about the arms I thought he must have to peel the coat from his body. A mere double chin was for amateurs, his was a treble, possibly quadruple. His cheeks had a perpetually stuffed look to them, the fullness of his face sinking his features in flesh, his mouth only noticeable by a bristling walrus mustache. His tiny, dark eyes took in the room, resting on each of us one at a time. Then he removed his hat with a flourish to reveal a gleaming pate spattered with a few strands of dark hair and announced himself as Detective Harrison J. Fullerton.

Instantly, our little band regained solidarity. Glances were exchanged: *This* was the famous Detective Fullerton? The terror of the Tenderloin, said to dispatch villains and reluctant witnesses with one blow from his mighty fist? The man who smashed the infamous ticket scalpers ring of 1909 and jailed a wily gang of pickpocket usherettes? In his waddling girth, he looked more enfant than terrible.

"A man is dead," he announced.

Shutting the door, he ambled into the center of the room and removed a small notebook from the tight confines of his coat pocket. "The deceased was one Sidney Warburton." He spoke with the deep wheeze of a church organ, which gave weight to every word, even as it suggested that word might be his last. "Mr. Warburton, I know, was a man of the theater. You were all his"—a pause to wetly inhale—"associates." Peanut cocked his head.

Leo stood to introduce himself, holding out a hand, which was not taken.

Detective Fullerton said, "I am told you argued with the deceased shortly before his demise."

"I did," said Leo.

"The subject of your . . . disagreement?"

"Work."

Even to my ears, this sounded evasive. Blanche Arden spoke up. "I assure you, Detective, it's very common for creative people to get passionate. What may look like a battle to some is just a healthy clearing of the air."

"Chairs were thrown," intoned the detective.

"Well, *a* chair," said Leo.

"And I would say toppled, rather than thrown," said Mrs. St. John.

"It just sort of fell over when he stood up," said Violet.

Seeing that Leo was protected by a web of feminine conspiracy, Detective Fullerton turned to a woman who had not spoken: Louise. He asked her name and she gave it as "Mrs. William Tyler." Then introduced me as her maid, "Miss Jane Prescott."

"Where were you when the shot was fired?"

"I was sitting at the table," whispered Louise.

"Did you witness the argument in question?"

"Not really." She kept her gaze averted from me. "Mr. Warburton had so many arguments with people, I didn't pay attention. Not to speak ill of the dead, of course."

"What Mrs. Tyler means," said Leo, "was that the deceased was a producer."

The detective turned to me. "And you, Miss Prescott? Did you hear anything of the argument?"

I confessed to being on the dance floor at the time. Rubbing his notebook between pudgy thumb and forefinger, Fullerton inquired, "Mrs. Tyler, was Mr. Hirschfeld at the table with you when you heard shots fired?"

Louise shrugged helplessly. "It was very crowded and very noisy."

This was true, but it was a poor excuse for not knowing whether someone was sitting two feet away from you. Fullerton let the silence stretch to make the point until Leo admitted, "I was upstairs. Warburt—Mr. Warburton keeps a room at the hotel. I . . . have a key."

Leo paused oddly before his confession concerning the key.

"Did anyone see you in this room?"

"Me," said Violet.

"And what was the reason you went upstairs to this room following your argument?" asked the detective.

". . . Personal," said Leo.

"Everything is personal, Mr. Hirschfeld."

"Husband and wife personal," said Violet. Who had the good grace to blush.

A ripple of irritation went through the room. The detective bunched his mouth. Unbunched his mouth. Then he turned to Mr. Harney. But before he could rouse the sleeping comic, Mrs. St. John said, "Mr. Harney was at the table the entire time, Detective. There's no point in delaying us all further by questioning him."

I glanced at her, unsure whether she was lying or mistaken. Mr. Harney had been rather dramatically unwell and it wasn't inconceivable that he would have lurched to the nearest men's room, say the one where Mr. Warburton had met his end. On the other hand, in his current condition, it seemed unlikely Harney could see straight, much less shoot straight. But he might have crossed paths with the killer. I wondered if there was a tactful way to inquire if anyone had seen a puddle of sick on the floor.

Swinging left, Detective Fullerton boomed, "Mr. Claude Arden!"

That gentleman had been sitting, head resting on clasped hands as if in prayer. Now he said, "Yes."

"Your whereabouts at the time of the shooting?"

"I was dancing with my wife." He extended a hand in Blanche's direction.

The Ardens had been dancing. But the burst of applause that greeted the end of their dance had come well before the shot rang out. Blanche had come back to the table. Claude had not.

"As a longtime associate of Mr. Warburton's, do you have any suspicions as to his killer?"

The Ardens looked at each other. "Well, he did run afoul of the Syndicate," said Claude.

"A group of men that controlled theater for many years," Mrs. St. John explained to Louise. "They owned most of the theaters. If you weren't with them, you simply couldn't get work. But Sidney bucked them by bringing actors to his side and won."

"We owe our careers to Sidney," Blanche chimed in. "But the Syndicate's all but died out. And I can't imagine Frohman or Klaw coming after Sidney with a gun."

The detective flipped through his notebook, then asked, "Was Mr. Warburton in financial difficulties?"

The Ardens looked surprised, Mrs. St. John intrigued. I recalled that heated conversation in Warburton's office. *What's the problem? Your investor getting cold feet? Or maybe they've had enough of the lies.* One article I had read suggested that his last show had been a failure, hence his eagerness to try something new. It raised the question: Where did Warburton's money come from? Who was this shadow investor? And what lies had he told them?

Then Leo said firmly, "The show is fine." He looked to the actors as he said it and I had the feeling it was reassurance for them, rather than information for the detective.

He added, "Detective, if you need financial details, I can arrange a meeting with Mr. Warburton's assistant, Miss Biederman. I'm sure she has all the documents you need."

Harriet, I thought. She would be devastated.

Then Detective Fullerton reached into his pocket with his handkerchief and took out a small pistol. At the sight of it, Nedda gasped. I knew nothing about guns, but even I could see it was a pretty thing. Small, easily concealed, with an engraved ivory handle and gold filigree on the barrel. It did not look like a serious weapon, although I had no doubt it could kill. It looked like a dandy's pistol, something for the man who prized style above all else . . .

"This was found on the floor of the washroom, not far from

Mr. Warburton's body. It is an unusual piece. Do any of you recognize it?"

No one answered.

"Anyone?" intoned the detective.

"Oh, for heaven's sake," Blanche said irritably. "We all know
whose it is."

Nedda Fiske sat up and fixed her with a hard stare.

"I'm sorry to point fingers at the guilty party, Nedda, but I'm
exhausted and I want to go home."

Mr. Arden joined his wife's cause. "Come now, it'll come out
sooner or later."

Mrs. St. John put a kind hand on the comic actress's arm.
"You can't protect him." Miss Fiske struck the hand away.

With a sigh, the detective said, "One of its more unusual features is an engraving. 'To Floyd . . .'"

Clapping a hand to her mouth, Nedda ran from the room.
There was unease as she left—ought we to stop her? But Detective Fullerton called to a policeman outside; Nedda was to be
detained, but treated kindly. Then he murmured, "Poor lady. Can
anyone tell me about the owner of this firearm?"

"Floyd Lombardo," said Claude Arden. "Also known as Lombardo LeRoi, also known as Nicholas Armisen, and Frederick
Rosenbaum. He's a gambler. With a singular talent for choosing
the lame animal."

"He is a lame animal," said Mrs. St. John.

"Does anyone know why Mr. Lombardo should wish to kill
Sidney Warburton?"

Leo answered. "Lombardo is a leech. He borrows, steals, owes
people money. He made himself a problem at the theater and
Warburton threw him out. Warburton also told Miss Fiske that
Lombardo had, uh, misbehaved himself, and that made her mad
at him. She was his only source of income, so I guess that left him

pretty desperate. Probably he thought with Sidney out of the way, she'd take him back."

"Does anyone know the man's address? Associates?" asked Fullerton.

"I believe there's a wife somewhere," said Claude. "Chicago, maybe."

"One in Florida as well," said Mrs. St. John.

"Ah, yes, Miss Orange Grove or some such."

Louise's eyes were enormous.

The killer identified, the exhausted group looked hopefully at the detective. Could we leave now? It felt selfish, but truthfully, what more needed to be said? Lombardo's gun had been found by the body. Certainly he had motive, although I wasn't sure how much was financial calculation and how much was revenge. He had not struck me as a thoughtful man, even in the best of circumstances. The swift decision, made on instinct, the grand gesture, bold action that risked all—that was his métier. Fortune favors the bold. With Louise's money in play, he must have felt the show would go on without Warburton. Probably he was well experienced in reducing Nedda to groveling by withholding affection and making her worry. How like him, I thought, to ruin his own ill-gotten chances by dropping the weapon at the scene.

I heard an odd bark, the rustle of clothes, and looked over to see that Roland Harney had emerged from the depths. For a moment, he gazed reproachfully at the group. "What's going on? Why are we here?"

"There's been a murder, Mr. Harney," said Louise. "I'm afraid Mr. Warburton has been shot."

"Shot?" Pouchy, bloodshot eyes darted around the room. "Which one of you bastards did it?"

7

"*Poor Miss Fiske*," lamented Louise as we made our way out of Rector's. "Do you think we ought to look for her? She shouldn't be alone at a time like this."

I was more concerned with getting Louise home than the heartache of Miss Fiske. Outside the club, we encountered a mass of reporters. At the sight of Louise, they pounced, shoving, shouting, desperate for a quote. I searched for any sight of the Ghost as I held tight to Louise and shouted, "Please, let us through. We don't know anything, please, just let us . . ."

Then I became aware of a body between us and the crush, heard a lower, kinder voice say, "Ladies," as we were redirected. I kept my head down and my feet moving as we maneuvered through the crowd. When the shouting had faded, and I could feel the warm breeze on my face, I looked to thank our deliverer and saw Michael Behan.

Louise was acquainted with Mr. Behan, having met him when

he visited me at her home following the death of George Rutherford. Sensitive to her anxieties, Mr. Behan had always been careful to show her the deference due a leading society matron, and he made a point of greeting her first.

To me, he said, "And the next time you're at a crime scene, for God's sake, make them take you out the side exit."

Then he smiled and I smiled back.

Louise thanked him for our rescue, then said, "You're not writing about Mr. Warburton's murder, are you?"

He reached for his notepad. "Well, I was writing about a shooting at Rector's. Now I gather I'm writing about Sidney Warburton's murder."

"Oh—please, Mr. Behan, could I beg you not to?"

"'Mr. Ragtime Musical Shot Dead'? The story's already out, Mrs. Tyler. Some of these fellows have waiters on the payroll."

Louise blinked. "That's terrible."

"A sign of the times," said Behan, raising his eyebrows at me, *Is she really that innocent?* I raised mine, *Yes, and let her be.*

Then I said, "But you won't mention Mrs. Tyler, will you?" I imagined Louise's mother-in-law reading the headline: MRS. WILLIAM TYLER FLEES RECTOR'S AFTER BROADWAY SLAY! No wonder Louise was nervous.

"No, Mrs. Tyler, I don't see any reason to bring you into it."

I smiled reassuringly, but Louise's brow was creased with worry. As the Ghost pulled up, she asked, "Mr. Behan, have you ever ridden in a Rolls-Royce?"

As it happened, Mr. Behan had not, but he settled in comfortably as Louise instructed Horst to take us on a scenic tour of Central Park. I perched on the jump seat opposite while she gave an account of her association with the deceased.

"So, you've invested some money in this show," said the reporter when she was done.

Louise bit her lip. "Quite a lot, actually."

Being tired, I allowed a small, shocked utterance to escape. Louise turned to me. "It's just I had no idea how expensive art can be. So much for the silk, a bit for new lights, a taxi home for the Ardens, well, you can't expect them to walk, steak for Peanut . . ."

Gin for his owner, I thought. Clearly, every member of the cast and crew had found a soft touch in their new patroness. This was just the sort of entanglement William had hoped I would help Louise avoid.

"And I *couldn't* leave poor Mr. Hirschfeld at the mercy of Sidney Warburton. It may have been his theater, but it was Mr. Hirschfeld's vision."

Behan's mouth quirked at the word "vision," but he nodded with appropriate solemnity.

"If you put Mr. Warburton being shot in a bathroom on the front page, it would hurt the show terribly."

"And there goes your investment."

"Yes, there goes my investment," she echoed.

Michael Behan let silence speak for him. He might like Louise Tyler, might feel some concern for my continued employment. But he had a baby on the way and his own employment to think about. A story had to be found.

"Perhaps," I suggested, "if you focused on the man suspected of shooting Mr. Warburton . . ."

"There's a suspect?" said Behan.

"There is. A ghastly man just drowning in scandal. In fact, it's a tragedy that such a distinguished man as Sidney Warburton—married with five children—should have his life ended by such a depraved character."

Behan glanced at Louise, a brief struggle between conscience, affection, and pragmatism playing out over his face. Happily, pragmatism and conscience came to an agreement, and he said, "Fine.

Warburton's an American treasure and the man who killed him a degenerate louse. And the man who killed him would be?"

"Floyd Lombardo," said Louise as Horst drew up in front of the Tyler home. "Why don't you come in for a cup of coffee, Mr. Behan? Jane can tell you all about him."

She glanced at the house where the first-floor light was on. William had waited up. I had a feeling she did not want me to hear what he had to say to her. Or she to him.

★ ★ ★

Michael Behan got his coffee. And a ham sandwich. Since I hadn't eaten all night, I got one, too. When we were seated at the kitchen table, he took an enormous bite, then asked, "How did you let a nice woman like Louise Tyler get mixed up in a bug-ridden disaster like this?"

"It's not a disaster," I said defensively.

"This show's been in trouble since the get-go. Warburton's a vaudeville huckster, he's got no business doing 'musical theater,' whatever that's supposed to be. The Ardens are a collective pain in the arse, Fiske certifiable. Their salaries probably put the costs sky-high, so Warburton tried to go cheap by using a composer no one's heard of. Then *he* drags in the wife of six months, the tempting Miss Tempest . . ."

Stung, I said, "Is that what the people call her?"

"So I'm told by those who know her least."

I bit into my sandwich with some savagery. "Well, it's Mrs. Hirschfeld now."

Behan examined me; I had the distinct feeling he was pondering the sum of two plus two.

"This composer—it wouldn't be the songwriter you were running around with last summer, would it? The one who needed a punch in the nose?"

"I said he *didn't* need a punch in the nose."

"What's your opinion these days?"

". . . Maybe a small punch."

Behan was quiet a long moment; a thought came to him and he jotted it down. Then planting a firm period on the page, he said, "That explains how Mrs. Tyler came to be in the exciting world of show business. Not to mention present at the scene of Sidney Warburton's murder. And on that subject . . . ?"

Taking a long sip of coffee, I said, "To be perfectly honest, I couldn't care less about Sidney Warburton's murder."

"Well, you might not care, but some of us have deadlines."

And others had investments. I couldn't imagine Louise had seriously endangered her vast fortune. But a financial disaster would not improve matters between husband and wife. And I didn't want Louise's first strike at purpose to end in failure.

"Floyd Lombardo?" Behan prompted.

"Floyd Lombardo is Nedda Fiske's . . ." I hesitated, disliking the melodramatic term "lover" but not sure what else to call him.

"Paramour?" suggested Behan. "Inamorato? Chum?"

"Millstone? Bad habit? He's a gambler. Owes people money. Married . . . possibly to more than one woman. She adores him, depends on him. She also pays his bills. Or did until recently. I overheard them fighting about it. He wanted money and she wouldn't give it to him. He sounded desperate."

"Why shoot Warburton?"

I told him the story of Floyd's banishment. "Lombardo's not a man to take insults lightly. And he probably thinks with Warburton out of the way, Nedda will weaken and take him back. They found his gun next to the body."

"You saw him at the restaurant?"

"No. But a place as big and crowded as Rector's, I could have easily missed him."

"Any idea who he owes money to?" I shook my head. "Know where he gambles? Cards or dice . . . ?"

"I've no idea. But please be sensitive to Miss Fiske. I can't help but feel sorry for her."

"And Mr. Hirschfeld, of course."

I recalled Leo's warning glance at Blanche and Violet's blushing confession. "Write what you like about Mr. Hirschfeld."

I asked if he wanted more coffee. He did. As I got up to get it, he composed headlines. "'Sidney Warburton, Lion of the Theater, Dies in Men's Toilet.'"

"Pants down, I'm afraid."

Eyes alight at that detail, he put pencil to paper, waiting for permission.

"Go ahead."

"You are a kind and noble woman, Miss Prescott."

Pouring more coffee, I inquired after Harry Knowles, a reporter who also worked at the *Herald*. Behan groaned. "The man can't write sober, can't write drunk; but there's a level in between where he's genius, and for some reason, I've decided it's my job to keep him there."

"That's good of you."

"Looking after Harry is good training for a father-to-be. He spits up. Throws tantrums. Been known to wet himself on occasion."

The mention of fatherhood reminded me. "Wait, I have something for you."

I had knitted Tib a pair of socks on the voyage back. Or tried to. Swelling seas hampered an effort already flawed by lack of skill. Still, I had produced something that could be put on a baby's foot. They were in my room, so I ran up the stairs, took the socks from my top drawer, and hurried back down to the kitchen.

They weren't wrapped, but I reasoned, better unwrapped than never.

Presenting the woolly bundles, I said, "For Tib. They're socks. I thought green went with either boy or girl and . . . Irish."

Michael Behan looked at the tiny tangles of wool, taking one in each hand with a bemused smile.

"Knitting might not be my forte," I confessed.

"No, they're . . ." Adjectives seemed to fail him. "I was just thinking of them on his feet. Or . . . her feet. The baby's." He looked up. "Thank you, this is very kind."

I smiled, pleased that he seemed pleased. Then it occurred to me that gifting his wife with socks made by a woman she had never met and likely never heard of might be awkward.

"If you want to say they're from someone at work . . ."

"No! No, of course I'll tell Maeve. She's a stickler for thank-you notes." I nodded in vague approval. "I can't believe you made something for him."

He held up one of the socks. "That's going to be on his foot. In two months. He'll be here and have feet. That need socks." He grinned, thrilled anew by the prospect of his child. Putting them in his pocket, he said, "And he'll have a fine pair."

"Or . . ."

"Or she will. And I'll . . ."

He paused and the pause became possibility. Then he nudged the socks deeper into his pocket with a brief smile and again said thank you. I said he was welcome. And that I hoped they fit.

I looked to the window to see the sky already lightening. Louise would not be rising anytime soon. But I didn't sleep well once the sun was up and I had two hours at best. Today would not be an easy day. Perhaps thinking the same, Behan said he should be going. I let him out the back door. He trundled down the steps, then turned.

"So, this show. You think it'll really open, dead producer and all?"

"Believe me, it'll take far more than a dead body to stop Leo Hirschfeld opening *Two Loves Have I*. Unless it's his own, of course."

8

"The show must go on" was first uttered in the last century during a circus performance in which the lion got the better of the tamer. In order to distract the audience from the blood in the hay and the arm that rested three feet from its former owner, the ringmaster shouted above the snarls of the still restive lion, "The show must go on!" Thus birthing the tradition that no matter what carnage transpires, entertainment will prevail.

This commitment to art—and the need for employment—brought Leo to the Tyler home a day later. He was admitted, given coffee, and obliged to repeat, "Yes, terrible," several times as Louise reminded him of the horrors of last night. I know this because the pictures that lined the wall of the staircase outside the living room were very dusty and required me to pause there for a lengthy period of time.

Finally, he said, "I am going to pay a call on Mrs. Warburton to express my condolences. I would be grateful if you would come with me, Mrs. Tyler."

"But I don't know her socially. Perhaps Mrs. Hirschfeld . . ."

"Violet has a headache. A terrible, terrible headache."

I smiled. The former Violet Tempest was not a personality suited to bereavement calls; soothing widows would not be her métier.

Soothing widows was not at the forefront of Leo's mind either. As he explained to Louise, "I'm afraid we have to persuade Mrs. Warburton that the best memorial to her husband would be the final show he worked on."

"Of course it would," said Louise.

"And that the show—this marvelous tribute to her husband— will not go on unless she consents to support it for just a bit longer . . ."

It took Louise a moment. "You're asking her for money."

"Yes, I am," he said fervently. "Also, that she doesn't throw us out of the theater. And I am hoping that as an investor, you will ask with me. Unless of course you're prepared to invest further—"

Louise made a noise of distress.

"—which I would not dream of asking you to do."

The subject having turned to money, voices were lowered and it was difficult to hear what was being said. But I could hear in the pitch of the murmurs—Louise's high and anxious, Leo's low and urgent—that Leo was winning his argument. This was confirmed when Louise opened the door and said she would be going out this afternoon and would I find something suitable for a bereavement call?

After lunch, as I buttoned a somber gray-and-lavender dress, she said, "Jane, I hate to ask, but would you come, too? I admire Mr. Hirschfeld greatly. But he's so desperate about the show, I'm worried he may say the wrong thing to poor Mrs. Warburton and I don't see how I could stop him. He'll listen to you, I think."

"Won't Mrs. Warburton think it odd, bringing your maid into her home?"

"She's theatrical, isn't she? I don't think they mind so much about those things."

* * *

On the drive over, Louise had a final qualm. It couldn't be right, could it? Discussing money with a grieving widow? "Her husband was just murdered, the poor woman must be devastated."

Leo said, "That is a reasonable assumption, Mrs. Tyler, but incorrect in this case. She liked being Mrs. Warburton. Sidney, she could take or leave."

Louise was right. Mrs. Warburton was theatrical. Also inconsolable. And she seemed to feel it fitting to express the second in terms of the first. If her feelings about her late husband were in any way ambivalent, it was not apparent. She received us in the parlor. Her mourning garb was the blackest of black, calling to mind famous widows such as Mrs. Lincoln and Queen Victoria. In the span of a few minutes, she made her way through as many handkerchiefs, casting the damp ones aside to be removed by a martyred-looking maid. At one point, having run through her supply, her hands fluttered, the display of grief hampered by a lack of props. Then Leo produced his own handkerchief and the weeping resumed.

The five little Warburtons were artfully arranged on a nearby settee in order of height, the baby in its bassinet on the far left. They were all dressed in black; even the bassinet bore a black ribbon. They gazed at their mother's distress as if used to it. For a while, we sat, with strained expressions, as Mrs. Warburton gathered the courage to speak. She seemed on the verge at several points, but then relapsed into tears. Her distress was infectious, at least to Louise, whose eyes brimmed as she suggested we return another time. The thought of losing her audience threw Mrs. Warburton into fresh paroxysms of anguish and all hope of escape was abandoned. Glancing at the clock, I thought it was possible we would not be home in time for dinner.

Leo was unfazed by the histrionics, patting Mrs. Warburton's hand and maintaining an expression of deep concern for longer than I would have thought him capable. He directed the maid to bring fresh handkerchiefs and a cup of tea (a wave of the finger suggested the addition of spirits), and threw around suitable Shakespeare—"We shall not see his like again," and so forth. Occasionally, he glanced at Louise to indicate *Not much longer.*

It was an awkward scene. Sitting in silence through so much noisy mourning became a strain. The first Warburton child pinched the second. The fourth slid its foot over the foot of the third and pressed down. The second dug vigorously in its nose. A sudden odor told us the baby had released its lunch, at which point, Leo called for the governess, who took the children upstairs.

Spotting a scrapbook open to a portrait of the man himself, Louise said, "Oh, Mrs. Warburton, may I look?"

Mrs. Warburton gulped. Then sat up. "It was my little hobby, keeping a record of Sidney's work for posterity. He's made so many careers, helped so many people. Given so much joy . . ."

Sifting through the pages with a reverent finger, Louise said, "Why, these are wonderful."

They were rather wonderful—photos, articles, and advertisements going back at least thirty years. One showed a young woman in tights sitting picturesquely on a motorbike, a banner over her head proclaiming, THE GIRL WHO FLIRTS WITH DEATH! The next was a dark gentleman billed as "The Egyptian Enigma" spewing flame into the air. Another showed a man in high collar and pomaded hair holding a duck. Louise, who loved animals, said, "Oh, how sweet."

"Yes, they sang together," said Mrs. Warburton.

Louise blinked, then pointed to a picture of three ladies standing with a large drum that bore the name "The Celebrated Cherry Sisters."

"What was their talent?"

"Nothing." Mrs. Warburton sniffed. "No, truly, nothing. They couldn't sing, couldn't dance, and they weren't funny. Sidney brought them to New York and billed them as the worst act in the world. Then he supplied the audience with rotten fruit and encouraged them to throw it at the stage. They sold out for ten straight weeks."

"That's a difficult way to make a living," said Louise.

"Sidney gave them their living," said Mrs. Warburton sharply. Then she sighed. "Oh, look, Mr. Warburton outside the Folly in Chicago. That's where we met, you know."

I looked at the picture, Mr. Warburton, his hair dark, surrounded by a full vaudeville troupe. It was a merry gathering: ladies in colored tights, tumblers with clown hats. The singer held his duck in his arms, a man in oversize shoes tipped a top hat. The musicians stood with their instruments, cello, trombone. My eye settled on a stout, serious man with a violin who, unlike the rest, refused to smile for the camera. There was something familiar in the shape of his face, but I could not place it.

Turning the page, Mrs. Warburton said, "And there's Zoltan the Mighty."

There he certainly was in a studio portrait that took up the entire page. An immensely muscled man holding his mighty arms aloft, his foot firmly fixed on an apathetic-looking lion. He wore nothing but laced sandals and the most minuscule of fig leaves. A clipping from a poster read, "The man who lifts train cars with his powerful pinky!"

"I saw him when I was a kid," said Leo. "Whatever happened to him?"

". . . Retired," said Mrs. Warburton, turning to a poster with several acts, one of which was a family group: father, mother, and two daughters with the largest hair bows I'd ever seen. Billed as "The Flying O'Briens," they were pictured grinning inanely as they flew, tumbled, and stood atop one another's shoulders. Opposite this was a photo of the Dancing Hollyhocks, "three lovely maids ready to dance into your heart."

Then Mrs. Warburton turned the page to reveal a poster of a dark-haired man striking a romantic pose. The headline read, HOW HE YEARNS FOR "SHE OF THE EMERALD EYES"!

Louise gasped. "That's Mr. Arden, isn't it?"

I said, "I suppose that was before he met Mrs. Arden," then worried I was not meant to speak.

But Mrs. Warburton took no offense. "Yes, it was Sidney who introduced them."

Recalling the lovely tale of eyes met across the footlights, I wondered how the producer had been involved. But maybe it was just habit for the Warburtons to take credit for things. *Romeo and Juliet? Yes, we introduced them. Such a shame how that turned out.*

It was another half hour before Mrs. Warburton turned to the final page, which was an image of Warburton and Leo shaking hands to celebrate their new partnership. Both men bent at the waist, heads meeting in the middle, one gray, one dark; whatever their feelings, they showed broad smiles to the camera. Behind them, the Ardens beamed. I was surprised not to see Violet or Nedda, but perhaps they had not yet been cast.

This gave Leo his opening. Taking her hand, he said, "It would be a tragedy if Sidney's legacy ended there."

"Sidney's legacy will never end! It will live on in his performers. They are his gift to the world . . ."

"Of course," said Leo, stemming the tide. "And if he had died in peace at home, that's just how people would remember him.

But he didn't. And you don't want his name linked to Floyd Lombardo's forever."

I could feel Louise holding her breath, nervous that Leo would mention the toilet. But the thought of shared billing had given Mrs. Warburton pause.

"If we could just keep the show going until it opens," said Leo.

"I know very little about business," she murmured. "You feel confident of its success?"

"Never more confident of anything in my life," he said, and I thought that that was probably true.

In the end, Mrs. Warburton agreed to continue supporting *Two Loves Have I* until opening night. There were conditions. The revenue breakdown between Leo and Warburton had been ridiculously uneven from the start. Now it was made more so. Also, Leo would write a song, an anthem in praise of her husband's generous pioneering spirit and the theater he loved. All royalties would be placed in trust for the five little Warburtons. So that they might remember their father.

★ ★ ★

Leo rode back with us to the Tyler house, full of praise for Louise's masterful handling of the conversation. "I knew it," he said. "I knew you would be the person to persuade her. Pulling out the scrapbook? Brilliant! If I'd been on my own, I would have botched it completely."

That had been Louise's concern and now she blushed as if found out. "Really, I don't see that I did anything much."

"No," said Leo. "You didn't *do* anything. You were simply yourself, that's why it worked, Mrs. Tyler."

I could see that the idea that she could be her natural self and accomplish things was heady stuff for Louise, as was Leo, ebullient and enraptured beside her. I was glad when we pulled up at the house and I could remind Louise she was due at the elderly Mrs. Ogilvie's for tea. Regretfully telling Horst she would go straight there, she let me and Leo out of the car. But she could not stop herself from asking when rehearsals would resume.

"Tomorrow," said Leo. "You'll be there, won't you?"

"Of course," she said with new certainty, and the Ghost rolled down the block.

Leaving me on the street with Leo.

As far as I was concerned, it had been a day of crying, lying, and nose-picking; I was not in the mood for further challenge. With a short, "Good day, Mr. Hirschfeld," I headed toward the back door.

"Well, at least now you're talking to me."

Angry to be accused of sulking—and unsettled by the car ride—I snapped, "I talk to you, Leo."

For a moment, I wrestled: dignity versus fury. Fury won. "But perhaps you don't hear me because I'm not wiggling down a staircase showing my rump to all and sundry." He opened his mouth; a compliment was coming. I shouted over him, "Something that, strangely enough, in all my years of domestic service, I have never once seen a maid do. Not even in France."

Seeing I couldn't be charmed, he opted for, "That was Vi's act before the show."

"Yes, I see why you married her. It's all quite . . . obvious."

"Don't discount the obvious. The obvious is pretty powerful stuff."

The shot landed, making me feel tired and hopeless. If it was all about that—and only that—why bother talking? I turned back toward the house.

"As you well know," he added.

Wheeling back around, I said, "Do you know what else is *obvious*?

That despite Miss Tempest's—excuse me, Mrs. Hirschfeld's—abundant charms, they're not enough."

"What are you talking about?"

"Forsaking all others, isn't that somewhere in the vows? For a year at least? I would have thought you could manage that."

Leo kept smiling. But his neck and ears went red. Usually, I liked being right. Now it gave me no pleasure at all.

"Just don't be a complete idiot and let her husband find out."

"Husband?"

He had not contradicted my charge that he had already wandered, but his confusion sounded genuine. Then again, I reminded myself, Leo said many things that sounded genuine, only to forget them when it suited. Given the peril the show already faced, a public affair with his leading lady, when his wife and her husband were also in the show, would not help matters. A betrayed Violet Tempest could be noisy, and she had friends in the press. And the prickly Claude Arden would not welcome the humiliation of having his wife's affair with an energetic young composer become common knowledge.

Nor, it occurred to me, would he welcome the knowledge that it was an affair and not just flirting. Some husbands were sanguine about infidelities. Mr. Arden didn't strike me as one of them.

"Anyway," Leo said with a bit of his old insouciance, "it's nice to know you care."

"I care"—I emphasized the point by giving him a sharp shove—"because you're spending Mrs. Tyler's money. That means your success is her success. And I will treat anything that threatens that success, including and especially stupidity on your part, in the harshest possible manner."

Going inside, I regretted I had not shoved Leo harder. My shoulders were agitated, my hands humming; I felt the need to do something. The word "care" jangled in my mind, discomfiting and accusatory. I thought of Louise's happy, eager face, Leo's red ears, my own snappishness. I had talked too much, said too much. And yet, I still felt the need to talk, talk, talk . . .

Quickly, I took up the telephone and asked to be connected to the number for Anna's family's restaurant. It was not time for the dinner rush, but her uncle sounded harried and so I kept my message short.

"Please ask Anna to call me. Tell her I'm sorry—she'll know why. I think. Only . . . please ask her to call. I need . . ."

I meant to say, I need to talk to her. But nervous and not wanting to keep her uncle, I finished, "I need her. Please tell her. Thank you."

The next day, rehearsals resumed under Leo's direction. It was important, he said, that the press see that the show was in no danger and that while "of course no one can ever replace Sidney," he was now firmly in charge. *Two Loves Have I* would open on schedule. Sensitive to Nedda Fiske's particular predicament, he gave her the first few days off, rehearsing instead the guest acts, mostly vaudeville stars who would be performing well-honed routines to presumably rapturous applause. Junie Nichols rolled out her comic bit of Baby WahWah, the juvenile relative of Nedda's character who ruins one date. Horrocks and Whey did their routine of two drunks whose shoelaces become entangled. And Bill Davidson played a waiter who "learned" the cakewalk by watching the Ardens dance.

I was happy to see Harriet Biederman in her customary spot in the second row—and concerned. She would have taken Sidney Warburton's death harder than anyone; I wanted to be sure someone had assured her of employment as long as she wanted it.

"How are you, Miss Biederman?"

She looked up, startled to be addressed. "Oh, Miss Prescott. I am sad. Like everyone. But . . ."

She gestured to the stage as if to say, *This is still here, what else matters?*

I asked if someone had spoken to her about work, and she answered, "Yes, Mr. Hirschfeld was very kind. He says I can work right up to the wedding." Her eyebrows jumped in imitation of Leo. "'And after! During, even!'"

"I'm so sorry. I know you held Mr. Warburton in high esteem. At least . . ." I groped for comfort. "You were not there when it happened."

Her smile dimmed. "I am very upset with myself for leaving. It was kind of Mr. Warburton to ask me to such an important dinner. To run out like that was disgraceful."

"You're being hard on yourself. I'm sure you had a reason."

She glanced at me, cheeks showing high color. "I thought so at the time, but it was not a good reason. I should have stayed and not been such a child."

Puzzled, I tried to feel out the source of her embarrassment. If she had left to please her bullying fiancé, would she call that childish? It seemed proper—wrongheaded, but proper. Perhaps something had offended her? There had been a fair amount of bad behavior at the table that night.

That phrase—bad behavior—reminded me: it was time to seek out and remove Mr. Harney's bottles. I said as much to Miss Biederman, adding, "It seems cruel somehow. Especially after Mr. Warburton's death. I feel I should leave him his comfort."

"If people cannot give up things that are dangerous to them, you take those things away." She met my eye as if to reassure me. "It's for his own good."

Then Leo called, "Did you get that change, Miss Biederman?"

Caught, she riffled through the notebook, coming to a fresh page so she could take down the new staging. I withdrew.

When I came to Mr. Harney's first hiding spot—behind the fire bucket, stage left—I found the bottle untouched and the comic chatting with Mr. Davidson, Peanut in the crook of his arm like a stuffed toy. Unlike the rest of the cast, Mr. Harney wore a black armband. This reminded me of his growling accusation. *Which one of you bastards did it?* His first thought had not been to accuse Floyd Lombardo, but one of his own colleagues.

Harney murmured compliments, Davidson condolences. The two men shook hands and parted. Thinking of the scrapbook, all those performers who owed Warburton their careers, I asked, "Did Mr. Davidson know Mr. Warburton?"

"Of course. Anyone who joked, sang, danced, or self-immolated onstage knew Sidney Warburton."

"Not everyone mourns him, though."

"No. Maybe they should, maybe they shouldn't, it's not my place to say. But there are some"—he nodded to the Ardens, now taking their place onstage—"who'd be digging ditches and scrubbing floors were it not for him. Sidney Warburton deserved far better than to meet his end at the hands of Floyd Lombardo."

Curious that he now acknowledged Lombardo's guilt, I said, "You asked which of us had done it, the night he was shot."

"I was drunk the night he was shot. Perhaps you noticed."

There was no disputing that. "I feel so sorry for Miss Fiske."

A heavy sigh. "Nedda Fiske, now there's a woman of genuine talent—and all the madness that goes with it. What she'll do when they catch Lombardo, I don't know. They'll give him the chair and that could be the end of her."

No sooner had he said Nedda's name than we heard it echoed by Leo in a tone that drew us out from the wings. Blanche and Claude had been dancing. Now the music came to an abrupt halt.

I watched as Nedda Fiske made her way down the aisle. Blanche broke away to say, "Nedda, what's wrong?"

This surprised me; Blanche Arden was not one to notice—or care much—about the suffering of others. But then looking at Nedda Fiske, I realized you would have to be blind not to notice and made of stone not to care. Her wonderfully comic mouth, usually so animated, was slack. Her hair was roughly put up and coarse from lack of care. Her face was heavy, eyes shadowed and staring. Normally, she was a stylish dresser whose witty fashion sense transformed her homeliness into what the French called jolie laide. But her clothes were not only drab, they were none too clean. Her coat was buttoned wrong, the heel of one shoe broken. Adele St. John would later say she looked like a dustwoman who'd gotten lost on her way to drown herself.

Now she stopped halfway down the aisle. "I just thought . . ."

She broke off as if she'd forgotten what she'd thought. Or that she could think. It occurred to me that she might be drunk.

Tentative, Louise said, "You don't look well, Miss Fiske. Please, take my car. Go home and get some rest."

"I don't want to go home."

From the stage, Claude Arden called, "If Floyd turns up, you'll want to be there for him, won't you? He'll need you, Nedda . . ."

"Floyd's not coming home."

"Nonsense," said Blanche. "He'll run back to you just as he always has."

"He won't," said Nedda, anguish seeping into her voice like acid. "He can't."

Her face began to crumble, her fists rising as she said again, "He can't." She repeated the phrase over and over. Then she struck herself, tore at her hair. Falling to her knees, she wailed, "He can't, he can't . . ." until grief became so great she could no longer form words. Leo ran over and tried to gather her up, but she beat him off, clawing at her face and wrists, desperate to do herself damage. Hurrying down the steps, I took hold of one flailing arm, catching a blow to the jaw in the process. Claude Arden took the other arm, and the three of us managed to subdue her. Prone, she twisted in our grasp, her back arching with each wracked "ah" of despair.

The doctor was called.

9

Floyd Lombardo had been pulled from the river. The police could not say how long he had been there—or how he had gotten there in the first place. That grisly determination would be made by the coroner at Bellevue.

The particular timing of Floyd Lombardo's demise weighed on my mind long past the hour I was dismissed. I pondered it on my bed, staring up at the ceiling, so lost in thought that I jumped when Ethel the parlormaid knocked on my door to say I had a telephone call.

"It's a gentleman," she said with a coy smile.

I took the call in the kitchen where the servants' phone was kept. It was late and Mrs. Avery had gone home. For a moment, I thought of turning on the lights, but there was a summer moon and so I left them off and settled myself on a stool by the phone.

It was a gentleman, a very tired-sounding gentleman by the name of Michael Behan. He was still at the *Herald*, writing up the latest on Mr. Lombardo, and wished to know: Had I just eaten dinner?

"No, why?"

"Because I heard from my friend at the morgue."

"And?"

"Lombardo was shot in the gut, which is a nasty way to go. The body was in a certain condition that indicates it had been in the water quite some time."

"How can they tell?"

"When they pulled him out, he was missing a few things. And when they cut him open, he was pretty ripe."

I pressed the phone to my stomach, inhaled. "It is summer."

"It is. Only—are you *sure* you want to hear this?"

"I'd like to know when he died and I'd like to be certain. So, go ahead."

"His skin was coming off him. That only happens after a few weeks."

The briefest vision of that vain, dapper man, his skin sagging off him like fat off a boiled ham. I swallowed sharply, called forth thoughts of meadow. Daisies. Birdsong.

"I see."

"I hope you don't, frankly. But tomorrow the city finds out Floyd Lombardo didn't kill Warburton. And that in fact someone killed Floyd Lombardo. The police know he owed money all over town. They're going on the assumption that one of his backers realized he had lost his main source of income in Miss Fiske and decided to be shot of him. I'm sorry, that was tasteless."

I reminded him we had started the conversation with the effects of water on dead bodies; taste was beside the point.

My mind went back to Nedda's fretting over Floyd's absence. *He hasn't been home in days.* Good riddance, we all thought about a man who might have been dead in the river as we smirked. How soon after his banishment from Nedda's life had Floyd Lombardo been killed? The question tugged at me, but before I could think why, Behan asked, "How is Miss Fiske?"

"Brokenhearted," I said. "Please don't put that in the newspaper."

"Come on, everyone knew she was running around with Lombardo."

"Leave her with some dignity, that's all I'm asking."

"This would be a woman who clutched a man's legs to be pulled across the stage?"

That had been one of Miss Fiske's signature acts at the Follies. How funny, I thought, onstage, she mocked the devotion she felt so deeply in real life. There were worse ways of managing, I supposed.

"I hear she's at home, under a doctor's care. Is she coming back to the show?" Like a dog, he had his nose to the ground, fixed on a new scent: the collapse of Sidney Warburton's last production.

"Remember Mrs. Tyler."

"You've now got two dead bodies and a missing star. Those who care for Mrs. Tyler might advise her to cut her losses and invest in swampland."

"Remarkably, she doesn't pay me for financial advice." Hearing the clock in the hall chime midnight, I asked, "Why aren't you at home?"

He sighed. "For a lump, Tib has remarkably refined tastes. His requirements are many and expensive. Hence old Dad, who gets paid by the article, is churning out the verbiage. Maeve's mother always thought Maeve made the mistake of her life marrying a grubby reporter. So, with Tib on the way, she's keeping a sharp eye on my ability to provide."

"Who was she supposed to marry?"

"Oh, there's an answer to that: Dermot Mulcahy, dentist of renown. You ask my mother-in-law, she'll be only too happy to tell you. He courted Maeve for years; she was all set to be Mrs. Dentist. Then I showed up."

Someone had once called Maeve Behan the most beautiful woman at St. John's parish and Michael Behan had not disagreed. It was a love match then. A defiant one. Maeve Behan had a chance to marry for money and had chosen love instead. And Michael Behan had persuaded her, because . . .

A vague comforting notion I had not even known I clung to disintegrated and fell away, leaving me with an empty feeling.

"Not to mention, poor Maeve's at the point where sleep is a distant memory and it's hot enough without me in the bed."

At the mention of the marital bed, I toyed with the phone cord.

He asked, "Just in case Miss Fiske doesn't return, what happens then?"

That decision had been made at the end of the day after a tense conference between the principals. "The world sees a whole new side of Violet Tempest."

"Really? And how is this new side of Jelly on Pins?"

Nervous, was my first thought. The news that Violet would replace Nedda as the factory girl had not been well received. The Ardens had demanded that the part should be cut altogether. Any one of the vaudevillians could fill the time. It had been one thing to expand the show to accommodate a star like Nedda Fiske. But now that she was gone . . . well, time to let the Darling Ardens take over. It would be madness to trust a buxom chorus girl with such an important part. Perhaps it was my imagination, but Blanche had seemed particularly annoyed by Leo's advancement of his wife.

Faced with such hostility and the prospect of doing more than descending and bending, Violet had been anxious. After the announcement, I overheard her ask Leo if he was sure. When he said yes, she said, "No, I mean really sure. With the singing." If he had a reassuring answer to that, I had not heard it.

The Ardens had won one concession. As the French maid was now consigned to oblivion, Claude Arden would sing "Why Not Me?"

"Enchanting," I said. "And on that, you may quote me."

"'Source closely connected to the production says, 'Enchanting, world to see Violet Tempest a whole new way. With actual clothes on.'"

I laughed. "Leave it at 'enchanting,' please." There, I had done Violet Hirschfeld a favor. I was not a jealous shrew in the slightest.

Then Behan asked the question I had hoped he would not: "So, if Floyd Lombardo didn't kill Warburton—who did?"

Images flitted through my mind. The eager faces that had greeted the stars on their arrival, even Leo, dressed as one of them, accepted as one of them. The handsome brunette, so breathy in her admiration. Excited whispers of Owney Davis's presence. The whirl and hubbub of the dance floor—why had that young man come to our table? The raging ragged lunatic who had accosted us outside the revolving door . . .

"It was a crowded restaurant, Mr. Behan. Full of people who knew Mr. Warburton and more than a few who had reason to hate him."

"But they found Lombardo's gun at the scene."

Lombardo's gun. I'd forgotten Lombardo's gun. Petulant, I made excuses. It was late, I was tired. Lombardo's gun—what did it matter?

Except if Lombardo was already in the river by that time, he could not have shot the gun—much less dropped it at the scene.

I need it, Nedda!

And I'm telling you, I don't have it!

That argument with Nedda Fiske. At the time, I thought he wanted money. But perhaps it was the gun? Lombardo owed money to impatient people. He felt a need for protection. And when that protection went missing, he had gone directly to Nedda.

Who had said she didn't have it.

A thought curled into being. I snuffed it out. Nedda Fiske had been heartbroken when Lombardo's body was found. Truly, genuinely . . .

Although she was an actress.

Not that good an actress. No one was.

I looked at the facts plainly: the person who shot Sidney Warburton had used Floyd's gun to do it. Meaning whoever it was had known both men.

I tried to reason a way out of the ugly implications. Lombardo could have dropped the gun on the street, had it stolen at a gambling den. Someone had mentioned a Syndicate, powerful financial interests who had reason to hate Sidney Warburton. It didn't *have* to be someone involved with *Two Loves Have I* . . .

"Thoughts, Miss Prescott?"

"Not at this time, Mr. Behan."

"Ah, remember when there were no secrets between us?"

Because it was late, he had slipped into his old teasing tone, the lazy charm that had no doubt gotten many a waitress, hatcheck girl, and yes, maid, to tell him stories. All in fun, just a joke, only he never quite got around to mentioning he was married. In fact, he had never told me directly; I had overheard him talking to his wife on the phone.

Something in the silence told me he had also heard the lapse— and regretted it. Which was to his credit.

Still I said, "No, I don't remember that. Good night, Mr. Behan."

★ ★ ★

I went to bed late and slept poorly, waking the next morning muddleheaded and irritable. After breakfast, I lingered in the kitchen with William's discarded newspaper. Detective Fullerton was careful in what he'd told the press. As a result, Warburton's death had been overshadowed by the gaudy slaying of Mrs. Lulu Bailey. At first, there had been some question as to who had shot Mrs. Bailey: it was either Dr. Carman, whom she visited after hours for an impromptu examination, or the doctor's wife, Florence, who had hidden a Dictaphone in his office, because she did not trust him with female patients.

I was wondering why Mrs. Carman had killed Mrs. Bailey since it was her husband who needed shooting when the doorbell rang. I couldn't think who would call at this hour and listened as Ethel answered the door. Hearing the wet, wheezing voice of Detective Fullerton, my heart sank.

He apologized for calling so early and asked Louise if she would prefer that her husband were present. Louise said she preferred her husband absent. Then amended it to say that in general, she enjoyed his company. But when police were investigating her connection to dead people, she liked him out of the house.

She did ask if I might be present. Detective Fullerton said he had been about to suggest that very thing.

Louise sat in her preferred chair by the front window. I stood behind her. The detective settled his bulk on the settee. Then he informed Louise that Floyd Lombardo was no longer a suspect. The police would now focus their inquiries on people who had been at Rector's that evening, especially those in the company of the deceased. *She,* he assured Louise, was not under suspicion. "Several witnesses have testified that you were seated at the table for the entirety of the evening."

He turned to me. "You, on the other hand, Miss Prescott, were not."

Louise said, "Jane was dancing, Detective. A very handsome young man invited her, and I couldn't ask her to refuse. She was in my sights the whole time, I assure you."

"Name . . . of this young man?"

"He said his name was Rodolfo," I said. "He worked at Rector's."

"Worked there?" Louise looked puzzled. I gave a brief smile to indicate this was one of life's realities I would explain in private.

"How well did you know the deceased, Miss Prescott?"

"Not well. Mr. Warburton didn't even consider me worth shouting at."

"I understand he shouted a great deal at . . . Mr. Hirschfeld. And that Mr. Hirschfeld shouted at him. In fact, they were shouting on the night in question."

Louise looked at me; I wished she wouldn't. It made us look conspiratorial.

"Mrs. Tyler, if you were at the table the entire evening, able to see your maid as she danced, then you must have heard the argument. What were the two gentlemen fighting about?"

Louise took a deep breath. "I believe there was a disagreement about the show. Really, Detective, it was almost trivial. Who would sing certain songs, things like that."

"'Sing certain songs,'" he repeated.

"Yes."

"Mrs. Tyler, are you aware that songwriters now make considerable money when their songs are recorded for phonograph?" Louise was not. "Then you are no doubt also unaware that the credit for the song dictates who receives the revenue? And that if a famous singer, such as Mr. Arden, say, consents to record the song, he may be credited along with the author? In recognition of the fact that the public is drawn to the recording for the sake of his voice, rather than the composer's words?"

Leo's earlier refusal to let Claude Arden sing "Why Not Me?" now made a great deal more sense.

The detective continued. "If a performer is well known, he may abuse the situation, taking more than his fair share of the profit—at least in the writer's eyes. I have been informed that there was a certain amount of ill will regarding Mr. Arden's recording of Mr. Hirschfeld's song, 'But on Fridays.' And that Mr. Warburton was the man who arranged for Mr. Arden to sing it."

And taken his own share for his troubles, I thought, remembering Leo's angry accusation: *I saw exactly what he did. And how much you and he made off it.*

"So, you see, Mrs. Tyler, arguments over who sings a song are not in the least trivial, amounting to significant revenue for the man who wins the argument. Was that the point of dispute the other night?"

"Oh, heavens, Detective, I don't listen to talk about business. I believe I was discussing clothes with Mrs. St. John." She smiled, inviting the detective to draw the conclusion that once a woman's mind was focused on clothes, all other concerns vanished. To his credit, Fullerton did not seem persuaded.

"You have no idea, then, why Mr. Hirschfeld threw a glass at Mr. Warburton?"

At heart, Louise was not a liar. Now she admitted, "I'm afraid that Mr. Warburton was insulting to Mrs. Hirschfeld."

This I had not heard and I glanced sharply at Louise. Fullerton inclined his belly forward. "How was he insulting, Mrs. Tyler?"

Louise went red. "I couldn't say."

"You didn't hear the words?"

"I heard them. I just can't repeat them."

"Perhaps you might whisper them to your maid. Then she can tell me."

Louise whispered. I listened. Then reported the substance, which roughly interpreted, likened Mrs. Hirschfeld to a bicycle that has gone flat from too many rides from too many owners.

"You can see why Mr. Hirschfeld took offense," said Louise.

For almost any man, the answer would have been a simple yes. But I had to wonder, would Leo take such umbrage at having his

wife's reputation attacked? The Leo I knew might not. He himself had ridden many a bicycle . . . or was he the bicycle? If so, I
had also ridden a borrowed bicycle—and was perhaps a tiny bit
borrowed myself. Which begged the question: Why was Violet
Tempest a bicycle and Leo not? Or if both were bicycles, why did
many riders make him seem carefree and dashing and her used
and worthless?

More to the point, did I believe Leo had stormed off because
Mr. Warburton implied that Violet Tempest hadn't been pure
before marrying him?

Not in the slightest.

So why had Leo stormed off?

Then the detective asked a rather interesting question. "Did
Mrs. Hirschfeld take offense?"

"Mrs. Hirschfeld was incapacitated," said Louise bluntly. "I
doubt she heard a word that was said."

"Do you know what led Mr. Warburton to insult Mrs. Hirschfeld?"

Louise frowned as she considered. "I don't. I was talking with
Mrs. St. John at the other end of the table and watching for Jane.
I only heard the bicycle part because it was so shocking. But you
must know by now, Sidney Warburton was a deeply unkind man.
He said all sorts of horrible things to people. Just ask his poor sec-
retary, Miss Biederman."

"By all accounts, Miss Biederman had left the restaurant by
the time the argument occurred," said the detective. "So, his wife
having been insulted, Mr. Hirschfeld threw the glass and left the
table?"

"Yes."

"His wife followed?"

Louise nodded. "I believe she went and found her husband—"

This brought us all to the memory of what Leo and Violet had been doing at the time of the murder. Louise asked the detective if he would like some more tea. The detective said that he would.

As I poured, Louise said, "Detective, you can't suspect Mr. Hirschfeld. It seems far more likely to me that some business associate of Mr. Warburton's committed the crime. Someone he'd treated badly or who had a grudge against him."

"Mr. Hirschfeld is a business associate of his."

Swiftly changing tack, Louise said, "We should ask Jane. She's known Mr. Hirschfeld longer, and she notices a great deal. You remember last year, those women who were murdered? Jane figured out who the killer was, even before the police did."

Fullerton smiled politely, not believing a word of this. Still he asked me, "What is your opinion of the relationship between Mr. Hirschfeld and the deceased?"

I took my time. "They did argue. But there is nothing on earth Mr. Hirschfeld cares about more than this show. Mr. Warburton was producing that show. I can't imagine anything that would provoke Mr. Hirschfeld enough to jeopardize that."

Detective Fullerton chewed on his mustache. "But of course, Mrs. Tyler is also financially involved."

Louise and I both blinked. She said, "Not to the extent that Mr. Hirschfeld could dispose of Mr. Warburton, I assure you."

"Also," I said quickly, "one of the first things Mr. Hirschfeld did after the murder was visit Mrs. Warburton to make sure . . ."

I had meant to underscore the importance of the Warburtons' financial support. Instead I had made Leo sound like a ghoul who bilked widows of their savings.

". . . that the family would continue to fund the show?" the detective said.

Recovering, I said, "Yes, but he wouldn't have done that if he'd shot Mr. Warburton in order to be free of his influence."

"Did the widow seem keenly interested in theater? The sort of person to give Mr. Hirschfeld advice?"

Louise and I glanced at each other. The question had to be answered honestly; Mrs. Warburton's interest in anything beyond the parameters of that couch and her bank account were minimal. "She does want a song in tribute to her husband," offered Louise.

"I see." Placing his hands on his vast thighs as if to signal to them that it was time to go, the detective rose.

Rising with him, Louise said, "Detective, listen to Mr. Hirschfeld's songs. Listen to 'Why Not Me?' The man who wrote that song isn't capable of killing anyone."

For all his reputation as a brute enforcer of the law, Detective Fullerton was not the sort to disabuse a lady of the notion that people who create beautiful things are incapable of ugly acts. Presenting her with his card, he said he hoped she was right, and should anything else occur to her, she should contact him at this number. Louise passed the card to me and said she would do exactly that.

I saw the detective out, then returned to the sitting room to find Louise pacing. Fist clenched in the other hand, she said, "We have to go back to Rector's."

"Why?"

"The detective thinks Mr. Hirschfeld murdered Mr. Warburton. We have to find someone who saw something that . . . points him in a different direction. A man like Sidney Warburton must have a hundred enemies. Mr. Hirschfeld told me in confidence that he'd been very difficult about money lately. Apparently, his last show was not a success. If Mr. Lombardo borrowed money from disreputable people, perhaps Mr. Warburton did, too."

And met with the same fate—the idea hung in the air between us.

"That fellow you danced with, maybe he saw Mr. Warburton there other times. Maybe he knows about other people who would have wanted to . . ."

Louise swallowed over the words "kill him." Then said, "Do you think he would be there now?"

Rodolfo's busiest time would be the evenings, especially the after-theater crowd. But Rector's also offered afternoon thé dansants or tango teas at which ladies could frolic without escort during the hours when their husbands were at work—a profitable opportunity for a tango pirate.

"He might this afternoon," I said reluctantly.

"Then we'll go this afternoon. You danced with him, he'll remember you. And I don't dare go alone."

I held back a groan. From what Michael Behan said, the busboys at Rector's did a nice side business in selling gossip to the papers. The story of Mrs. William Tyler chatting with a taxi dancer would send thrills of approbation through New York society.

"Mrs. Tyler, if Mr. Hirschfeld didn't kill Mr. Warburton, the police won't find any evidence that he did. His wife gave him a very memorable alibi. I think we should just let things proceed . . ."

"I know he hurt you."

"He didn't hurt me, Mrs. Tyler."

"But you must care a little about his work. After all, he wrote 'But on Fridays' for you."

Had Louise Tyler been Anna, I would have laughed. Laughed and said, *Yes, and he wrote "But on Mondays" for the ticket taker at the Odeon and "But on Thursdays" for his uncle Hesh's secretary.* Most likely, there was a drawer full of songs "written for" girls all over the city and possibly New Jersey.

But Louise Tyler was not Anna and thinking of "But on Fridays" took me back to Leo's visit last year when I had been badly bruised and frightened and he had burst into my room with promises of Delmonico's and dancing and reminded me that I was alive and life had many wonderful things to offer. He was good at that, reminding you what life had to offer. His songs did it, too, full of his greedy, eager spirit that said, Why not? *Why not?*

And even if he said why not too often and not always wisely, he hadn't killed Sidney Warburton and he didn't deserve that cloud hanging over his first show.

Still—there was one last concern. "Mr. Tyler will be home at five thirty. What will you tell him if we don't get back in time?"

Louise turned her ring round her finger. "After Rector's, we'll stop off at Lord & Taylor. That way I can say I was shopping and I won't have lied."

For some reason, her words brought back Leo's proud boast that *Mother Hirschfeld never lies. I hear her son takes after her.* To which I had always said, *Omits.*

Louise, it seemed, had learned to omit.

10

On the ride over, Louise was full of plans, all of which involved the word "you" to an alarming degree. "Now, when you find him, maybe you shouldn't ask about Mr. Warburton right away. Instead, you . . ."

"Mrs. Tyler, the gentleman isn't going to have any interest in speaking with me."

"You mean, he'll only want to dance?"

I took a deep breath. "No. I mean he'll only be interested in engaging with a lady who can pay him."

Louise went still. "By engaging, you mean . . ."

"Talking. Dancing. Lighting her cigarette." I widened my eyes to indicate metaphor.

"Heavens, I don't smoke," said Louise.

Despite Louise's aversion to nicotine and innuendo, Rodolfo managed to spot us in short order and make his silky way to our table. A brief glance between the two of us; which was the customer? But when Louise said, "How lovely to see you again," he gave her his full professional attention.

"Such excitement the other day," she said when he had sat.

"This day for me is already far more exciting."

Had the young man not been so beautiful, this statement would have provoked giggles. But there was something about his almond-eyed gaze, the way he held his mouth, even the elongated posture that seemed to offer his body for intimate perusal, that made one intensely aware of the many and varied meanings of the word "exciting." Louise looked as if someone had just offered her a cigarette—and she was no longer certain she didn't smoke.

For the sake of discretion, I wanted as few words as possible exchanged between Louise and Rodolfo. Therefore, I would ask the questions. I began with, "Have the police spoken with you?"

With minimal movement, Rodolfo's bearing indicated he was no longer open for business. The chair did not shift, but it felt as if he had put a distance of several feet between himself and us. As if I were smoothing the tablecloth, I slid a five-dollar bill under the napkin nearest him. His shoulders relaxed, his lips parted, his eyes did a strange sort of . . . smoky lingering. Placing a well-manicured finger on the bill, he tucked the rest of it under the napkin with a small, serene smile.

"My employer has an interest in discovering who killed Mr. Warburton," I told him.

"We all do, it is a loss to the world . . ."

"It's financial loss she's concerned with." Louise was embarrassed, but I sensed we were on the clock and I didn't want her money wasted on continental dramatics. "You knew who Warburton was. He'd been here before."

"Of course, he often came."

"With people."

He nodded. "Always, he has many guests, as he did that night. Many people wanting to talk to him."

Louise leaned forward. "What sort of people?"

Rodolfo made his living by pleasing. He could sense Louise wanted a particular answer, but was unsure as to what it was. He began by guessing. "Theater people. Businesspeople. Rich people . . ."

"There are all sorts of rich people these days," I said. "Did these people make their money legally?" I was careful not to bandy the name Owney Davis.

"I could not say."

"Perhaps they lent money to Mr. Warburton," Louise suggested. "Perhaps they—"

Before she could pronounce Sidney Warburton and Floyd Lombardo the victims of criminal assassination by loan sharks, I shook my head.

But Rodolfo understood her meaning. Idly turning over a heavy silver knife, he said, "Forgive me. I thought the police already knew who killed Mr. Warburton. The companion of Miss Fiske."

"As it happens, Mr. Lombardo was killed well before Mr. Warburton."

This interested him. "*Was* he? Ah, she get tired at last."

"What do you mean?" asked Louise.

The briefest glance of assessment. "I make mistake. The pronouns. He, she . . . Lombardo made many people angry. No surprise he's dead."

"Were any of those people also angry at Mr. Warburton?" I asked.

Rodolfo made a dismissive wave. "Warburton is a successful man, everyone wants something from him. Not everyone can have, so of course they are angry."

"Can you remember anyone in particular?"

"Who was angry with Warburton?" He gestured all around the room. "The waiter he yells at, the actress he does not hire. The man who threw the glass. His wife . . ."

"Mr. Hirschfeld's wife?"

A contraction of the beautiful brow. ". . . Pronouns. Mrs. Warburton. There is a Mrs. Warburton, yes?"

"Yes," I said. "Why would she be angry?"

He chuckled. "I can only say that if you wish to find people who are angry with a man like Sidney Warburton, look first for the wife. And then for the husbands."

It took us a moment to unravel this. "You mean there were other women," said Louise.

"He is a successful man," Rodolfo repeated as if this explained everything. Which, sadly, perhaps it did.

I asked, "The women he dallied with, they were all married?" Rodolfo nodded. "Who?"

"You want names?" He looked mournfully at the napkin. I looked at Louise, then laid my hand over Rodolfo's, a second five-dollar bill in my palm. Turning his liquid gaze upon me, he embraced my hand, one finger sliding suggestively across the palm. Then he pocketed the bill.

It was money well spent. Rodolfo had an excellent memory, and his desire to attract Warburton's attention meant he had watched the producer's movements for some time. He reeled off the names of several ladies of the stage, three society ladies— Louise gasped when a fellow Dumb Friends committee member was named—and indicated there were others too dull to recall. Afterward, we were silent a moment in tribute to the dead man's stamina. Then I asked the only question that was both suitable and relevant: Had any of the ladies—or their husbands—been present the night of Warburton's murder?

Three of the actresses had, one society lady.

"And the husbands," I pressed. "Were they here?"

A fraction of hesitation. Then Rodolfo said, "I do not pay so much attention to gentlemen. I did notice that Claude Arden and the beautiful Mrs. Arden were having one of their . . . tiffs."

"About what?" asked Louise, oblivious to the fact that Mrs. Arden had been flirting wildly with Leo that night. Although, I wondered, if Claude had noticed her theatrics, he would have also seen that they were directed at the other end of the table, and not at Sidney Warburton, who was sitting next to her. Which argued against him shooting the producer in a jealous rage.

Rodolfo then suggested that perhaps a lady had discovered that she was just one of many and acted according to the rules of melodrama.

Louise said, "But we should remember, Mr. Warburton was murdered in the men's washroom." She turned pink. "A lady would never go in there."

Why a lady with adultery on her conscience and murder on her mind would stop at the men's room door, I wasn't sure. But Louise had made an interesting point. Leo had said Warburton had an apartment, which he probably used for his assignations. A lover wanting to shoot him would have asked to meet him there. Whereas a gentleman might not have been aware he had such a room and thought a bathroom stall the best place to catch him at close range and still get away.

On impulse, I said, "Could I see the washroom?"

Louise coughed my name.

"It's where he was killed, Mrs. Tyler," I said apologetically. Then suggested she wait in the car while I had a look.

The washroom where Sidney Warburton had died was not the palatial men's salon on the lower floor where men enjoyed a respite from female company. This one was functional and somewhat out of the way. It lay at the end of a circuitous hall-way, accessed from the dining room by swinging doors that were also used by the waitstaff going to and from the kitchen nearby. The chance of anyone noticing me was remote. But I couldn't simply walk into a men's washroom, so I asked Rodolfo to take me to the kitchen. I waited until the swinging doors were calm then darted inside. I soon spotted what I needed, and exited with the complete anonymity that only a woman carrying a mop and bucket can achieve. I also noticed that the kitchen had a door that opened to the street for deliveries. Given the chaos of the after-theater dinner rush, it was possible a gentleman could have exited through here and not be seen.

It was early, but already men headed to the washroom with looks of consternation. Stepping in front of the door, I said, "If you wouldn't mind using the facilities down the hall, sir. I'm sorry to say someone's been ill." There were two gentlemen inside, but once I made it clear I mopped without regard for calfskin, they left.

When I had the washroom to myself, I stepped from one stall to the next, trying to see where Sidney Warburton had died. Rodolfo had said I would know it when I saw it and he was right. The stall closest to the kitchens had no door and was missing tiles above the toilet. The brick underneath had the distinct dent of a bullet. I brushed it with the tip of my finger. I half expected a shock of some kind. But death had left only this ugly little pock-mark.

Closing the next stall door, I leaned down to judge how much you would see with the door closed. Only the feet and some pant leg. How could the killer know he was shooting through the right door? Of course, Sidney Warburton could be identified from his famous yellow spats. Although Leo had also been wearing yellow spats that evening—and was possibly also engaged in a dalliance with a married woman. I dwelled on the unpleasant implications for a moment before remembering that Leo had disappeared with Violet. If someone had wanted to shoot him, they would hardly have looked for him in this washroom. Hence the likelihood that the shooter knew who sat behind the stall door because he had followed Warburton in here.

There was a quick knock and I turned to see Rodolfo stick his beautiful head around the door. "This interest in toilets, it's a little disgusting."

Motioning him in, I asked, "Do you use this bathroom?"

"If I have to."

"Why would you have to?"

He rolled his eyes as if it was obvious. "It's close. But I prefer the one downstairs."

I saw what he meant: a flight of stairs could be uncomfortable for an overfull bladder. This was the emergency bathroom—plain, anonymous, a place to void, no more. I could imagine even the staff went here from time to time.

If you came from outside and made your way through the kitchens, this would be the first private spot for killing you came to.

But how could that person from outside be sure Sidney Warburton would use this bathroom? Most gentlemen would have retired to the more palatial washroom downstairs. Certainly a man of Sidney Warburton's stature would have. And that night should have, but he had been unable to wait and so made a fatal choice.

Could someone from the outside—Louise's hoped-for gangster—have known he would make that choice?

No. It was clear that the killer had followed Warburton here from the dining room. But how had he escaped Rector's without notice? The washroom had one small window and it was high up. Perhaps you could reach it if you stood on a toilet, but it would be quite the feat of agility and only a very slim man could fit. Or . . . a small and particularly flexible woman.

Stepping outside, I looked up and down the hall. In front of me, the hallway leading back to the dining room. To the left, the kitchen. To the right, an elevator.

Pointing to the elevator, I asked, "Where does that take you?"

"Upstairs. The kitchen staff uses it to get to the hotel rooms."

How much time for escape would the killer have had? The shot had not been understood right away. Noise from the band, the kitchen, hundreds of merry inebriates. It had taken at least a few minutes for the next man in need of relief to enter and discover Sidney Warburton's body. In that time, the killer could have easily reached the street through the kitchen's delivery door. Or taken the elevator up to the rooms and hidden in an odd closet.

Or . . . simply returned to the party.

Where had Claude Arden been when the police herded us into that room? For that matter, where had Mr. Harney been? Leo, we knew. But all of those men, I realized, came to Rector's regularly. They would know about this washroom. Especially Mr. Harney; it was an ideal place to be sick. As he had been that night . . .

Rodolfo tapped his foot. "If you're done, the dinner rush is starting."

I returned the mop and bucket to the kitchen. As we walked back to the dining room, I said I was sorry Mr. Warburton had died before I could make introductions.

He shrugged. "I am going to be in pictures. Already I have made one in Brooklyn. *My Official Wife.* It's about a plot to kill the czar of Russia."

"What part do you play?"

He looked sulky. "I am in the background."

Before we went our separate ways, I pondered the discovery of Warburton's affairs. The vision of Warburton as Lothario struck me as odd. Why? He was not unattractive and he was influential.

Many a hopeful actress had probably had to make do with much worse. And yet I rarely saw him flirt and he had never cast his eye on me.

Was it arrogant that I thought that strange? Perhaps he wouldn't bother with the woman who cleaned Mrs. Tyler's clothes. But in my experience, most men who dallied widely approached everyone with a certain . . . warmth. Even in an exchange as banal as passing off hat and gloves, the eye could linger. Such men wanted, at all times, and that wanting created an unmistakable frisson. Sometimes it was odious, sometimes not. Leo, for example, turned that particular energy on everyone, seeing the excitement of possibility in pretty and plain, young and old, rich and poor, men as well as women. And he made them feel it, too.

All I had ever felt from Sidney Warburton was rage.

I said as much to Rodolfo, and he nodded. "Warburton, he did not so much like women as he hates other men. It is them he wants to insult; men understand this. When he chooses a woman, it is not for her beauty, it is to say to the husband, I have her. I took her from you. He is an ugly little man. And yet he is able to steal their women."

I nodded, then remembered Rodolfo's one unpracticed response. *Ah, she get tired at last.* Did he really forget pronouns?

Before I could ask, he took my hand. "One last thing I must tell you. I could not say before in front of your boss . . ."

Liquid eyes locked on mine, making my stomach and other parts do strange somersaults. "Yes?"

"One of Warburton's women?"

I nodded.

"She was sitting at your table."

A swift kiss on the back of my hand. Then, pleased with his performance, he went off to work.

It was nearing five thirty when I returned to the car and gave

Louise the unhappy news that an unknown killer had not come in through the kitchen to shoot Sidney Warburton—and that the murderer had followed him from the dining room.

Louise frowned. Then rallied. "All sorts of disreputable people dine at Rector's, don't they? It needn't have been someone from our table."

Thinking of the gangster Owney Davis, I conceded that was true. I wrestled with how to tell Louise that one of the women at our table had been carrying on an affair with the producer when she directed Horst to drive to Lord & Taylor.

Surprised, I said, "Are you certain? It's been a very busy day."

"I told William I was out shopping. He'll think it odd if I come back empty-handed."

"Yes, but . . . perhaps you're tired."

"Why on earth would I be tired?"

Our eyes met. I saw nothing in hers that suggested she wished me to be truthful.

★ ★ ★

That evening, surly at the change of dinner hour, Mrs. Avery slapped a grease-stained piece of paper into my hand. On it was Anna's name and a number I didn't recognize.

I waited until the Tylers had retired to call. Anna had never kept regular hours, I wasn't afraid of waking her. Wherever she was, it did not seem to be a home—at least not an average home. I had to speak to several people in order to reach her: the woman who answered the phone, a man who was asked if he knew where Anna was, who then shouted to a third unseen person. For a few moments, I heard only the rumble of distant conversation. Finally, I heard Anna's voice.

"Hello!" I said, with a brightness that sounded empty even to my ears.

". . . Oh," she said after a moment. "Yes, hello."

"You're busy."

"No. But it's very noisy. Hard to hear."

"Perhaps we should have dinner."

This had been our habit, dinner on my day off—one I had abandoned over the summer to make time for Leo.

"Dinner."

"It's been so long. My fault."

"What?"

"My *fault*," I said, raising my voice as high as I dared in the Tyler house. "I think . . . I've been working a lot, I think Mrs. Tyler would give me an evening off. Could you meet tomorrow?"

There was silence. I knew my friend, knew her silences. She was not calculating whether or not she was free to meet tomorrow night. She was deciding whether or not she wanted to.

Then she said, "Tomorrow, yes."

As I went upstairs to my room, I heard muffled voices coming from the Tylers' bedroom. The words were unclear, but the timbre was high, the pauses too long. This was not a pleasant before bed chat. I had the feeling the Lord & Taylor story had not satisfied William. Nor should it have. It was a harmless lie, I told myself. But a lie nonetheless.

In bed, I pondered the nature of attachment. It had taken Anna two phone calls and two days to call me; if she had reached out to me, I would have been on the phone in an instant. But, I reminded myself, I had disappeared to go dancing with Leo first. Although she had disappeared many times over the years and I hadn't taken offense. Maybe, I thought querulously, she just didn't like the tables turned. People could find betrayal in the mildest slight or neglect if they chose to.

Which brought me to "Warburton's woman"—such a strange way to put it—and that jealous husband who might have stalked the man who wronged him and taken his life. Was that an act of love? Or power? Or money, I thought, hearing voices suddenly raised and shrill from downstairs, there was also money to consider. Security. *It's for the good of the family business.*

Family shouldn't *be* a business, I thought. Love shouldn't be a business. You should be able to count on them, trust them . . .

And then I laughed at myself because nothing in the world worked that way.

But it wasn't pleasant to be reminded. Rejection. Jealousy— they could make you feel . . .

Or do.

Some very ugly things.

11

"*Good morning, Miss Biederman.*"

"Good morning, Miss Prescott."

"Are these for washing, Mrs. St. John?"

"Please, Jane."

"You look lovely, Mrs. Hirschfeld."

"Gee, thanks."

"Your tea, Mrs. Arden."

"Claude, darling, I'd like to try it down left."

The next day as I made my way around the theater, I brooded over the discovery that Sidney Warburton had enjoyed the privilege claimed by many powerful men: the favors of women not his wife. Specifically, women who were the wives of others.

One of whom had been sitting at our table the night of the murder. Which meant she was at the theater today.

There had been seven women at our table, including Louise, whom I discounted. Three of the six remaining had husbands. I began with Violet Hirschfeld. Rodolfo's list had been comprised of women of a certain stature: they were either great beauties, married to prestigious men, or both. Warburton would have taken pride in their seduction. Whereas he had described Violet as a bicycle. His contempt did not suggest an enamored swain— although perhaps a rejected one. Violet did not strike me as a woman of deep feeling, but she was attentive to her new husband and young enough that she may have rejected the little producer as "old"—and been tactless enough to say so. But if Warburton's nastiness toward Violet did stem from rejection, Leo would have no cause for jealousy, at least when it came to his wife. Jealousy over control of the show was a different matter—and that I set aside as irrelevant to the question at hand.

Adele St. John? I had never heard a single reference to Mr. St. John, but someone had given her the title of "Mrs." She seemed altogether too forthright to get entangled with Sidney Warburton, except in the business sense. Also, too tall. But perhaps the unseen Mr. St. John was jealous of the time she spent at the theater? Perhaps he disliked her career—unorthodox for a woman of her station.

Also, it needn't be a husband, I realized. Harriet Biederman had a fiancé. Nedda Fiske, an unstable lover. I had never sensed even a whiff of eroticism between Nedda Fiske and the producer. Her devotion to Lombardo seemed all consuming. Not to mention Lombardo had been floating in the river at the time of Warburton's death, as unassailable an alibi as you could want.

Harriet's fiancé on the other hand was not only alive, he was bullying and bad tempered. His dislike of her career was well known, and such a man would not have approved of his fiancée's presence at a place like Rector's—or her working extra hours. Many men expected their women home at the hour of their choosing, and he had shown up at the theater once before when she was late. Maybe torn between two bullies in her life, Harriet had defied the butcher by going to dinner, then panicked and run home? Even as the butcher was on his way to her boss's favorite restaurant in order to drag her out by force? Or to shoot the man who seemed to enjoy more of his fiancée's devotion than he did?

And if Harriet had changed her mind about giving up her career in the theater? What would the butcher's reaction be then? It would be helpful to know how close he lived to Harriet, how much he was able to keep track of her comings and goings.

Hearing a change in melody, I looked up to see the Ardens take to the stage to begin the scene of their first meeting. This part of the show, unlike so many others, was fine. But Claude was a taskmaster, insisting they rehearse numbers long since perfected over and over again. I watched as they moved through their bright, chipper patter into their bright, chipper dance—so precise, so sure. One had no anxiety watching them. But today, their expertise offered very little pleasure. It all felt rather mechanical. As opposed to Blanche's ardent trills of a few weeks ago.

The music stopped. I looked up to see the Ardens in their classic final pose: the ecstatic dip. Claude was dripping sweat, the expression on Blanche's face was strained.

"Lower," barked Claude. "More arch in the neck."

Blanche tried, the cords of her lovely throat visible. Her extended arm trembled.

"More length in the back."

Teeth gritted, she said, "Claude, I am as low and as long as the good Lord made me, I can go no further."

Her husband flung her to the floor, presumably to prove that she—and he—could go quite a bit lower. Blanche cried out, then swung a fist at her partner's knee; it didn't land, it wasn't meant to. She took a deep breath, seeming on the verge of tears.

"You can go lower, and you know it," said Claude.

Leo scrambled onstage. With care, he pushed Claude away

from Blanche. Then he helped the blond dancer to her feet. His hands stayed protectively on her arm and shoulder, a familiarity that Blanche seemed to find in no way objectionable. Drawing Claude into a small circle, he murmured to both of them. All heads were down, and I couldn't hear what was said. But I knew the sound of Leo cajoling. Claude mumbled something that sounded like an apology and Blanche responded with a distant acceptance. The circle loosened, heads rose. Hands on both stars' shoulders, Leo looked into Blanche's eyes, then Claude's, asking each if they were all right. Truly, were they? Because he needed them to be, he was counting on them, they were the heart of the show. To my surprise, both smiled sheepishly, embarrassed by their row and lulled by Leo's attention.

"Good," said Leo. "Good." He rubbed Claude's shoulder. The hand on Blanche's shoulder lingered.

Then it dropped as he said, "Violet."

The arrival of his wife spurred Leo into fresh jaunty energy. Striding to the piano, he said, "Claude, you stay, let's run 'A Girl Like You.' Blanche, you go. I command you to eat. Or sleep. Those are your two choices. You have no others."

As I watched Blanche leave the stage, I wrestled with my suspicions. Blanche was the most beautiful woman in the show, the one most likely to lure a man who seduced to bolster his own sense of power. She was, to put it crudely, a prize in the way that none of the other women at the table was, not even Violet. And while her husband might speak lovingly of her, his actions did not always match his words. Did his cruelty stem from jealousy? Remembering his complaints about Nedda, I realized he was also prickly about his dignity as a performer. Had professional humiliation and personal cuckolding—both at the hands of Sidney Warburton—made him snap?

But I just could not see Warburton's appeal for Blanche. Not as clearly as I could see Leo's appeal for her. Claude had seen her flirtation with Leo that night. Had he gone to the bathroom, seen only a pair of yellow spats—covered shoes below the bathroom stall door, and shot, thinking he was aiming at the nobody songwriter who dared to dally with his wife—and nag him about royalties—rather than his longtime employer?

Rodolfo had been clear: one of the women at our table was Sidney Warburton's lover and I could not discount his statement. After rehearsals, Warburton often retired to Rector's with his stars, especially the Ardens and the Hirschfelds. Rodolfo would have had a chance to observe them on many evenings. If Blanche were misbehaving with Warburton, he would know.

But might he have seen Blanche flirting with Warburton to cover up her affair with Leo?

There was of course the possibility that she was involved with both men. Warburton being Blanche's lover did not mean Leo had not also been invited to the Arden dressing room on occasion. Really, until I knew who had inspired Blanche's operatics that day, I couldn't know anything.

Who might know of Blanche's clandestine involvements? In whom would she confide? The sight of Louise chatting with Harriet gave me the answer. A lady has little to hide from the woman who dresses her. Settling Peanut into his basket, I went in search of Adele St. John.

I took myself down to the workroom and found Adele St. John contemplating the last act dress. This was a marvel of blue-gray chiffon trimmed in gray fox. From its straight simple structure, I knew it would be worn with a minimum of undergarments and the length showed not only ankle, but calf. I had seen dresses approach this style, but this was the next step and I sensed that Louise's entire wardrobe might have to change a year, even months, from now. I said as much.

Adele St. John had never spoken much to me beyond *Do this* and *Don't get in my way.* Now she said, "Yes, she's still all bunched at the waist and the ankles. I detest that shape. Tiny waist, enormous bosom, bulging bottom. Why would any woman in her right mind want to be squeezed into some grotesque mockery of the female form? Only a man would think it wonderful to hobble a woman so she can't even walk. Your Mrs. Tyler is marvelous. Tall, slim, wonderful long lines. When I'm done here, we're going to create a new, modern look for her."

Immediately, I thought of William's mother, who would not welcome a modern daughter-in-law. I always thought strict adherence to the rules of fashion gave Louise confidence. She was unquestionably "right" for today, as defined by the Tylers and the Armslows. But Mrs. St. John was looking beyond today and to a Louise who did not need to worry so much about mothers-in-law.

For myself, I wasn't sure I would do well in a fashion landscape where waist and bosom were irrelevant. While short hair was enchanting on Blanche Arden—and now that I thought of it, might suit Louise—I was rather proud of my hair. I had always thought that if I got the chance to show it off down, the effect might be quite captivating. Leo had begged me to do that, take it down just once. Mindful of the trouble of putting it back up—and the fact that trailing tresses looked best on naked shoulders—I said no.

I looked up to see Mrs. St. John gazing at me with an amused smile. I had the unsettling thought she knew exactly what I was thinking.

"There's stockings to mend over there if you've nothing to do," she said. I took up needle and thread, she took up her sketch pad, and we worked in companionable silence. It was so harmonious, I was reminded of my interest in matters matrimonial and when I had finished three stockings, I asked, "Does Mr. St. John enjoy the theater?"

A pause as she decided whether I was worth answering. "He does."

I was about to say that must be nice, a shared interest, when she added, "His passion for theater stems from his passion for its practitioners. Italian for choice, although Spanish will do. Occasionally German for variety. When I last heard from him, he was 'enjoying' the theatrical season in Rome. That was several weeks ago, he may have moved on to Vienna by now. Is that what you wanted to know?"

Before I could even conceive of an answer, much less utter it, we heard shouting from upstairs. Sighing, "Oh, dear," Mrs. St. John set aside her pad and headed up to the stage. Mending basket in hand, I followed, to find Peanut yapping furiously in the wings and Mr. Harney drinking with great purpose from a flask. Returned from lunch, Blanche gave a bored wave of the arm. Louise sat tense and watchful in the front row. On the stage stood Claude, fists fixed to his hips, and Violet, who looked lost.

Settling next to Harriet, I whispered, "What happened?"

Troubled, she looked up. "It's . . . not good."

From the piano, Leo said, "Let's try that again. First—Harney, can you come back, please?"

The comic wandered unsteadily onto the stage; it was the first time I had seen him tipsy in performance. I could see Leo knew it as well, yet he insisted on going through the father-daughter song, "The Gutter's Good Enough for Me," followed by Claude's song, "A Girl Like You."

It took only a minute to see that Harriet was right. Whether it was the lack of stairs, which were her métier, or the memory of the happy howls that had greeted Nedda's performance, Violet was . . . I didn't want to use the word "bad" . . . tentative. Which unfortunately was the same thing. The scenes with Mr. Harney, once a highlight, were now stiff and awkward. She embraced Mr. Arden with all the passion of a woman cleaning drains. Violet could sing, she could dance, she could almost act. She just didn't do any of it well. Worse, she seemed to know it. Her performance felt like one long apology: *I know I'm not good. Please don't be angry.*

Claude Arden was angry. He kept his contempt for his costar barely under control as they rehearsed the silly patter that followed the song. The lines needed deft timing and Violet could not keep up. She mouthed in anguish as she struggled to remember, finally calling, "Line!"

Arden threw up his arms. "Oh, for—"

"I'm sorry," she whimpered. "It's just the new lines . . ."

"They're the same ones we've had for months, God help us. How do you not remember them?"

Leo said, "Take it easy, Claude."

"Oh, yes, that's an excellent idea. Opening night is a few weeks away, but I shall certainly take it easy." Storming to the edge of the stage he stage-whispered to Leo, "I know she's got you by the cods, but even you must see we have a problem."

There was a short, uncomfortable pause as we all realized Leo had no answer. Taking this as permission to quit for the day, Claude marched off the stage and headed toward the door.

"It's not like you were so happy working with Nedda," Violet shouted, embarrassed by her husband's failure to defend her.

Over his shoulder, Claude called, "Well, I'd sacrifice camels at the full moon to have her back now."

After a moment we heard a thud as he left the theater. Blanche and Mrs. St. John followed, promising to bring him back. Her mind perhaps on future business, Mrs. St. John asked Louise if she might join them; the patroness's voice would be useful. Louise looked to Leo, who nodded, then left with the two women.

Eyes on the piano keys, Leo said, "Vi, how about we work through a few scenes? I'll do Arden's lines."

But Violet had not forgotten Leo's failure to defend her. Stomping down the stage steps, she said, "I'm exhausted. I'm going home."

"You can't go home," said Leo. "We need to work on 'The Gutter's Good Enough for Me.'" He gestured to Mr. Harney.

"Get Peanut to do it," she said, marching past the actor and up the aisle.

"He is a pretty good-looking dog," shouted Leo after the door had slammed. "Okay, Harney, I guess you have the afternoon off."

As Harney left with Peanut, Harriet asked, "Do you need me, Mr. Hirschfeld?"

For a moment, he hesitated; was he going to give up all chance of working? Then he said, "No, thank you, Miss Biederman. Take a long lunch."

I didn't ask if I could go. I didn't ask if I could stay. I simply took up another stocking and started mending. Leo sat at the piano, shoulders slumped, fingers idling on the keys. A note sounded, then another. A ripple, then nothing.

Now he said, "I would give a considerable amount of money to not have everyone hate me. But unfortunately, I'm broke."

I looked up, prepared to snipe. But Leo's face was drawn. There were dark shadows under his eyes. I couldn't remember the last time I had seen him eat. His jaw was tense, his neck strained. He looked beaten. Seeing him at the piano, I remembered the evenings he had been unable to get off work at the movie house. I had kept him company in the darkened pit as he played through eight showings of *Mabel's Awful Mistake* and *The Scimitar of the Prophet*. Acting alongside the images on the screen, I had swooned, taken fright, fought off villains, and, at the end, reunited with my sweetheart. Leo had enjoyed the performances enormously, and afterward when we had the theater to ourselves, he whispered, "Having rescued the damsel from the railroad tracks, the hero receives a kiss of undying gratitude." I noted that in the original play, the gentleman had been tied to the tracks and saved by the heroine. He said kisses of undying gratitude worked for him either way.

"I don't hate you, Leo. Mrs. Tyler certainly doesn't hate you."

He smiled slightly. "Mrs. Tyler is a very nice lady."

"She thinks you're a genius."

"And such a smart lady."

"Even Peanut thinks you're tolerable."

Taking my basket, I moved to the front row. Delicately, I trod into deeper waters. "Honestly? Isn't life a little easier without Sidney Warburton?" Leo rolled his eyes to suggest *infinitely.* "Aside from the small difficulty of who killed him."

Leo repeated the producer's name, adding an expletive. "There must have been fifty people at Rector's that night who wanted him dead. I don't worry who killed Sidney Warburton. If I ever meet him, I'll buy him a drink."

"Was he in financial difficulty?" Before he could deny it, I added, "I overheard you arguing about money. You mentioned an investor getting cold feet."

"Sidney's wife has plenty of money. He just cried poor to get his way."

So Mrs. Warburton was the shadow investor. And the lies Leo had mentioned no doubt concerned the women the producer dallied with.

"The police think it might have been a jealous husband." Saying "the police" made it sound more impressive than Rodolfo at Rector's. "Apparently, Mr. Warburton had a fondness for other men's wives."

Leo shrugged as if the subject held no interest for him.

"Or perhaps it was someone with a particular dislike of yellow spats."

He looked at me.

"With the stall door shut, one wonders how the jealous husband identified his wife's lover. Mr. Warburton was wearing yellow spats. But then so were you."

"You think someone meant to kill me and shot Sidney instead?" He started playing again.

"I think Blanche Arden is keeping company with someone not her husband."

"How could you know that?"

"Because I heard them." The briefest break in the music. "Or heard her, the gentleman was discreet. Claude was onstage at the time. But I didn't see you anywhere."

"And you think I was the gentleman in question. That's very flattering."

"Were you?"

"Would you care if I was?"

"Answer me, Leo."

He played a definitive chord. "Despite the cooing and hair pulling, Blanche Arden has no real interest in me. What you heard was good old Sidney giving direction and Blanche making sure the costume budget stayed generous. Just another example of the joy Sidney Warburton brought to people's lives."

He sounded bitter—against Warburton or against Blanche? The use of the word "real"—did that imply pretense that he had believed at one point? Reciprocated?

It didn't matter, I realized. What was important was that Leo had just confirmed that Blanche was Warburton's woman.

"Isn't it possible Claude found out?"

"And *shot* Sidney?" He shook his head. "Sidney was Claude's bread and butter, he wouldn't mess that up."

I wasn't so sure. Men didn't always credit their fellow men with the capacity for deep emotion. Given Blanche's protests that it was just business, Claude was clearly not as quiescent about the affair as Leo thought. Another thought came to me. Florenz Ziegfeld had fallen in love with the singer Anna Held, but she left him last year after he dallied with chorus girl Lillian Lorraine. Powerful men in the theater were often drawn to actresses as partners. Why should Sidney Warburton be any different?

I said, "Actually, Blanche is Claude's bread and butter. Without her, he goes back to singing 'She of the Emerald Eyes.' No more Darling Dancing Ardens. Maybe Warburton was tired of Mrs. Warburton—that's not hard to imagine. And maybe Blanche liked the idea of a partner who wouldn't throw her on the ground."

He frowned at that. Then shook his head. "I'm sure you noticed, Blanche didn't shed any tears when Sidney was killed."

"No, she was too busy making eyes at you." I demonstrated, stroking my throat elaborately and sighing.

He perked up. "No, don't stop, that was very . . . poignant. More sighing, maybe let the finger stay at your lips . . ."

I punched him hard in the shoulder, causing him to howl. Rubbing his arm, he shot me several reproachful looks. But his mouth curled upward as he said, "Maybe I should give my regards to Blanche Arden. I'm not doing so well with the other women in my life. You're angry with me, Violet's furious . . ."

"She's not furious, Leo, she's just . . ."

Untalented. Frightened. Childish.

". . . tired."

"She does get tired easily, that Mrs. Hirschfeld," he said, returning to the piano.

Annoyed, I returned to my stockings. Then said impulsively, "I don't know what you were thinking."

"I'm not sure how much thinking had to do with it."

"Your mother must be pleased." Mrs. Hirschfeld had liked me well enough, but made it clear she had different hopes for Leo.

"Ida Hirschfeld is *not* pleased. But then Ida Hirschfeld's happiness was not at the forefront of my thoughts. She was already mad at me for how things turned out with Clara."

I shook my head, not understanding.

"Some neighborhood busybody saw me with Violet and said, 'Oh, Clara, I saw Leo with a girl, I thought for sure it was you.' Two weeks later Clara is engaged to her professor and Mother Hirschfeld isn't speaking to her youngest son. So, I thought, fine, everyone wants me to be married, I'll get married. Violet isn't hard on the eyes. Everybody seemed to think that a married Leo Hirschfeld solves all the world's problems—why not?"

There was something odd in his use of the word "everybody." But before I could ask, he said, "My father keeps forgetting. One time we went to dinner at the family's. He took me aside and said, 'She's very pretty, but you don't marry that.' I said, 'Pop, I did marry that.' On the bright side, my brothers are all very jealous."

I tried to tell myself that Leo Hirschfeld had done this to himself and deserved not an ounce of my sympathy. He wasn't even asking for sympathy. He hadn't said a single word about being lonely. And there was no reason to believe that he was. Except that it was clear that he was.

An eruption like that of a small volcano or Peanut coughing up a rat's tail sounded from the back of the theater. I turned to see Detective Fullerton looming.

"Detective!" called Leo. "Do you have good news?"

"I . . . do not." The cumbersome detective made his way down to the front of the theater; no seat would accommodate him, so

Leo invited him to sit on a nearby chair. The detective wondered if Leo would prefer that I not be present; what he had to say was of a private nature.

"Jane knows all my worst secrets," said Leo cheerfully. "Well, most of them. No, stay. Please."

I had gotten up to leave. But Leo's request was serious and I sat back down.

"Does Mr. Hirschfeld need a lawyer?" I asked.

"I don't know," said the detective. "Do you need a lawyer, Mr. Hirschfeld?"

"Why don't you tell me your bad news and then we'll decide?"

The detective adjusted himself on the chair. "It has come to my attention that the deceased, while a married man, engaged in several dalliances."

"I would think 'several' is putting it low," said Leo.

"Mr. Warburton took his position as a license to abuse the trust of young ladies hoping to enter the theatrical profession. He *also* engaged the attentions of several married women."

Leo nodded.

"Including, I am sorry to say, your wife."

A man so musically gifted, it was rare that Leo Hirschfeld missed a beat. He missed one now. Then recovered. "Yes, I know that they enjoyed each other's company in the past."

I looked at him; had he known this?

"Would you consider the week before Mr. Warburton's death the past? A waiter reports seeing the two in a compromising position outside Mr. Warburton's apartment."

My jaw fell. No wonder the rest of the cast was so contemptuous of Violet: not only was she Leo's wife, she was the producer's girlfriend.

For his part, Leo smiled, seemed to withdraw. I had the feeling he was addressing his thoughts to the dead man. And words. None of them pleasant.

I said, "Detective, maybe we could continue this conversation at another time. You can appreciate this is a shock . . ."

"I can." The little eyes flicked between me and Leo; I had the sudden ugly sensation of assessment. "And you can appreciate, I hope, that I have more questions."

Leo crossed one arm around his middle and massaged his forehead. "I think Miss Prescott is right, I'm not . . ."

The detective rose from his seat in a fit of prosecutorial fury. I had never seen an actual grizzly bear unfold itself from all fours to its full height, but now I imagined it would look something like Detective Fullerton as he went from wheezing buffoon to terrifying threat. Still seated on the piano bench, Leo looked six years old.

"You were seen arguing with the deceased on the night of the murder," he bellowed. "Several people have reported your business dealings as acrimonious. You wished to be rid of his interfering, both with your wife and your work. You cannot account for your whereabouts at the time of the murder . . ."

"On the contrary," I said, "Mr. Hirschfeld accounted quite vividly for his whereabouts. And his wife confirmed it. As for acrimonious dealings, you could say the same of any number of people. Mr. Warburton was not a well-liked man."

"But he was a powerful man. Many people depended on him for their livelihood."

"Including Mr. Hirschfeld . . ."

"Except that recently, he had brought in another investor. Hadn't you, Mr. Hirschfeld? Buoyed by Mrs. Tyler's riches, you no longer had to endure a man who berated you, cuckolded you, humiliated you . . ."

It was at this point that Leo did the worst possible thing: he smiled. Instantly, he put a hand over his mouth. But from his eyes, you could see that he was beaming with suppressed laughter.

"A man is dead, sir!" Fullerton thundered. "Do you find this amusing?"

I could see Leo weighing a criticism of Fullerton's dialogue and wisely deciding against.

"No," he said. "I don't find it amusing. I don't find it especially tragic either—of course, my wife may feel differently."

His quip made me recall Violet's tears in the aftermath of Warburton's murder, her ludicrous statement that he had committed suicide. Did she suspect Leo of murder? Certainly, she had been very ill-tempered toward him.

Just then we heard the squeak of hinges and the muted thud of a padded door as Louise and the Ardens returned from lunch. At the sight of the detective, they stayed warily at the back row.

"Are you arresting me, Detective?" Leo wanted to know. "Because we have to get on with the second act."

What one might call a dramatic pause followed. Then the detective rumbled, "Not at the present time, Mr. Hirschfeld. But I would appreciate it if you did not leave the city."

"How can I leave the city? The show opens in two weeks." Then waving to the cast, he said, "It's all right. The detective here was just letting me know I'm a suspect. Can we start with 'The Gutter's Good Enough for Me'? Oh, Vi's not here. Fine, let's go with the club scene."

12

"How can Mr. Hirschfeld be so calm?"

It was the sixth time Louise Tyler had asked this question as we waited for Horst to bring the car around to the front of the theater. I had tried a variety of answers ranging from "I don't know" to casting doubts on Leo's sanity. Now I tried what I believed to be the truth.

"If the detective had threatened to shut down the musical, then you would have seen Mr. Hirschfeld agitated. I don't think anything is real to him beyond that opening night. If they put him in handcuffs at the final curtain, he'll be perfectly happy."

"But you don't really think he killed Mr. Warburton?"

"No, I don't." Although why I didn't, given the many motives Fullerton had listed, was puzzling.

Louise said, "Mr. Hirschfeld's right. It could have been anyone at the restaurant that evening. I don't know why Detective Fullerton is so focused on him. It seems very lazy to me."

This struck me as loyalty bordering on delusional. But then I remembered that Leo had not chosen to share with the cast the precise reason he was a suspect, leaving them to assume it was the argument and thrown glass that spurred the detective's suspicions.

I said, "Apparently, Mr. Warburton and Mrs. Hirschfeld . . ."

It took Louise a moment. She showed all the appropriate signs of shock: dropped mouth, wide eyes, the swiftly exhaled, "No!"

"A waiter at Rector's saw them in circumstances less than ideal."

"Oh, poor Mr. Hirschfeld!"

Louise's faith was such that I felt it impossible to note that this gave "poor Mr. Hirschfeld" a very good motive, save for the fact that he had been keeping intimate company with his spouse at the time of the murder—and he himself could be free with his attentions, which argued against possessive jealousy of said spouse.

The Ghost pulled up to the curb and Horst got out to open the door for Louise. She stepped inside, then looked confused when I did not follow.

"Oh, you have the evening off, don't you?"

"You were kind enough to give it. I'm meeting my friend for dinner quite near here."

"Have a lovely time."

"Thank you, Mrs. Tyler. I hope you have a nice evening as well."

I was by no means sure I was going to have a lovely time. For days, I had been certain that I would feel better if I could spend several hours with my oldest friend, picking apart recent events. But I was also aware that my time with Leo had caused a rift and it might be better to start with something less fraught. So I had asked if she would like to see a movie. To my surprise, she said yes and so we met just a few blocks from the Sidney Theater.

I could not remember a time I had seen Anna above Houston.

As I saw her walk out of the subway at Forty-Second Street, I realized that I had hoped for glad cries, outstretched arms, and overlapping questions: *How is? No, you, I was going to ask . . .* I did get a smile when she saw me. And she walked faster to reach me. There was a long embrace. But when we agreed we were glad to see each other, there was a touch of awkward relief, as if we both knew that might not have been the case.

I said, "I haven't seen you in so long, I feel terrible."

She nodded. But she did not say that she too had been busy.

I don't know whether it was provocation or appeasement that I chose the movie about assassination in Russia that Rodolfo had claimed to be in. But Anna was particular about how she spent her time; a movie about nihilists, I reasoned, would appeal more than one of Mr. Chaplin's comedies.

As we took our seats in the theater, I realized I had never seen a movie in this way; in all former viewings I had been looking up from the orchestra pit while Leo played the score. To put it politely, I had been caught up in other things. Now as the house lights dimmed and the whole world became a spectacle of light and shadow, I forgot everything else, even myself. I had the odd feeling that I was the one who had become insubstantial; only the images on the screen mattered.

Part adventure, part love story, *My Official Wife* told the story of Arthur Lennox, a New Yorker who traveled to Russia and fell under the spell of the "so infamous Helene Marie." The beautiful Helene Marie tried to assassinate the czar with the tiniest gun I had ever seen, then duped another man into helping her escape. When her new lover tried to embrace her, she sneered, "Love you! I? You poor fool! I loathe you and all your kind. Yet you are useful sometimes." The lover, perhaps feeling it was not enough to be useful, killed her. The ending was quite spectacular, with a ship blown up by torpedo. Sadly, I did not see poor Rodolfo in any of the crowd scenes.

As we left the theater, Anna said, "Well, that felt very realistic and true to life."

Widening my eyes in imitation of the film's star, I said, "'Love you? I?'"

Anna tossed her head. "'You poor fool!'"

"Still, it was sad she had to die in the end."

"She insulted her comrades and failed in her mission. She deserved to die."

Our habit had been to eat at her uncle's restaurant, where the food was excellent, abundant, and served without charge. That evening, as we were far uptown, we ate at Maxl's, which served up schnitzel, pickled cabbage, and boiled potatoes in large quantities on thick white plates. Anna asked how the trip to Europe had been, but nervous about irritating her, I just said that the houses were cold and the trains smoky. In return, I asked the questions I always asked. How were her aunts? Were her brothers working? Business at her uncle's restaurant was good? She answered, but the brevity of her response communicated more than the words. I tried to think of feints around our stiffness, teasing, shared memories, inquiries about people she would not think I'd remember. But nothing worked.

Finally, I said, "Where are you living now? Your uncle didn't tell me."

"I had to move. I'm staying with friends."

Taking in her wording—*had to move*—I thought to ask why, but amended it to, "When?"

"Last summer."

The words left silence in their wake; if I was going to settle the matter of last summer, now was the time. Picking at my veal, I said, "And I didn't know. I didn't know, because I didn't ask." I looked her in the eye. "I wasn't a good friend last summer. I'm sorry."

"Why are you sorry?" She sawed at her veal with her knife and fork. "I told you to go dancing, you went dancing."

This was true. Anna had been the one to say I should dance with Leo Hirschfeld as long as I enjoyed his company and stayed clear-eyed. She was my oldest friend, I thought with a trace of resentment. She should have known that might not be so easy for me as it was for her.

But resentment was not what the situation required. "I was hardly dancing so much that I couldn't have talked to you."

She shrugged, leaving me in the position of feeling my presence hadn't been missed—and yet I had still wronged her.

"Well, no more dancing." I offered a smile. "As a matter of fact, he got married."

I waited. If she gave me another shrug, I would call for the check.

Anna frowned. "I thought he said marriage wasn't for him."

"Funny, that's what I remembered, too."

It all came spilling out, in far greater detail than anyone should have patience for. As I spoke, I was aware that I was boring my oldest friend with the very thing that had led me to neglect her. And yet I couldn't help it. I wanted so badly for someone to take the jumble of feeling and regret, and find some sort of . . . hope. Or redemption at least, for me.

Anna was quiet throughout my rambling account. When I finished with a weak apology for talking so long, she said, "So you told him to go get married."

"If he couldn't go more than a few days without seeing another girl, I wasn't going to hope he could wait nine months."

"So you told him to get married."

"I said that he could . . ."

"And then you're horrified when he does. How dare he?"

"If he had married Clara, I would have been perfectly happy."

"Ah. If he had married the girl his mother chose for him, you could feel he was being a dutiful son, and consoled yourself with the knowledge that in his heart"—she laid a hand over hers—"*you* were his one and only love. The girl who got away, the one he couldn't have, whom he would never forget. He would lie awake at night, wondering, *Why, why did I let her go?*"

My stomach knotted. Sullenly, I pushed my plate away.

"Admit it."

"I will not."

"It's true."

"I didn't say it wasn't true. I just said I wouldn't admit it."

Anna laughed. "I'm sorry. I'm sure sometimes, at night, he feels like a complete fool."

She tore off a piece of bread. "Then he makes love to the chorus girl and forgets all about it."

It was meant as a joke. I was supposed to laugh. I tried—and failed. Remorseful, Anna reached across the table. "I went too far. My aunts always tell me, Anna, after I'm sorry, close the mouth. Really? It hurts that much?"

"Perhaps I just feel like an idiot."

"Well, love makes you stupid."

I was about to remind her we weren't talking about love, just one of its flighty cousins. Then I realized a more interesting subject had been raised.

"Why do you say that?" I asked.

Anna drank her wine, pointedly not giving an answer.

"It's not very kind, leaving me to feel foolish all alone."

"Maybe someday you'll introduce me to Mr. Hirschfeld. I would like to meet the man who made Jane Prescott feel foolish."

This was deliberately obnoxious; she was trying to throw me

off the subject. But it worked. I had wanted to talk about the shooting of Sidney Warburton, have her assure me that Leo might be guilty of being exactly the man he said he was, but not of murder. Now it seemed best to drop the subject of Leo entirely. Dispirited, I asked where she was working these days. In an equally subdued voice, she said, "The same."

"The IWW?"

". . . in some things."

Here it was again, that tactic of allusion without admission. *I will not tell you things, but I will tell you I am not telling you.* Frustrated, I turned to the matter I had vowed not to raise and asked what she had heard about the Lexington Avenue disaster.

"Why do you call it a disaster?"

"Four people dead? I don't call it a success."

"If you mean that it didn't work . . ."

"Well, a bomb is meant to kill people, it achieved that, I suppose."

"It was meant for one person, not four," she said quietly.

"And if it had killed that one person, it would be a triumph?"

"It would have been justice."

Justice—the word landed like a massive block of marble: inarguable, implacable, so weighty and pure, it banished all doubt, all questions. In my experience, causing someone's death, or what some might call murder, was never so clean, its motives as chaotic and disturbing as the bloody aftermath.

Sensing my mood had turned, Anna said, "You weren't here. You don't know what it felt like."

"Then tell me. *Talk* to me."

"The talking doesn't work."

"And the alternative does?"

Anna cried, "Rockefeller has killed two women! And eleven children. But because he is rich enough to pay other people to do it, you are disgusted with people who try to hold him accountable."

"I am disgusted by killing, Anna." My voice had risen, as if struggling to pass the knot in my throat. "I want answers other than killing."

"And we have tried to find them. But this is where we are."

That left us with nothing more to say and I asked the waiter for the bill. When he brought it, I worried that Anna would slap her money on the table and leave. But she waited.

"Where are you going now?" I asked when we left the restaurant.

She said she was getting the train. I said I would walk with her, even though I knew ultimately, we would go in opposite directions. Heartsore at how at odds we were, I said, "Because I'm stupid, just tell me . . ."

That you weren't one of the plotters the police are still looking for. Tell me you have no idea who Michael Murphy is. Or where he is.

Anna asked, "What do you want me to say?" I opened my mouth to say the truth, but she cut me off. "If I say no, you won't believe me. *Why,* you will think, *didn't she say that before?*"

"Say it now and we'll see."

"And if I say yes, then what? Speeches about peace and the sanctity of life?"

Just such a speech had been sounding in my head. But now I said, "No."

"Then what would you say? If I crossed that river and went where you think I should not go. If I am that person that it frightens you to think I might be, what then? What do you say to me then?"

Taking two quick steps, I put my arms around her and held on. My head to hers, fingers to the sharp blades of her back, I breathed in the smell of my oldest, dearest friend.

"I say, be careful."

And then I let her go.

★ ★ ★

Afterward, in need of distraction, I dawdled by a newsstand. The night was extremely warm, the air so humid, you could hardly call it air; every few seconds, it seemed, I had to tug at my collar or swipe my wrist across my brow. The papers were full of the divorce of the duchess of Westminster. Yet another leader was out of power in Mexico—although he, unlike his predecessor, was still living. A color illustration of daredevil Pearl White beamed on the cover of the latest edition of *Photoplay*, the new magazine devoted to movies—Blanche Arden's favorite magazine, in fact. The murder of Lulu Bailey was still on the front page, as was the murder of Sidney Warburton. So far, there was no report of his liaison with Violet and I wondered how Fullerton had managed to keep the chatty waiters of Rector's quiet. The police were still looking for others who may have taken part in the bombing; it was believed someone had helped Michael Murphy leave the country. The financiers were anxious about the difficulties between Austria and Serbia.

Taking in the miasma of headlines, I had the curious sense of approaching disaster. But when I searched inside myself for energy to resist, to say, *No, we shall do this and not that, we shall change course,* I felt numb exhaustion. It was late, probably later than I thought.

Really, it was clear where I should go. The Tyler home was not far. The elevated would take me. A streetcar would get me close. I could even walk, the streets were bustling enough for safety. And yet I found myself in front of the Sidney Theater. When I rang the bell at the stage door, I was not surprised when Leo opened it. It occurred to me to ask why he was there. But then he pushed the door wider and I simply went in.

The theater was dark and empty. Leo had set up a work lamp by the piano. On the stage, there was a phonograph; a record lay on top of the piano in a paper envelope. Leo sat on the edge of the stage, legs dangling. And sighed.

"What isn't working?" I asked, leaning on the piano.

"What is working? I'm trying to decide what should happen at the end."

"Who gets Claude?"

"I know it has to be Blanche. But I want Nedda to have . . ."

He shook his head.

". . . want Vi to have a moment where the audience will think, *No, he should have chosen her.* It's a song. She sings it, not him. But I can't hear it."

"Do you have anything?"

He came to the piano, played a melody. It was brief, melancholy, and uncertain.

"That's how it begins?"

"That's the whole thing. I know, it's not much of a moment. More a . . . crawl off the stage and die."

"Why don't you go home? Maybe you'll be inspired."

Leo's eyebrows had always been expressive. Their message now was that inspiration did not lie at home.

"I'm sorry about . . ." I knew of no tidy way to refer to Violet's affair with Warburton. "It must hurt."

"Terribly," he said flippantly.

Tired of casual talk about feelings, I said, "I don't think there's any shame in admitting you don't enjoy hearing about your wife with another man. It has to be a shock if nothing else . . ."

"Well, it would be a shock if I hadn't known all along." He

played a pretty string of notes. "Sidney and Violet went way back."

"How way back?" He shook his head. "How way back, Leo?"

"Before me. During me. And before you ask, no, I didn't mind. I was the piano player with one hit song. If Violet Tempest wanted to try and make her married boyfriend jealous by playing around with me, I wasn't going to say no. Sidney was getting tired of her—both onstage and off. He booked a bigger star to come on right after Vi's act. The big star wanted more time, which meant Violet got less. Vi's whole act is, she goes down the stairs slow and the audience gets a good look, right?"

I agreed that did seem to be the whole act.

"But to please the big star, Sidney made Violet go down the stairs faster. Too fast. One time she tripped and she let him have it. He was yelling, she was yelling. I felt bad for her, so the next time she did it, I played the song slow. After rehearsal, Violet came over to the piano and said, 'Stop by the dressing room later, I want to show you something.' Said it loud enough so Sidney would hear. I went by and she showed me something."

"How on *earth* did you end up married?"

Here he hesitated. "Violet wanted Warburton to leave Mrs. W and all the little Ws. It wasn't going to happen, but Violet, as you've noticed, doesn't always think things through. So she tells him there's a sixth W on the way. He gives her some choices, none of which involve matrimony. Then he suggests she tell me it's mine and I better do the right thing. She says, he won't believe it, which I wouldn't have, because . . ."

This involved a level of detail best left to the imagination and I cleared my throat.

"At any rate, Sidney comes to me and we have a very frank conversation about my bright future and Violet's role therein. I end up married and writing the score to his new show. Not a bad deal all in all."

"But she was so upset when he died. How on earth can she still care for him?"

"You don't understand. Violet and Sidney—whatever he did, she forgave. After he gave her the good news that she would be getting married, only not to him, she was mad for a few weeks. For the 'honeymoon' he sent us to some dump in Niagara. I worked, she complained about Sidney. It was extremely romantic. But on the train back, she says, 'Did I ever tell you about the time he met me in the hotel lobby with a single rose?' I said, 'Vi, you hate this guy now, forget the rose.' She goes crazy, starts hitting me. 'How dare you, Sidney and I are special, I will never forget that rose.' *Why* are you laughing?"

I covered my mouth, mumbled, "I'm sorry." It had been the image of Leo dodging blows on the train.

Then remembering their frequent absences, I observed that he seemed to have made the best of things.

"Half the time, I was trying to calm her down because Sidney had been rotten to her."

"And the other half?" He shrugged. "Once you knew there was no baby, why stay married?"

Swinging his leg over the bench to face me, he said, "I'll do you a why, Miss Prescott—why did you leave?"

Startled, I said, "I had to go with Mrs. Tyler for her sister's wedding. In *Europe*."

"Why did you leave me?"

His antic face still for once, and for a moment, I felt remorse. Then reality asserted itself. "Oh, you would have stood at the docks, pining . . ."

"Yes."

"For all of five minutes."

"At least ten. Maybe even fifteen."

"Don't pretend your heart was broken, Leo Hirschfeld."

"Fine, it wasn't broken. But you put a good dent in it. Why do you think I wrote 'Why Not Me?'"

"Because there's a certain pleasure in maudlin self-pity."

I had meant to sound light, theatrical. But Leo launched himself off the bench and demanded, "Why are you so angry at me? What the hell did I do?"

Well, I thought, that was a grave strategic error on his part. I took a deep breath, preparing to elucidate in full.

Only to find the words wouldn't come. It was not so clearcut, what Leo Hirschfeld had done or hadn't done. Except that everything he did made me feel one way, while everything he said made me feel foolish for feeling that way. He never pretended I was the only girl and made it clear marriage held no interest for him. Therefore, what was given should be given freely. At the time, it felt like there was a certain honor in that. But he had been honest to my face and lied to my heart. Or the other way around, I couldn't tell. Dancing, it had started with dancing and it should have stayed with dancing. Moonlight, Luna Park, the movies . . . I should have known better.

Hands in his pockets, he said, "I took out my old summer pants for cleaning the other day. There was still sand in the cuffs."

Somewhere in my room was a straw hat, the band still stiff with salt from the sea air—a good summer hat, if I changed the band. Yet I hadn't.

He slid the phonograph record across the piano. "Look what I got today."

I picked it up, read "But on Fridays" on the label. Under the title: "Sung by Claude Arden."

"The mouse type at the bottom, Leo Hirschfeld—you squint, you can just see it. Almost as minuscule as my royalties. You want to listen?"

"All right."

He climbed onto the stage and put the record on. After a few scratches, the melodious voice of Claude Arden floated into the air. "A working girl's life is endless toil . . ."

"It used to be 'a maid's,'" I said, absurdly disappointed.

"Arden's change. It's how he got half the royalties. Sidney got most of the rest."

Then Arden sang, "They . . . dance," and Leo held out his hand. There seemed no point in refusing.

Perhaps because we were worn out, neither of us felt inclined to hop, trot, or wiggle. Instead we held. And swayed. And occasionally dipped, which for some reason we both found comical. Then not comical. There is risk in dipping; both parties can only go so far before losing balance. If one person is careless, the other can fall, or both can if arms flail and feet go out from under. At the very least, pride is endangered. And yet you cannot remain planted firmly on the ground, you have to allow for flight. And trust that the other person has you and knows what they're about.

Then Leo pulled me up, holding my hand to his chest. The hand on my back slid to my waist. I was aware of his open shirt collar, the smell of him; of roughly similar heights, we fit well. I had missed that, fitting well, fitting easily. He was starting to kiss along my hairline, nudging gently so I would look up. I looked up.

Of the kiss, I expected the sweet, the familiar. It was neither. Was it the time apart? The difference between a boy with a crowded calendar and a married man? For all his eagerness, Leo had never been one to push. There had been a few game attempts, a few light removals and refusals. Now there was an urgency, a neediness I hadn't felt before . . . from him. It was all coming from him, this new intensity, wasn't it? He stopped for a moment, as if surprised himself. It was the point to step back, to say, *Well* . . .

But we didn't. And had Violet Hirschfeld not walked in, I am not sure what would have happened.

But she did walk in.

And then she walked out.

The following morning Violet went to see Detective Fullerton and told him that on the night of the murder, she had been very unhappy. She had had a great deal to drink. So much so, that while she had been with her husband, she could not be entirely certain that she had been with him at the time of Sidney Warburton's death. In fact, there was a stretch of time where she had no idea of his whereabouts.

As Leo said, you could hardly blame her.

13

Detective Fullerton may have terrified the waiters at Rector's into silence, but he was helpless in the face of the press's infatuation with Violet Tempest. Having subsisted on the detective's deliberately dry and dull reports, the newspapers were gleeful at this revelation from Jelly on Pins. Violet was not directly quoted, but Leo's original alibi and her confession that she had been too drunk to "know if it was morning or midnight" was reported in correct and sober language. The cartoonists were bolder. One showed Violet, tipsy and confused as she tripped over Sidney Warburton's body. Another depicted her in a boozy embrace with her husband—gun in his pocket—asking, "What's THAT, honey?"

I was horrified that Leo had been publicly announced as a suspect and terrified that my lapse in judgment would make its way into the papers. But few took Violet's accusation seriously. A murder investigation could not rely on the testimony of a chorus girl who had overindulged in champagne. Feminine spite was assumed. As was feminine stupidity.

The morning after the story broke, conversation at the Tyler breakfast table was all too audible as William demanded to know just what was going on with "this theatrical fiasco" of Louise's while Louise said it was all a silly misunderstanding and the newspapers looking to make things up.

"How on earth," William demanded, "do you misunderstand a man shot dead in the washroom?"

That, Louise conceded, was true. But the show was going just fine without him, better, really, and . . .

"How can the show be fine if Mr. Hirschfeld is going to jail?"

"He's not going to jail."

"His own wife says he's guilty."

"She didn't say he was guilty, she said she wasn't sure where he was at the time of the murder. She's not the sort of woman who thinks clearly in the best of circumstances, and she was far from it that night. We made that very point to the police."

"So now you're talking to the police about drunken chorus girls."

Throughout, I paid great attention to my eggs and toast, well aware that William had had a telephone call from his mother the day before. The senior Mrs. Tyler had made her views on Louise's activities abundantly clear. Tyler women did not dine at Rector's. Tyler women did not associate with theater people. They certainly did not involve themselves in business and while patronizing the arts was all very well, such interests should be restricted to the opera or orchestra. In short, Tyler women listened to their mothers-in-law and came to Oyster Bay when they were told to.

Then I heard Louise say, "I'm sorry, William, but I won't give it up."

Mrs. Avery grunted over her coffee and Ethel looked gleeful.

Somewhat belatedly William said they should continue this discussion later.

"Later," said Louise, "I shall be at the theater."

★ ★ ★

I would not be at the theater. When I had confessed my unfortunate role in Violet Tempest's about-face, Louise had been understanding. She had also made it clear I was to get out the broom and start sweeping up the mess I had made. And that for the time being, my presence at the Sidney would be more hindrance than help. She would explain my absence to Mrs. St. John.

Certainly, there was work to be done at home. Shoes to be cleaned, hems mended, fall wardrobe to be inspected, jewelry to be sorted. Louise's room had not been tidied as she liked it for weeks. Ethel had done a passable job, but the trained eye could spot problems. As I shook out the satin coverlet of Louise's bed and tucked her pillows just so, I thought, really, it was a good thing I had been banished from the theater. This was where I belonged.

Just as I was tutting Ethel's arrangement of Louise's shoes on the floor of her closet—what had possessed her to line them up by color as opposed to purpose—the young lady herself appeared at the door and said, "Phone for you."

Hurrying down the stairs, I took up the phone and waved Ethel off. Then I said, "Hello?"

And heard, "Exactly how much did Miss Tempest, excuse me, Mrs. Hirschfeld, excuse me, about to be *former* Mrs. Hirschfeld have to drink that evening?"

"Enough that her word on anything should be taken with a grain of salt and several aspirin. You'll notice that Mr. Hirschfeld is still at large."

"For the time being. Is the missus still with the show?"

"I've heard nothing to the contrary."

"As fine a 'no comment' as I've ever heard. I don't suppose you could come out to lunch?"

My spirits rose at the word "out," also the word "lunch." "Why?"

"Because I may have found the man who killed Floyd Lombardo."

★ ★ ★

Louise was already unhappy with me. Stepping out for lunch with a reporter, even one she liked, wasn't likely to get me back in her good graces. But any evidence that might connect the murder of Floyd Lombardo to that of Sidney Warburton and clear Leo—who had no grudge against the flamboyant gambler—should be welcome. At least that was my reasoning as I joined Michael Behan at a bustling Ukrainian café that served large bowls of hot meat borscht and platters of pierogi, neither of which seemed desirable on a humid August day. I was surprised he had chosen to meet so far downtown and said so.

"We'll get to that," he said, using his spoon to cut a chunk of meat in two. "Do I remember right that you said someone had busted Floyd Lombardo's hand?"

I nodded.

"And that he'd been acting panicky about money?"

I nodded again. "That was why he needed the gun. The people he owed were impatient."

"Which either means he was behind on his payment schedule or he lost big and owed them more than usual, and they were worried about getting it back. Guess what sporting event happened about a month ago?"

Why did men assume everyone was as obsessed with sport as they were? "The Pig Aquatics Meet. I don't know, Mr. Behan."

"Belmont. Exactly the sort of event where idiots bet big and lose big. Didn't you say Lombardo said he broke his hand playing polo?"

"Yes"—and I remembered Violet's joke about Owney Davis's interest in horses.

Behan ran a piece of dark bread around the rim of his bowl. "So, I asked some of my friends who dabble in ponies . . ."

"How do you have friends who dabble in ponies?"

"I am an appreciator of the elite athlete, Miss Prescott, equine and human."

"Is that a nice way of saying you bet on horses?"

"Getting back to ponies . . . my friends confirmed that Lombardo was a conspicuous presence at this year's race. Furthermore—are you going to eat that?"

He pointed to my bowl. I slid it in his direction.

"Thank you. Furthermore, Lombardo was shot in the gut. Why shoot someone in the gut? It makes no sense."

"Shooting doesn't make sense."

He paused, spoon halfway between bowl and mouth. "Well, it does if we concede that the goal was to stop Lombardo from breathing."

I conceded that had been the goal.

"Still, I thought: Why not head? Why not chest? Gut's messy, takes time to die. Lombardo was tall, right?"

"He was."

"Lombardo tall, shooter short—there's your bullet to the gut."

Warburton had been short, I thought uneasily. Mistaking my unease for confusion, Behan gestured with his spoon. "Horses, short men . . . adds up to jockeys, don't you think?"

"It could. But why would a jockey shoot Floyd Lombardo?"

"Very good question. One I put to my friends at the track. Racing is a hard sport. Not everyone makes enough to retire well. They get desperate. You put that together with people who make money off the desperate, well, you might find a hand smasher. Or worse."

I knew more than one boxer whose ability to turn grown men to pulp had led to different employment after he left the ring. Still, I said, "There are a lot of desperate people in the city, Mr. Behan."

"Sure. But remember, they outlawed betting on races for a few years. Belmont closed and the sport nearly went under. Now that it's back, it's a relatively select group of individuals who've managed to worm their way back into the sewer level of the business. My friend remembered one particular fellow. Never very good, rode drunk more than sober, and didn't hold back with the whip—even after the race. Some people love horses better than people, but he didn't love either, apparently. Mainly he made a living riding better jockeys into the rails. That caught up to him though and he had a bad fall that left him a little off in the head. A few years back, there were rumors that he knifed a promising jockey for pay. Year ago, he pulled a gun on someone. Turns out, he lives in New York. Got a sister out in Queens."

"So, we're going to Queens?"

"We're looking for a mean ex-jockey and a drunk, Miss Prescott. We're going to a saloon."

Saloons where a man might drink himself to death were plentiful on the Lower East Side. Saloons that catered to men whose business was butchery, also plentiful. But saloons where a murderous ex-jockey could drink and pick up the odd job—those were few. And so Michael Behan and I found ourselves standing outside the Nag's Nose and arguing over whether I should go in. In the reporter's opinion, it was a low place and he didn't want his nose broken when some drunk made a grab. I wasn't dressed to do business; what reason did I have for being there?

"You're a reporter," I said. "I'm your . . . secretary. Say it with a wink and nobody will think twice. If they can think at all."

Still grumbling, he put a hand on my back to suggest familiarity and guided me through the door. The Nag's Nose hearkened back to the time when families had run saloons out of their front parlor while living at the back of the apartment. It was a rough space, with raw wood planks for floor, a low ceiling, and an odd assortment of tables, chairs, and stools. The bar was pocked with rings and scuffed by a thousand drunken kicks. A few drawings of horses hung on the wall, alongside framed photographs of famous jockeys. The air was stale, redolent with beer and unwashed bodies. Yet, even in the middle of the day, thirty or so men had gathered in this dismal place to pour forgetfulness down their throats.

The hum dimmed a bit as we came in, but we were soon absorbed into the crush at the bar where Michael Behan ordered beers for the both of us. Then he talked loudly about the money he'd won on a recent bet. That attracted attention. A round of drinks made him friends. A second round of drinks and he was the most popular man in the place. He was even given a stool. At which point, he announced himself a racing fan, particularly of those jockeys who had the guts and common sense to do whatever it took to win. He became very Irish as he swapped bits of racing lore with the other men, pointedly praising the efforts of riders with Irish names. A portly man teetering on a nearby stool shouted, "They've made it a gentleman's sport. Not a circus, where the monkeys ride the horses!"

Enchanted by his own wit, the gentleman saw fit to repeat the joke several times, inviting Michael to toast this happy progress. Which he did, his smile growing pained over time. Then he said, "Speaking of gentlemen, my father took me to a race when I was a boy and I'll never forget one of the riders. Now he wasn't pretty, but he found spaces, squeezed through, and got the last bit he could out of the nag. That man rode to win."

"Rode to win," slurred the other gentleman.

"Name of Jimmy Galligan. I always wondered what happened to him."

At this, the man went still, then roared, "Wondered what . . . why he's sitting right over there!" He pointed to a dim corner at the far back of the saloon, where a man sat alone at a table.

Affecting awestruck admiration, Behan whispered, "Do you think he'd mind if I went over?"

The beet-faced man lowered his voice. "I'd go over quiet if I was you. Jimmy's had a tender head for the last few years. Gets prickly if he's disturbed."

"How's he been faring?"

"Well, it's not a fair world, as we've been saying," said the gentleman. "But lately, he seems to have had a bit of luck."

"Has he?" said Behan.

"He has. And he's drinking it down as fast as he can."

★ ★ ★

Whatever Jimmy Galligan had been in his youth, life had taken him ruthlessly in its grip and wrung him out until all that was left was a twisted, grimy rag of a human being. His mouth was set at an odd angle and had few teeth left. His nose was broken, his skin pocked. His face was mottled with rage and drink; his hair, rough and pulled, stood up in greasy patches on his skull. Behan's friend had spoken of his brains being knocked around, and the wary gaze that greeted us told me that this was a man who saw enemies everywhere. He accepted Behan's drink and compliments, but made it clear we wouldn't get anything from him in return and we were suckers if we thought otherwise. His gaze narrowed as I sat down and I knew he was one of those men who hated most people and disliked women even more.

Perhaps for this reason, Behan settled for a quieter approach that drew on one of the few passions that still burned in this wasted man: grievance. He asked Galligan about when he'd worked with horses. In reply, Galligan spat on the floor.

"Shame," said Behan. "A man of your talents. How do you make your living these days, Mr. Galligan?"

"Who says I do?"

Behan glanced at the bottle of whiskey. "Would that be a gift from an admirer, then?"

"I'm useful from time to time, I suppose."

Feeling the man would mumble us into submission, I asked, "In what way, Mr. Galligan?"

He squinted at me the way you would vermin: disgust and incredulity that I was present and had made myself known. I would have to make the oddness of my presence an asset. Was there anything a woman might have to offer a man like this? A discarded newspaper with a headline about the trial of Mrs. Carman for murdering her husband's lover gave me an idea.

Planting my clasped hands on the edge of the table as a signal I wished to do business, I said, "For example, if a lady decided she wished to be rid of her husband, could you be of use to her? Or it needn't be a husband. Just a gentleman of her acquaintance."

Galligan's poisonous little eyes slid in Behan's direction. "Nice. Doesn't even wait till you're out of the room."

"He's not the gentleman I wish to be rid of. Obviously."

The eyes flicked down to my hand. "Don't see a ring."

"Women can get entangled with the wrong man in all kinds of ways. I'm sure you're familiar with the sort of man I mean. A leech. Parasite. Never worked a day in his life, still feels entitled to the worldly comforts better men can't afford. He lives off women. Borrows. Doesn't pay his debts. He has a certain charm, but it wears thin. And one day, the lady—or someone else—grows tired of him. And they decide it's time for him to pay up. Once and for all. So they find a bill collector. Is that your line of work, Mr. Galligan? Bill collection?"

I could see he recognized Floyd Lombardo from my description. But he was still unsure how much to trust me. The bottle was close to empty. From what the gentleman at the bar had said, Galligan was running through funds quickly. He didn't want to talk to me. But I could feel his neediness. He was close to death, but not quite ready to go and wanted to enjoy himself—or numb himself—before departure.

"Answer me, Mr. Galligan—are you useful or no?"

"Don't care for the kind of man you describe," he grunted.

"Have you known such men?"

"Maybe."

"Held them to account? Made them pay what's owed?"

"Held them to account, let's say."

"I'd want it clean. What's your method?"

"River cleans up most messes."

"What if the gentleman dislikes water?"

"Bullet usually gets them over it."

It was a sorry statement on our times, but Floyd Lombardo was probably not the only man who had been killed in the past month for nonpayment of debts. And yet I couldn't ask Galligan for references or specifics of past work.

Glancing at the bottle, I said, "Right now, you look like a man of leisure. When was the last time you worked?"

"Sometime in the past two months." That squared with his unusual cash flow.

"I'd need to know you can handle resistance."

"I can."

"You're not a big man. I need more than your word."

The reference to his size provoked as intended. Pointing a

shaky finger, Galligan growled, "You go over to Bellevue, ask for a gentleman of the name of Armisen. He'll give me a reference."

Armisen. That was one of Floyd's aliases. Working to remain calm in light of the fact that I was sitting across from a confessed killer, I said, "I think I know the man. At least I knew one of his friends. A Mr. Warburton?"

I saw no recognition of the name. Stupid to hope Galligan had killed both men, but at least I had tried. A question came unformed. I knew there was something more to ask, but before I could get at it, Behan nudged me: *Time to go.*

"I'll be in touch, Mr. Galligan."

"I'll be here. Or I won't be." Then tilting a grimy glass at Behan, he said, "Best of luck. Me, I'd put a pillow over her before she does the same to you."

So advised, Michael Behan kept a careful eye on me as we left. A few times, he opened his mouth, then either judged we were not far away enough for easy talk—or he was as yet uncertain what he wished to say. After the bile of the Nag's Nose, I felt a need for clean wind and open space. So I led us toward the piers where the stench of despair and the thud of glasses was replaced by the smell of fish piled high on tables and the screech of seagulls. I listened to the creak of ships and the shouts of employed and busy men. Then I took in the vast expanse of blue sky and breathed deep, feeling I had escaped.

Then Michael Behan announced, "That is a side of you, Miss Prescott, I have never seen before and wish never to see again. 'I'd want it clean.'" He shuddered.

Ignoring his theatrics, I said, "Well, now we know who killed Floyd Lombardo. But I didn't see any sign that Galligan was connected to Sidney Warburton."

"Doesn't seem much of a theatergoer," agreed Behan.

"Also," I realized with sinking heart, "Warburton was a better investment than Floyd Lombardo. Even if he did borrow money from the likes of Owney Davis, there would be no reason to shoot him until the show failed."

"So . . ."

So I would not be able to give Louise glad tidings that someone unconnected to the show had killed Sidney Warburton.

On the other hand, I would be able to tell her that Nedda Fiske had not shot Floyd Lombardo. Something some might say she had every right to do.

Whether or not she shot Sidney Warburton was still in doubt. But why would she, unless she knew Lombardo was dead and she blamed Warburton for his killing?

We walked along the edge of the island. Behan asked, "Any thoughts as to who *did* kill Warburton? Mrs. Hirschfeld seems to have put her husband in a difficult spot."

Disliking this subject, I kicked at a discarded tobacco tin. "Oh, I don't care. Let the police handle it."

We came upon a bench and Behan said, "You seem out of sorts, Miss Prescott. Would you care to sit? Perhaps your feet hurt."

We sat. I stared out at the glittering gray ribbon of the East River, letting my eye wander to the Brooklyn Bridge in the distance. Behan made notes. Brought down to earth by the scratch of his pencil, I said, "Are you writing about Warburton?"

"Not unless you're willing to be more forthcoming. The detective is running an unusually professional investigation and news is hard to come by. But there's something in Galligan. Ugly side of racing . . ."

"How did you come by your passion for horses?"

"My father. He was the real expert. He taught me to read with the sports pages."

I smiled. "No."

"But yes. He would put me on his lap, and say, Michael, find me Isaac Murphy on this page. Find me Oliver Lewis. I'd figure out the sounds and point to what I thought it was, and if I had it right, he'd quiz me. Time of his fastest race, horse he rode in the Kentucky Derby, things like that. As long I got the right answer, I could stay up. First wrong answer, off to bed. I didn't get to see him much, so . . ."

"So you wanted to find those names."

"I did." He tapped his notebook. "There's a good story here. I might even get a byline out of it."

"How so?"

"If you write something beyond the daily dose of misery, something special like, say, a wonderfully evocative portrait of a jockey gone wrong, sometimes the *Herald* gives you credit." He drew a finger over the cover of the notebook. "'By Michael Behan.'"

"You'd be famous," I said lightly.

He tucked the notepad back in his pocket. "Just be nice to have my name on my work for a change."

That brought an image of him with Tib on his lap. *All right, now, find me Michael Behan on this page.*

"Of course. And you should."

I thought of Adele St. John's gorgeous fantasia of a dress—her name would be on that. Claude's name on that record. Leo's name in all those newspapers as the composer of "But on Fridays." Then imagined "This pair of shoes selected by Jane Prescott." "This brush moved to its proper place by Jane Prescott." No, it wasn't work you'd put a name to. Which had never bothered me before. And yet I couldn't escape feeling somehow . . . lesser. Ninety-nine percent of the world lived and died without the rest of the ninety-nine percent knowing who they were. Why should it bother me to be one of them? Why did I suddenly feel that unless I was someone with my name on things, someone *known*, there wasn't much point?

"Should we tell the police about Galligan?" I asked.

He squinted into the distance. "I suppose we should but we don't have proof and the man'll be dead inside a year anyway. I don't have the sense the public is clamoring for the capture of Floyd Lombardo's killer."

Nedda Fiske would be, I thought. There was still something that nagged me about Floyd Lombardo's death, some vague tendril that reached toward Warburton's killing. But I felt sure Owney Davis hadn't sent Galligan, or another of his ilk, after the producer. And beyond that, I couldn't see what would tie the two men's deaths together.

A dockyard worker pushed a cart stacked high with crates through a nearby puddle, splashing our shoes with muck. It seemed a sign to go. As we rose to make our way to the train, Behan asked, "Mind if I ask a difficult question?"

"You'll ask it anyway."

"What'll you do if your man did it?"

I was about to ask how desperately he needed a story when he added, "Only you've been known to have a bit of a soft spot for people who kill people."

Anger rising, I said, "I don't recall feeling anything remotely soft for George Rutherford."

"Point taken. But Mrs. Hirschfeld's sudden recollection of what she can't recollect is problematic, don't you think?"

"Mrs. Hirschfeld is lying."

"Lying implies she can remember what happened and construct its opposite. Why would she lie?"

"Because she and Mr. Hirschfeld had an argument."

"So she ran off and told the police her husband was a murderer?"

"It was a . . . very bad argument." Actually, there had been no argument. Some attempt at an apology by Leo, but the door had slammed shut between "I'm" and "sorry."

There was a long pause as Michael Behan tried to fathom Leo's actual crime. Then he said, "Ah. Which one, Arden or Fiske?"

I truly, truly did not wish to be honest with him. But neither of those women deserved to be dragged into scandal because I had been an idiot. "Neither Arden, nor Fiske."

"Don't tell me he made a play for Louise Tyler. She's got a good six inches on him."

"It was not Louise Tyler and if you write anything that implies it was, Mr. Tyler will sue your wretched paper and I will break every one of your fingers."

At this, he let out a long, quiet exhale and looked down the street. Explanations and excuses came to mind. It wasn't, it was only, he needn't think . . . Then the stubborn thought that I didn't owe Michael Behan excuse or explanation.

"At any rate, that's why she's lying."

"Oh, *she's* lying. *She's* the one who's got it all wrong."

"Well, it's certainly a convenient time for her to remember she had no idea where Leo was."

"I'm not sure you can be called a disinterested witness when it comes to Jelly on Pins, Miss Prescott."

He disapproved. The smug Irish . . . prig disapproved. He had judged me as a conniving interloper casting aspersions on a wife who had been carrying out an affair throughout her entire marriage. And yet *I* was the scarlet woman who couldn't be trusted.

He observed that I had picked up some Parisian habits. I observed that he was a jackass.

Then I left him there on the street.

★ ★ ★

That night, I informed Louise that Michael Behan had it on good authority that Floyd Lombardo had been killed over his debts by people who probably had no idea who Sidney Warburton was—much less any interest in killing him. Louise sighed and expressed the hope that the detective would hurry up and find that anonymous killer who had slipped in and out of Rector's unseen. I said I hoped so, too.

Then she informed me that I could return to the theater. "Mrs. St. John insists."

"Was she told why I didn't come today?" I asked, apprehensive.

"Well . . . yes. Mrs. Hirschfeld was rather vocal about what happened. I think she wants sympathy. But they all seem to be taking Mr. Hirschfeld's side."

I said I would make a point of apologizing to Mrs. Hirschfeld first thing.

"Do thank Mrs. St. John as well," said Louise. "And Mr. Harney, he said Peanut was pining for you."

I smiled.

"Oh—and Mrs. Arden." Louise widened her eyes to show surprise that I had received support from this quarter. "She told Mrs. Hirschfeld that she was overreacting, especially given that she . . . with Mr. Warburton."

Curious, I asked, "Mrs. Arden wasn't upset that Mr. Hirschfeld and I . . . ?" We were having difficulty with verbs, I noticed.

"No. She said it's very common for people to get caught up when they're doing a show. Nothing to be taken seriously."

My first reaction was indignation at being dismissed in this way; I had not gotten "caught up." My second was to wonder, how would Blanche Arden know? To her husband, she had insisted that her flirtations were a matter of business; certainly Sidney Warburton was not a man to inspire genuine ardor in a woman such as Blanche. Whereas the little scene she played out with Leo in the wings had been more . . . skillfully acted.

Mother Hirschfeld's son never lied. If Leo told me he believed

Warburton to be Blanche's lover, then he sincerely believed they were the pair I had overhead that day.

But he did omit.

With whom had Blanche gotten caught up? Had she, in fact, been caught?

And had Sidney Warburton paid the price?

14

The next day, I returned to the show. It was not a warm welcome back. When I said good morning to Harriet Biederman, she was correct but nothing more. Mr. Harney handed over Peanut for his walk with a gentle look of reproach. The Ardens ignored me as usual. Mrs. St. John passed off a basket of soiled clothing and vanished before I could thank her. Studiously, I avoided Leo and just as studiously, he avoided me.

I kept myself below in the wardrobe room. Whenever my work for Mr. Harney and Peanut took me to the theater level, I tried to be inconspicuous, so as not to give offense. Not surprisingly, Violet and Leo were not speaking; all direction from him was communicated to Miss Biederman who relayed it to Violet, who as often as not ignored it. Her visit to the police having given her the whip hand, Miss Tempest was not in the mood to be directed—in anything. She had a new and bold approach to the role: overact beyond what I would have thought humanly possible. A happy musicale was now played as if Medea was its heroine.

At lunchtime, with dry mouth and roiling stomach, I knocked on the door of Violet's dressing room. I had given a lot of thought as to how to best approach this meeting. In some ways, it felt silly to apologize for kissing Leo when the marriage was a matter of business. But if there was little love involved, there was pride. Position. Violet was already resented and I had embarrassed her. No wonder she was acting up.

She asked who it was. I identified myself. The door opened.

Mindful of ears around us, I whispered, "Mrs. Hirschfeld, may I please speak with you?"

For a long moment, she hesitated; the urge to slam the door in my face was clear. Then she stepped back and let it swing open. Not specifically invited, I waited a moment, then went inside, saying, "I would like very much to apologize. And to explain . . ."

Violet had taken refuge in a corner chair. Picking at a loose thread as if it were an act that required great concentration, she said, "You don't have to explain. It's not complicated. He got an itch, you were there."

I swallowed the insult. "In any event, if my being here causes you distress, I will ask Mrs. Tyler to relieve me of my duties on the show."

She shrugged. "I don't mind if you stay."

Her nonchalance was frustrating, in part because I didn't believe it. Her averted gaze and crude assessment of the situation told me she was angry. Which she had a right to be. I found myself wishing she would scream, throw things, even slap me. I wasn't sure how to manage this mumbling hostility. Several lines of melodrama came to mind. I settled on bluntness. "I don't want your husband, Mrs. Hirschfeld."

Again, the maddening half shrug.

"And I don't want to embarrass you or cause more gossip."

Progress—she looked at me. "I just thought . . . maybe you were someone who didn't think I was a joke."

Setting aside all the times I had thought exactly that, I said, "I don't."

She plucked the thread loose, began winding it around her finger. "I'm guessing you and Leo had something before I met him; he's had something with half the girls in New York. I mean, even on this show . . ."

I had told myself Leo was telling the truth when he said he was not Blanche's lover. Alternatively, I had told myself that I would not care if he were. Now I discovered neither was true and felt a dispiriting wrench of misery.

"And I know you know about me and Sidney."

"Yes. I'm sorry. For your loss. It must be very difficult."

It was an awkward condolence, but she appreciated it, murmuring, "It is. I miss him. He wasn't always kind, but he knew what was best for me and I trusted him."

I marveled that she could feel so much for a man who'd been so cruel to her. But then, Nedda Fiske suffered from the same malady. And there were those who might say my attachment to Leo didn't show the best judgment, myself included.

"Leo, I feel like the only thing he cares about is the show. He's not taking care of *me*. So I have to."

I indicated that that was always a wise strategy.

"I'm the star now. I don't need people laughing at me." I nodded, braced for dismissal. "But you don't have to go."

I must have shown my surprise, because she added, "I'd appreciate a little help with my costumes. The old battle-ax forgets there are two women in the show."

"Of course."

"Everyone around here wants me to fail. I could use a friend."

She looked at me uncertain: would I be that? What she had said was true; her old protector was dead and her new one . . . distractible. I nodded. Then remembered I had come with a purpose beyond making amends to Violet Tempest.

"Mrs. Hirschfeld, you do know that your husband didn't kill Mr. Warburton."

I had advocated for Leo too soon. Alerted to the fact that I had concerns other than her, Violet became wary. "I only know what I told the police. And that was that I didn't know."

This was pure Violet Tempest idiocy. "But you told them after . . ." I indicated myself. "You were hurt, I understand. But—"

"It wasn't about that," she said, feigning indifference. "But when someone lies to you, you remember that it's important to tell the truth. I never felt right, telling that lie. I didn't want it on my conscience."

She was so simple, it was difficult to know if she had genuinely convinced herself her act had no malice in it. It occurred to me that her generosity to me had also been calculated: I was to be the ever-present reminder of Violet's visit to the detective. One wrong word from Leo, one critique too harsh, one piece of staging changed to favor the Ardens, and she would go straight back to the police.

Biting through my tongue, I said, "But the police won't look for the real killer if they're focused on Mr. Hirschfeld. You must want that person brought to justice . . ."

Her expression hardened, losing its bewildered lamb softness. "Oh, I know who killed Sidney and after this show, that person is going to pay, believe me."

For a moment she sat, lost in anger. Her jaw was set, her shoulders rigid, the hands in her lap clenched and powerful; she was not a delicate woman, I realized. And not a ridiculous one. Fleetingly, I saw a very different Violet Tempest, a far more compelling one than Salome on Stairs.

Then she looked down at a pile of discarded clothes on the floor, as if to remind me that I had responsibilities: rumpled stockings, a discarded corset, a chemise yellow with sweat. Standing, I gathered them into my arms to show I knew my place.

Taking Violet's clothes to the sink near the wardrobe room, I wondered if the actress truly suspected Leo of murdering her lover. She hadn't said it was Leo, but whom else would she need through the show and then no further? I ran hot water into the sink as I thought of Harriet, silent as her eyes brimmed. Adele St. John swearing Mr. Harney never left the table. Claude Arden, who had not returned to the table with his wife. I liked all those people far more than I liked the dead man.

All of a sudden Warburton's nasty joke about bicycles came to mind, with its hint of warm, damp seats and tires flabby from overuse. That slur reminded me of Michael Behan's curt observation about Parisian habits and I felt a mix of rage and shame so scalding it brought tears.

Then I saw I hadn't put the plug in the sink and all the water had run out. I let out a cry of frustration, punctuated by a well-chosen epithet. This brought Claude Arden up short as he came down the hall and I had no choice but to present myself as the tearstained, red-faced misery I had become.

Digging in his pocket, he handed me a handkerchief. "What happened? Was he unkind?"

Stunned that the haughty Claude Arden should show interest, I said, ". . . No. We haven't spoken."

"That's probably best for now. The show didn't need the first love triangle, Lord knows we don't need a second. Not that I'd call what's between the Hirschfelds love."

He advised me to blow my nose. I did.

"You seem like a sincere young woman. Think twice about getting mixed up in this." He gestured around the theater.

"It's not a place for genuine feeling. In here? Best to wear your armor."

Touched, I remembered Claude's yearning gaze at his spouse, the way he had spoken of that "one girl" he loved. I very much hoped he had not been driven by genuine feeling to do something terrible.

I promised I would wash the handkerchief and have it back first thing in the morning. Then leaving the clothes to soak, I went in search of Mrs. St. John. I found that excellent woman in her lair, contemplating Blanche's last dance dress. As I came in, she gestured to a pair of pants Mr. Harney had split and shoes of Mr. Arden's that needed buffing. "There's also a factory girl costume that needs letting out around the bust. If I can rely on you not to stick pins in it."

I started with the pants. "I want to thank you for speaking on my behalf."

A quick glance over her shoulder. "You're welcome. But really, it was Mr. Harney. He went into a decline and the dog was leaving its business everywhere. Desperate times, etcetera."

"I'll thank him as well."

Sitting down on a stool, she took up her sketch pad. "I hear you and the missus had a chat."

"I thought she deserved the opportunity to throw something at me." Mrs. St. John's mouth twitched. "Also I was hoping I could talk her into telling the police the truth. It's my fault she changed her story and put the show in danger."

"If you want to talk anyone into anything, talk Mr. Hirschfeld into calling her bluff and firing her before she ruins the show."

Remembering Violet's statement that everyone wanted her to fail, I was curious as to how deep the hostility went. "Someone has to play the part."

"Do they? The public has never had a problem with just the Ardens before."

"Perhaps Miss Fiske will come back."

"She's only marginally less vulgar."

So the Ardens did not want Violet and they didn't want Nedda Fiske. They wanted the factory girl gone. What had Claude said? The show didn't need the first love triangle and certainly not a second? It occurred to me that getting rid of Floyd Lombardo had been the first step in Nedda's collapse and withdrawal from the show.

But Jimmy Galligan had killed Floyd because of unpaid debts, making the Ardens' dislike of Nedda Fiske irrelevant.

But their affections for other people, I reminded myself, were not.

Striving for lightness of tone, I said, "I envy you, being so close to the Ardens. What are they like, really?"

Eyes on the sketch pad, she said, "That's not a question, it's a request. Is this something you want from them or something you wish to know about them?"

"I suppose I'm looking for inspiration. It's a happy marriage, isn't it?"

"Mr. and Mrs. Arden are ideally suited," she pronounced. "A more harmonious pair you could not imagine."

"And they . . . only harmonize with each other?"

Now she looked up with narrowed eyes. "Oh, dear. What newspaper is paying you?"

I was startled by the swiftness of the accusation. "None."

"Just casually interested in the state of the Arden marriage," she said. "Nothing in it for you. Well, if it's Mr. Arden you're hoping for, I'm afraid you'll be disappointed. He's quite devoted."

"I know. I know he loves Mrs. Arden very much." I did not like what I had to say, but knew it had to be said. "I don't see the same devotion from her."

She drew swift sharp lines on the page. "I cannot think what's gotten into your head, but I am tempted to slap it right out."

"At Rector's, Mrs. Arden was flirting quite visibly with Mr. Hirschfeld . . ."

"Aren't you the jealous little squit?"

Fed up with her protectiveness of her patron—and not a little stung—I stated in blunt terms what I had heard in the dressing room that day. "Mr. Arden was onstage. But two gentlemen were not: Mr. Hirschfeld and Mr. Warburton. I asked Mr. Hirschfeld . . ."

"And he of course was completely honest with you."

"He claimed it was Mr. Warburton. Who did have a reputation of enjoying the company of other men's wives and who was shot two days later."

Slapping down her pencil, she said, "Why on earth would Claude Arden shoot the man who has promoted his career for decades? The man responsible for producing this very show? Dear God, don't be such a child."

I was just young enough for that insult to hurt. Losing my temper, I said, "Mrs. Arden was harmonizing quite loudly with someone not her husband. I don't think it was Leo Hirschfeld and you say it wasn't Mr. Warburton. She would never have had anything to do with Floyd Lombardo and I think we can agree Mr. Harney is out of the question. So who was it?"

No doubt Mrs. St. John meant to accuse me of lying. Or say she didn't know. Or, even at this late point, challenge me on whether or not I had in fact heard Blanche Arden. Why not Nedda Fiske? Why not Violet Tempest? They could have easily borrowed her dressing room—it was the largest.

But she did none of these things. She just sat there with a small, resigned smile.

Until I said, "Oh."

I looked at the wonder of a dress. "It's so beautiful, I should have . . ."

"It's beautiful because I have skill and I like to make beautiful things and get paid handsomely for doing so. Love has nothing to do with it. But in every other respect, yes."

I wasn't unaware of women who loved women. There had been attachments at the refuge; some of the women went on to share apartments and lives. On the Lower East Side, the occasional couple was bold enough to walk arm in arm. At Mrs. Armslow's there had been a cook and housekeeper so emotionally partnered, we joked that they were married—and perhaps they were in a way. Yet I was surprised; Blanche Arden and Adele St. John were handsome, wealthy women, able to choose anyone they wanted. So they were, I realized, and they had chosen each other.

Still. Adele St. John had trusted me with a secret that was not hers alone to keep. It felt right to exchange confidence for confidence.

"I guess I am a jealous little squit."

Mrs. St. John observed that Leo Hirschfeld was a poor mate for anyone with a jealous temperament—and if they didn't have one to start, they soon would have. Just then Blanche Arden put her lovely head around the door and sniffed. "This smells doomy."

Mrs. St. John waved her in. "I'm explaining that Claude did not kill Sidney in a fit of cuckolded rage."

She tilted her head to suggest that she had explained a few other things as well.

"Oh. Truth telling." Blanche turned to me. "A gentle reminder: if you run off to the newspapers or decide to entertain your pals in the scullery with the scandalous goings-on of theater folk . . ."

"I wouldn't do that, I promise."

"No, you truly won't do that. Because I like Mr. Hirschfeld

and I'd hate to tell lurid stories about him that are none of anyone's business."

Her tone made it clear that I would be included in those stories and she would use every ounce of skill in the telling. I would
be unemployable.

"I wouldn't," I said again. "I won't. Mrs. St. John has been very
kind to me." It was an odd thing to say of that brusque woman,
but true.

Settling in beside Mrs. St. John, Blanche said, "Well, that's
true, she is kind. But I'm not and you remember that."

We sat in silence a long moment. Then Mrs. St. John said,
"She's wondering if Claude knows."

"Oh, and if he *cares*. Claude does care—passionately."

Pained, I nodded.

"About a dreary little woman who lives in Rocky River, Ohio."

I blinked.

"Claude's beloved is named Ruth Stobitz. They were childhood sweethearts in the days of yore. Ruth's father owned a mill.
Ruth wanted Claude to work in that mill. Ruth wanted Claude
to sing in church and church only. Be respectable. Steadily employed. Claude loved her, but he did not love mills. Or Rocky
River. And he knew he had the talent to be something more. And
so he broke poor Ruth's heart and became the man who sings
'She of the Emerald Eyes.'"

So, this was the "one girl" who had Claude Arden's heart.
"Does Ruth have emerald eyes?" I asked, hopeful.

"I haven't the faintest idea. Claude won't give up performing,
but he loves Ruth still. He even writes to her when he's feeling
exceptionally desperate and I gather she writes back."

"Why didn't she come with him?"

"And leave Rocky River?" said Blanche, as if aghast. "Leave
the dear old mill? For something as disreputable as the theater?"

"But isn't it difficult for you?" The whole conversation had become so improbable; we had entered a wholly different realm, where truths were told, souls bared, and nothing deemed shocking unless it was cruel. Or tacky.

"Oh, Lord no. Sidney put us together. My old partner got herself in the family way in Detroit. I could dance. Claude could sing. I needed a partner, he needed a new act. The Castles have made matrimony so bankable, and Sidney wanted a double act, so he insisted we get married. Claude made it very clear to me that he would never 'love another,' as he put it. I said that was fine with me as long as he didn't expect me to play by those rules."

She looked fondly at Mrs. St. John. Then said, "The only thing I do mind is that he gets so gloomy. Deep down, I think he feels the sacrifice of Saint Ruth is only worth it if we become the biggest stars in the history of the stage."

"He does seem in bad temper at times," I said.

"Claude is not a natural dancer and he gets very anxious with a new show. The only way for him to cope with the stage fright is to do it again and again and again, work it into the muscle to the point where we could do it in our sleep. Not to mention, this has been a fairly fraught production. Dalliances I'm used to. But this is my first dead producer."

Peering at me, she asked, "What on earth made you think Claude had shot Sidney?"

Not wanting to mention her romantic interlude, I said, "I overheard you and Mr. Arden arguing on the dance floor. You said something about the family business, so I thought perhaps he was jealous." Blanche looked puzzled. "Both men were wearing yellow spats, you see, Mr. Warburton and Mr. Hirschfeld."

"You had been putting on a show for Mr. Hirschfeld," Mrs. St. John reminded her.

"I had not," said Blanche. "I was putting on a show for you, my darling. But yes, Claude assumed it was Mr. Hirschfeld and said I was making a scene. He was worried Sidney wouldn't like it. Sidney was jealous of Mr. Hirschfeld, I think. All that youth and talent."

She said this with a warmth that made me remember that interlude in the wings. I didn't want to hurt Mrs. St. John, but I wanted to be sure. "You're certain Mr. Arden didn't think you were . . . dallying with Mr. Hirschfeld? At times, you seemed not unenamored."

"It's never a bad idea to have a talented man aware of your charms," she said crisply. "Besides, don't you think it's possible you were seeing things through a rather green-eyed lens?"

It was possible. Even likely. And several other things had now become distinctly unlikely. I couldn't think of any reason for Blanche to shoot Warburton and if the Darling Ardens were a fiction and the "one girl" was back in Ohio—there was no reason for Claude to have shot him either. This left me with a list of names that made me very unhappy.

Mrs. St. John said, "You seem distressed."

"I admit I was attached to the idea of Mr. Arden killing Mr. Warburton in a fit of jealous passion because it cleared Mr. Hirschfeld."

Blanche's eyes brightened. "That would make a wonderful movie. Sidney as a dirty-fingered cad, tormenting a hopeful young actress. One day, he goes too far, she screams. Her costar, secretly in love with her, races in and shoots the villain . . ."

"And goes to prison where he is hanged," finished Mrs. St. John. In love with the dramatic Mrs. Arden she might be, but I could not imagine her killing to defend her honor; histrionic proofs of devotion—they, too, I realized, were make-believe. Too bad, they sounded fun.

"So who *did* kill our dirty-fingered cad?" Blanche Arden wondered.

Three pairs of female eyes met: how candid were we to be?

"Mr. Hirschfeld does have motive," said Blanche. "Sidney was horrible to him, slept with his wife . . ."

"If you shot everyone who . . . ," drawled Mrs. St. John. Blanche shooed her quiet.

"He's a rather romantic boy in his own way. Remember how he stood up for Violet every time Sidney insulted her?"

"I remember he was enraged to be called a drooling chimp. Come to think of it, what about Mrs. Hirschfeld?"

"I'd love to get rid of her. But with everything she'd had to drink that night?" Blanche shook her head. "I can't imagine her handling a gun in the best of circumstances. At any rate, why? She enjoyed playing one man off the other. You can't do that if one of them is dead."

Guiltily, I thought that an imprisoned Violet Tempest *would* solve a host of problems. But remembering her savagery when she spoke of Warburton's killer—and my promise to be her ally—I said, "I think she loved Mr. Warburton. She may really believe Mr. Hirschfeld killed him."

"Nonsense," said Mrs. St. John. "But she's lost one meal ticket and when she saw the two of you the other night, she realized she was about to lose another. Hence her sudden memory lapse."

Leaning her head on her hand, Blanche asked, "What's he like, little Leo?" Probably like Peanut, Mrs. St. John opined, but more attractive.

Wanting to be off that subject, I asked them, "Did you know Mr. Warburton for a long time? Mr. Hirschfeld said he'd made a lot of enemies along the way."

Both women shook their heads. "I'd say other than Claude, Roland Harney has known him the longest," said Mrs. St. John. "You could ask Miss Biederman. Maybe she keeps a list of Warburton's enemies in that book of hers."

"If anyone *should* have shot him, it's Miss Biederman," I said. "He was so cruel to her."

I had meant it as a joke, but Blanche took it seriously. "Was she even there that night?"

"Ran out early to keep the fiancé happy," said Mrs. St. John. "I can't see it. A loyal servant to the last."

The issue of loyalty raised, I recalled Adele St. John's sudden—and untrue—defense of Roland Harney. She had said he was at the table the entire time when in fact, he had disappeared to the bathroom. I was trying to think of a polite way to raise the subject when our conversation was interrupted by the sound of shoes clattering down the stairs and shouting from Violet: "Miss Biederman, kindly inform the director that until Mr. Harney is sober, I shall not go on!"

Then, from a distance, Leo's rejoinder: "Miss Biederman, will you kindly tell my wife that if we wait until Mr. Harney is sober, she will never go on."

Then "That's fine with me!" from Violet and a slammed door.

Blanche whispered, "Dare we hope that was the last straw?"

"I doubt it," said Mrs. St. John. "She's got Mr. Hirschfeld over a barrel and she knows it. Right now, she might be playing 'I was too drunk to remember,' but one firm accusation from her and the detective puts him in handcuffs."

"I don't understand why she wants to stay," I said with more petulance than was ideal. "She isn't good and the critics will be cruel."

Blanche Arden laid a hand on my arm. "She's an actress, dear. And it's a part. A very, very good part."

The grip tightened slightly.

★ ★ ★

At the end of the day, I was on my way to rejoin Louise in the theater when I passed by the office and heard Leo on the phone.

". . . No, Mrs. Warburton, I wanted you to hear it from me personally. Sidney meant the world to me. I would never, never have harmed him. I miss him every day, I swear to you."

Then he caught sight of me and waved frantically that I should come in. As I did, he said, "Yes. My wife is . . . well, she'd had a little too much to drink. She was confused."

There was a pause as he listened to the reply. From her tone, I had the sense that Mrs. Warburton was not unaware of Violet's connection with her husband. And not disposed to think well of her. Leo made noises of faint objection, but did not defend his wife.

Finally he said, "I can't wait for you to see it. Yes. Sidney's song, you're going to . . . bring several handkerchiefs, that's all I can say. Yes. Good-bye. Yes."

Hanging up, he set his hands against his forehead, then pulled his hair straight up, eyes popping as he did so. Then coming around the desk, he said, "I'm sorry, I'm sorry, I never meant for you . . ."

His arms were open, I felt intent to embrace. I had promised Violet not to embarrass her, promised Louise not to cause more trouble.

I put a hand between us. "It was mutual stupidity."

He stopped dead. "That's . . . no, you're right, stupidity's a good word. I guess. I—"

I felt questions in the air, ones without easy answers. I dispelled them with a simpler one: "Did you convince the widow Warburton you didn't kill her husband?"

"I think so. She's not Violet's biggest fan."

Retreating behind the desk, he said, "I suppose I should ask— do you think I shot Sidney Warburton?"

"No."

"That was fast."

It had been fast. I turned the "no" over in my mind. Warburton had insulted Leo, insulted his wife. That might drive some men to murder—not Leo Hirschfeld. But Warburton had posed a threat to the thing that mattered most to him. When we first met, Leo had brashly predicted that one day, all Broadway would be one big Hirschfeld production. This show was the first step. Warburton had given Leo that chance—but he had also threatened to take it away in every way that mattered. I had to allow for the fact that dancing with a man or other intimacies didn't tell you everything there was to know about him. In fact, they confused the issue considerably.

There were very good reasons for Leo Hirschfeld to shoot Sidney Warburton. Why weren't any of them good enough?

"If you're going to call the police, at least have the courtesy to give me a five-minute start."

I turned to him. "Mother Hirschfeld never lies. I hear her son takes after her."

"Yes, he does," said Leo quietly.

"He does omit facts."

"From time to time."

"Did you shoot Sidney Warburton?"

"No."

"Well, then." I crossed my arms. "I'll tell you another reason you didn't shoot Sidney Warburton: you're arrogant. Ridiculously arrogant and it's an insult to your talent to have to shoot someone who stood in your way. Delusional or not, you think your songs are too great not to be successful. Killing Warburton would mean a lapse of faith in your talent. And I can't see that ever happening. 'Warburton? What's Warburton? I'm Leo Hirschfeld, damn it.'"

"I really am madly in love with you."

"The question is what do we do about it?"

"About . . . ?"

Hope was in his eyes. I doused it with a snap of the fingers. "Finding Warburton's killer."

"Oh, that." He waved a hand. "I told you, a thousand people wanted to kill Sidney. Anybody who ever worked with him."

"You wouldn't happen to have a list of those people, would you?" I asked sarcastically.

Then I remembered: there was such a list. At least a record. With pictures. People who had worked with Sidney Warburton, only to vanish except as a faded piece of paper in a book. Perhaps one of them had returned.

"Call Mrs. Warburton back."

"Why?"

"Tell her you need that scrapbook. Inspiration for the song you're writing. Tell her I'll be by this evening to pick it up."

Intrigued, Leo took up the phone.

15

Early that evening, I arrived at the Warburton home to the sound of screams. Alarmed, I put my head close to the door; a woman's screams . . . but more in rage than terror. Two women? No, a woman and a child. Shriek after shriek, each punctuated by an explosive *No!*

I rang again. Heard shouts and the pounding of feet. Then the door was yanked open and a young woman, her hair in disarray, stood before me. It was the sullen maid from our first visit.

"I'm so sorry," I said. "Mrs. Warburton said I could come for the book."

"She's not at home."

No, judging from the chaos behind her—rugs askew, lamps overturned, chairs on their side in the hallway—the house had been surrendered to the five little Warburtons who were now pillaging at will.

Fearful that Mrs. Warburton had forgotten her promise, I said, "Did she leave it . . ."

"Yes, she left it," snapped the maid. "And now Simon has it and won't let go of it." She gestured toward the stairs. "He's in his room, you're welcome to try. I have to give the baby its bath." And with that she stomped off.

Gingerly I made my way up the stairs, following the path of rejected clothes, discarded towels, and thrown toys and books to the third floor. Stepping over a pillow that had been used as a weapon judging from the flurry of feathers, I saw a five-year-old boy sitting on a stripped bed, his arms wrapped around the scrapbook. With a riot of dark curls and a scowl on his tearstained face, he looked like a small Beethoven. He was either the nose-picker or the one whose foot had been stepped on. Seeing me, he screamed, "No!" as a warning shot.

I asked if I could sit on the bed and was informed, "No!" But when I asked if the book in his arms was about his father, I got a sulky nod.

My feelings about children—especially screaming ones—were ambivalent. Part of me wanted to unbuckle his little hands and take the book without further ado. But I knew that would upset him. And I was reluctant to do that.

"You will get it back," I promised him. "We just want to look at all the wonderful things your father did, so Mr. Hirschfeld can write a song about him."

He shook his head, not wanting to be bargained with.

"You'll get to hear the song," I tried.

He lifted his chin off the book. "At the theater? Will he be there?"

"Who?"

"Papa."

A rush of sorrow as I realized hearing the word "dead" did not make a child understand its permanence. The little boy had decided that if his father was not home, he was where he usually was: working. At the theater.

"Will you show it to me?" I asked him. "I'd love to see."

Slowly he set the book in the middle of the bed. I was allowed to sit. He opened the book and began discoursing with great knowledge about the performers. I asked his favorite: the fire-eater. His least favorite: Claude Arden. When I said perhaps when he was older, Simon wrinkled his nose.

Then pointing to Zoltan the Mighty, he said, "He lifts trains." He lifted his own arm and scowled in imitation of the strong man.

I was about to ask if he had actually seen Zoltan lift this train when he added, "He got run over."

Unsure as to what "run over" meant to a child, I said, "That's horrible. Did you know him?"

A sharp shake of the head. Simon was too young to have seen Zoltan, but the strong man's end was something terrible enough to be remembered—and repeated. Or . . . was it his end? Simon had not used the words "killed" or "dead." Then again, he was still under the impression that his murdered father was some-where, presently out of reach, but not gone.

In the end, he relinquished the book, on my assurance that it would be returned to him before opening night.

"Promise," he said. "Or I'll run you over."

Unsettled, I looked at him. "First, I don't let people run over me. Second, you're a gentleman and gentlemen don't run ladies over. They don't run anyone over. Third, I'm bigger than you."

I held out my hand. "But I promise to give your book back."

He took my hand and we shook on it.

* * *

That night, I sat alone at the kitchen table and gazed at the past. The first page of the scrapbook was dominated by a handsome studio portrait of Sidney Warburton himself. Taken close up to give the illusion of height, the photograph captured the bold theatricality of his high, silver hair, his large protuberant eyes that focused like stage lights, the full mouth ready to pronounce, the arrogant tilt of the chin. Beneath, one might expect the legend: "The Great Man."

How many careers had Sidney Warburton made? How many lives had he ruined? And was the person who had ended his life somewhere in these bright, happy images?

Faces flickered as I turned the pages of the early years: the Cherry Sisters. The gentleman who sang with his duck. The lovely girl on her motorbike, a man who played drums with his feet. All gone and forgotten, except one: Claude Arden, first as the man who yearns for "She of the Emerald Eyes," then reborn as half of the Darling Dancing Ardens.

But where was everybody else? By all accounts, Roland Harney had worked with Warburton for years. Why was there no image of him in these pages?

Or like Claude Arden, had he been reborn? And if so how? And why? Looking at the lively, painted faces, I couldn't find anyone who resembled Roland Harney as a youth. True, many of the images were drawings, but I could not envision him as the Egyptian fire-eater or Buncey, the Man Made of Rubber. For a long while, I gazed at the father in the Flying O'Briens, but it was difficult to imagine Roland Harney ever flying through the air. Or having a wife and children. He seemed a confirmed bachelor. One of the posters did have a drawing of a flop-eared dog that resembled Peanut. But it was possible there had been a few Peanuts over time.

I found the picture of the troupe standing outside the theater. Warburton in top hat and greatcoat was off to the side, dancers and clowns were allowed center place. I peered at the crowded back rows, mentally subtracted years and pounds. This one? Maybe. That one? Perhaps? The dour man with the violin caught my eye, as if he had cleared his throat to request my attention. I looked deeply at his face, but it gave me no answers. He was shorter than Mr. Harney, his face fleshy in the wrong way.

Finally, I turned to Zoltan the Mighty, the man who lifted trains with his powerful pinky. The two men were not dissimilar in looks, but many years had passed and a bald head and handlebar mustache could make almost any two men look alike. It was hard to imagine the taut skin and bulging muscles melting into the ample, sagging flesh, but age was not kind. Simon had said Zoltan had been "run over." Mr. Harney's signature lurch: years of drinking or a catastrophic accident?

Turning back, I looked again. It was there, I saw it now. But the faces, past and present, had begun to blur. This one became that, that one connected to the other. Yes, there was a resemblance. But what did it mean?

"Family portraits?"

I looked up and saw William standing at the door. "Mr. Tyler."

"Good evening, Jane." Seeing the scrapbook, he leaned over to see the pictures, only to utter a quick noise of disgust. I closed the book.

Going to the icebox, he poured himself a glass of milk, then took the chair opposite. "Just I'm rather tired of the theater these days."

"Mrs. Tyler only wants you to be proud of her." I wasn't sure it was the only thing Louise wanted, but it seemed the politic thing to say.

"Does she? I wasn't under the impression she cared much about my opinion one way or the other."

There was subtle stress laid on "my" and he met my eye as he said it. I told him he was being silly. "When you see the show, you'll understand her excitement."

Slipping laced hands over his shin like a boy, he said, "I don't know if I can. Louise's father is traveling to Washington. Wants me to come."

"Well, tell him you can't."

"When you worked for Mr. Benchley, did you ever tell him 'no'?"

The answer was no, I hadn't. But I wasn't his son-in-law, and I made that point.

"The last time we were in Washington"—last year, William and Mr. Benchley had spent months in the capital, fighting the new income tax—"I felt terrible leaving Louise so long. Now she's always out and about and I'm at home or with her father like a young lady with a protective family."

Sensing wounded pride, I was about to suggest he come to rehearsals with her; but William Tyler was an earnest, gentle young man. It was difficult to imagine him in the scrabbling, madcap world of the theater.

Nodding to the scrapbook, he said, "Louise insists Mr. Hirschfeld had nothing to do with killing the producer. Says it was some unknown character who made his way into the restaurant and vanished without a trace."

He waited for me to agree with that. I agreed that the killer was not Mr. Hirschfeld and was as yet unknown—to us.

"But I think it may be someone Mr. Warburton knew. And for a very long time. Someone to whom he did great harm."

William peered at the album. "And you think he's in there?"

My mind went to the image of Zoltan, arms raised, his oiled body exuding virility. Then to Mr. Harney, slumped over his own ponderous belly.

"I don't know."

★ ★ ★

Only two people had worked with Sidney Warburton closely enough that they might know his history with Mr. Harney: Claude

Arden and Harriet Biederman. Despite his kindness the other day, Claude Arden was unlikely to give me much more of his time and I did not expect to find him helpful. Miss Biederman, on the other hand, was helpful to a fault. I decided to start with her.

Leo had coaxed Violet back to rehearsals and so Mr. Harney started work first thing that morning, a fact that could not have pleased him. However, he seemed not only sober, but dedicated. Kindly, he underplayed, allowing Violet center stage. For her part, Violet faced front, addressing only the imaginary audience, leaving her partner high and dry.

With some tact, I slid into the seat next to Harriet. I was offered a small nod of acknowledgment, but her eyes remained on the stage. Rehearsal was in progress. And I was no longer trusted; I had put my own feelings above getting the job done. I had not known Harriet long, but I knew her in this. If she could put up with Warburton's abuse for the sake of art, why couldn't I keep my hands off Leo Hirschfeld?

Still, she was not a spiteful person and her natural friendliness soon asserted itself. At first we exchanged glances of pity for Mr. Harney, then dismay when Violet sang sharp and insisted Harney was throwing her off. A new key was suggested. Harriet dutifully wrote it down. Thinking the change wouldn't last five minutes, I asked, "Do you write it all down? Every change, every disagreement?"

She smiled noncommittally.

"It would be interesting to see the show as it was. I imagine it's changed."

Here, she placed a protective hand on top of the book. "These are Mr. Warburton's thoughts. And Mr. Hirschfeld's. Some they shared with the cast, others they did not. Their ideas need privacy. If people find out there was ever a question, a doubt, they will say, *Yes, it should be that way.*"

Then she nodded to the book in my lap. "Is that Mrs. Warburton's scrapbook?"

"It is."

"Many times, she has demanded, 'Harriet, I need this poster!' 'Harriet, I need this picture.'"

Her complaint meant we were friends again. Turning to the picture of Zoltan, I said, "Did you work with Mr. Warburton back then?"

". . . Not work."

But knew, was implied. That made sense. Harriet was only a little older than I was; she couldn't have been Warburton's secretary at the turn of the century. Although she was probably every bit as efficient as a child. Before I could ask how she came to work for the producer, Leo interrupted to relay instructions to his wife via Harriet. From now on, Mr. Harney would stand three feet from Mrs. Hirschfeld at all times. While Harriet wrote this down, I turned pages. From time to time, she glanced over, her expression indicating nothing beyond polite interest. Until I came to a photo of the full troupe standing outside a theater.

Harriet's face convulsed in misery. Clumsily, she wrestled herself from her seat, pen and notebook gathered close to her chest. In her haste, she knocked over the bottle of ink that always stood under the seat. For a moment, she stared at the spreading black pool, clearly compelled to wipe it up in spite of her own distress. But then she turned and hurried from the theater.

Leo called for a break. Coming to me, he asked, "What happened?"

"I think I revived an unhappy memory."

I saw comprehension in his face.

"What happened, Leo?"

". . . Nothing. I don't know. Just . . ."

Raising his finger to forestall further questioning, he went after his wife, who had stalked off in a huff at the interruption. Mr. Harney would be expecting me and taking up the scrapbook, I headed up to the dressing rooms. It was Mr. Harney's habit to strip down to the bare decencies, flop into a large overstuffed chair—to which he bore some resemblance—and place his feet in ice water. He was fond of this routine and would be annoyed by my lateness.

As I went, I rehearsed in my mind how I would open the scrapbook to Zoltan's picture and inquire: had he, by any chance, known the man?

But as I came to the dressing room, the door swung open and a fully dressed Mr. Harney hurtled into the hallway.

"Jane. Would you do me a kindness and fetch a taxi?"

"Of course, Mr. Harney. Shall I tell the driver where you're going?"

Basset face impassive, he said, "You shall not."

I fetched Mr. Harney his taxi. Standing at a short distance from the curb, I was able to hear the address he gave the driver. Going back inside, I saw Louise, who asked, "Where on earth is Mr. Harney off to?"

I repeated the address. Did she recognize it? She did.

"That's where Nedda Fiske lives."

★ ★ ★

The rest of the morning was spent on the technical rehearsal. I went to wardrobe and asked Mrs. St. John if I might be of use. Directing me to a pair of boots worn by the factory girl, she said, "Mrs. Hirschfeld claims they pinch. Perhaps you can do something with them. Feel free to employ needles, pins, shards of glass . . ."

Sitting down with the shoes, I said, "She's being so unkind to Mr. Harney."

"I know," she said shortly. "I saw."

After yesterday, Mrs. St. John and I had a new bond of trust. I did not want to jeopardize it by presuming to challenge her. But if her answer would help Mr. Harney, I felt it was worth the presumption.

I began tentatively, saying I was very fond of Mr. Harney. She said she was rather fond of him herself, the old sauce bag.

"Has he had a very hard life?" I asked. "Is that why he drinks?"

Turning at the waist, chin on a single finger, she said, "It is when you sound like a six-year-old girl inquiring as to the existence of Santa Claus that I am reminded you're anything but. What are you asking me?"

"You lied to the police the night Mr. Warburton was killed. You said Mr. Harney never left our table. I saw him do just that. And he was headed toward the men's room where Mr. Warburton was killed."

She gave a half shrug. "I honestly didn't notice."

"Yes, you did. You see everything down to the smallest detail. And if you hadn't noticed, you wouldn't have said anything at all."

Sighing, she dropped down on the edge of the stool. "I suppose it was stupid. But for goodness sake, the man had gone off to be ill. He was staggering. He would have been incapable of killing anyone except himself."

"Then why lie?"

"Because I knew he hadn't killed Warburton, but I also know the police can be very rough. It was sentimental, I suppose, but the thought of poor old Harney being bullied and shouted at by detectives gave me chills. Especially with Warburton dead. Say what you like about that man, but he was one of the few people still willing to employ Roland Harney. When this show closes opening night—as it will—what will he do? Where will he go?"

"Someone will give him a job," I said doubtfully. "Peanut's very popular."

"Anyone can be ignored by a dog. Most New York producers will feel he's just not worth the trouble and he's too old to go out on the circuit again." She looked at me. "So, perhaps you understand why I didn't relish the thought of him in a prison cell, even for a night. He wouldn't have survived."

I hadn't known Roland Harney's future was so dependent on Sidney Warburton. It did argue against him as the killer. On the other hand, how had he come to be such a wreck?

I asked Mrs. St. John that very question and she waved a hand. "Terror, rejection, despair—the actor's life. I'm sure I don't know the particulars."

As she got up, the stool shifted, one of the legs rattling the pages of a magazine that had fallen on the floor. It was *Photoplay*, the new one. No doubt left behind by Blanche.

Noticing that the picture of Pearl White on the cover faintly resembled the blond actress, I said, "Mrs. Arden seems very fond of movies. Would the Ardens ever make one?"

"I wouldn't know."

Her tone suggested she did know—and was not happy. I said, "They do make movies in New York."

"Most of the studios are going out west. Better weather, easier to film year-round."

"Movies need beautiful costumes, too."

"Movies are made quickly and cheaply, two words I detest. Along with deserts and palm trees. My life is here."

I had the feeling she had made this very point to Blanche. Who had bought the magazine nonetheless.

"Then we have to pray *Two Loves Have I* has a wonderful long run."

An outburst of shouting—Mr. Arden this time—drew our attention upward.

"I'm not a believer in miracles," said Adele St. John.

16

That afternoon, Leo had scheduled a full run-through of the second act with the orchestra. But Roland Harney was nowhere to be found. Claude Arden suggested we search the saloons. Blanche suggested gutters. Both agreed either was preferable to sharing a stage with Violet Tempest. Louise, who knew where Mr. Harney had gone, removed herself to the far end of the theater where she was deep in conversation with Leo. I lingered, but withdrew when she met my eye in a warning not to approach.

At loose ends, I went to wait with Peanut in the wings. There I found Harriet, who was talking with one of the stagehands about the slowness of a scene change: a divan had not been where it needed to be. I was struck by the difference in her manner. Normally quiet to the point of invisibility, she was clear and exacting in her demands; it was not *would you*, it was *you will*. He tried to make excuses, but she would have none of it. When she had made him swear the divan would make it onto the stage before Violet had to swoon upon it, she turned and our eyes met. Hoping for fellowship, I offered a bright, approving face. Hers stayed closed.

Leo had returned to the piano and was calling places for Claude and Violet when the lobby door swung open and Roland Harney barreled in with his odd, jerky gait, shouting, "My apologies! My apologies! Where are we?"

I saw from Leo's expression that he was considering a rebuke. But either because Harney had put up with a lot from Violet or there was simply no time, he clapped his hands and said, "Let's start."

When Harney had finished his scenes and Peanut had finished his, I collected them both and went up to the dressing room. I took the scrapbook with me as well, laying it on a table as Mr. Harney fell into his sprung chair. As I put the basin of ice water in place and started to remove his shoes, he pulled a bottle from his coat pocket and took a swig. I let him have one more, then took the bottle and set it aside. He frowned, but did not object.

Then he asked, "Did they ask for me?" I nodded. "What did you tell them?"

"That you'd gone out. I didn't say where."

"You didn't know where."

"I heard the address you gave the driver."

He waited for me to ask, accuse, something. When I didn't, he waved his hand and said, "Anyway, nobody misses the clown."

"I missed him." He gave me a look of droll disbelief. "You get tired of the lovers; all they think about is themselves, their grand romance. The clown is for the audience. He wanders into the mess and makes us laugh at it. If you don't happen to be a lover, he's the one you root for."

We shared a smile, at which point I chose to ask, "How was your visit with Miss Fiske?"

Sadness came over his face like a shadow. "Unsuccessful."

"Is she still mourning Mr. Lombardo?"

He heard the question under the question. "Let's just say she wants something that it is not in my power to give." Sinking back, he said, "God, I miss Sidney. He would have her back here, dead lover or no dead lover."

His phrasing was both callous and curious. I was reminding myself that one could miss someone and still be the reason they were absent when he noticed the scrapbook, laid carefully open on the dressing table, and exclaimed, "Dear God, is that Arden? What a peacock!"

He reached out his hands. "Let me see, let me see . . ."

No longer exhausted, he settled the bulky volume on his lap, murmuring, "Don't remember him, do remember her—unfortunately." Broad smiles and claps of delight greeted old friends. Sneers and insults indicated lesser talents—or rivals. For fifteen minutes, he regaled me with stories: which theaters had been lovely, which hell—most were hell. Towns with the best audiences were fondly remembered. Acts that had gone on to fame and fortune. Acts that had not. Listening, I thought he would never be so eager to talk about the past if the solution to Warburton's death lay in his own hidden identity. Nonetheless, I watched as he came to Zoltan the Mighty. Beyond a faint look of derision, I saw nothing.

"Are you in here?" I asked.

"Probably."

"Which act?"

He gave me something like a smile and handed me the book. "Find me."

I made a good show of looking, perusing the group shot once again before hesitating at the strong man's picture. When I did, Harney gave a hearty chuckle that seemed beyond the artifice of even the most skilled actor. Still I said, "It's not impossible."

"Don't be absurd." Taking the book back, he turned back the pages. When he found the Flying O'Briens and the Dancing Hollyhocks, he tapped the girl in the middle of the dance trio.

"There's me."

And it was, I saw it now. True, he was much thinner, clad in a resplendent parlor gown and wig. But the smile was the same and I had seen him extend his arm in the same graceful way, tilt his chin just as he did in the photograph. That sweetness and generosity with an audience, it was all there.

"You're lovely."

"Thank you for the present tense."

"*Are* these your sisters?"

"Good God, no. The Hollyhock girls came to my town in eighteen . . . well, you don't need to know the year. I was fifteen. I had never seen anything so marvelous, the way they moved, the way they looked, the dream they created for the audience. It was everything I wanted. After the show, I went 'round to the dressing room and said I would do anything to join the troupe, clean up after the goats, anything. Luckily, they'd just lost their third girl to a bassoonist in Des Moines. What people called impersonators were popular in those days. Once they figured out I had no qualms about the dress—and that it fit—they went straight to Sidney. Nettie and Virginia"—he indicated the picture—"were wonderful. Although, I was widely considered the most graceful dancer of the three. Many a stage-door Johnny came calling for Eugenia Hollyhock."

"And where is Eugenia now?"

He sighed. "After a few years, Nettie decided she was done with the business. Tired of six shows a day, changing in toilets, and sleeping on trains. She took her savings and opened a boardinghouse. Virginia became a magician's assistant, got sawed in half and pinched black and blue every night. None of the other acts wanted Eugenia and she couldn't quite make it on her own, poor thing. That's when she started to . . . slip away. Everything did, the drink will do that. One night, I took a bad fall. Something went snap and my dancing days were done. I spent a week pickling in my rooms, trying my best to poison myself. At the end of it, Sidney came to my room and said he was going to have to leave me behind—unless I could keep the gin in check. If I could do that, he'd find something for me. It so happened, the other half of Peanut's act had just met an unfortunate end in a saloon. So I switched to dogs. And trousers. Adieu, Eugenia. Hello, Roland."

He gave his name a sour twist and for a long moment, sat with his loss. Then said, "Sidney was brutal to a lot of people, make no mistake. But he knew my only home was this"—he gestured to the stage—"and he found a way for me to keep it. Some people might say he got what was coming and maybe he did. But from some of us, me, at least, he deserved enormous gratitude. He literally saved my life."

"The night he was killed, you said someone at the table did it."

He waved a podgy, red-veined hand. "The night he was killed, I was drunk."

"Being drunk makes us indiscreet, not fantasists. You were headed to the washroom, weren't you?" He nodded. "Mr. Warburton was killed there; perhaps you saw the murderer."

Closing the book, he handed it back to me. "I will only say that on that night, I saw an individual who had very good reason to want Sidney dead."

I showed him the group photo, and I said, "He wouldn't be in this picture, would he?"

I watched as recognition came into his eyes.

"When Miss Biederman saw this photograph, she became very upset. Why?"

"Well, you must see the resemblance."

I looked at the scowling violinist, the only performer who did not smile for the camera. "Is it . . . her father?"

Mr. Harney nodded, then leaned back in his chair. "I only worked one tour with Erich Biederman. Unpleasant man, and that's putting it kindly. Came to this country full of himself and expecting to join an orchestra. Dragged poor little Harriet all across the coast looking for one that would take him. The wife ran off. Still, he refused to take any job that wasn't classical. He took pupils, lost pupils. She worked so he could pursue music. Sidney heard him playing outside a train station one night, gave him a job playing in the band. But a steady job wasn't enough for the great Erich Biederman. He kept nagging Sidney, 'Let me perform real music.' One night, the magician went sick and Sidney let him perform."

"It didn't go well."

"A record amount of produce was flung onto the stage. It took Harriet ages to get the tomato stains out of his ratty old tails."

"Did he quit?"

"Quit? He and Harriet would have starved. No, Herr Bieder-man performed Bach for the masses for the next two weeks— every night with the same results. I suggested something a little more popular, a jig perhaps. No, no, wouldn't hear of it. Then in Boston, Sidney took on a new act to replace the magician. A performing baboon. Guess what instrument it played?"

"Oh, no."

He nodded. "The audience loved it. The beast took five curtain calls. I spent the entire night's performance wondering when the explosion would come. But Biederman made it through the evening without complaint. As we left for the rooming house, he said he'd left something in the theater. When he didn't come back, we sent Harriet to find him. He'd hanged himself from a heating pipe."

"My God, how old was she?"

"Fourteen. Now, to his credit, Sidney took her on. Gave her a job keeping track of the luggage and hotel bookings. That was Sidney's gift, you see. He knew talent, knew how to put it to work."

I did not think it to Warburton's credit that he humiliated Erich Biederman to the point of despair, then hired his daughter to work tirelessly on his own behalf. I knew Harriet Biederman placed great value on art; there was nothing she admired more and she readily forgave those who created it, even for the worst of crimes. But what must she have felt all those years? Where had she put the grief and rage?

Just then there was a swift knock at the door. I opened it to find Louise.

"Jane, would you come with me, please?"

Puzzled by her urgency, I followed her up the stairs. Louise had put on her hat and jacket. Clearly we were going somewhere. Under her arm, she carried a paper envelope. My suspicions were confirmed when she led me to the lobby and asked me to fetch Horst. She was uncommonly brisk, a manner that did not invite questions.

When the Rolls arrived, she said, "We'll be stopping by Rector's."

The stop at Rector's was brief. Louise sent me inside, telling me to give her name and they would know why I was there. So instructed, I presented myself to the maître d' and was given a brown paper bag, redolent of seafood and garlic. I made my way out through the famous revolving doors—they seemed less magical without the twinkling lights of Times Square at night.

As I came out, I caught sight of the shaggy old tramp who frightened us all that night. In daylight, he, too, looked average. Small. Sad. Mumbling and waving an agitated hand—he was talking to someone, but no one that I could see—he swung his ruined leg as he rounded the corner.

A sharp knock on the window reminded me I was needed. Careful to hold the bag upright, I got in the car. Then Louise gave Horst an address—the same one Roland Harney had given the taxi driver.

As we rolled out of Times Square, I said, "May I ask what's in the envelope?"

"Something for Miss Fiske," was the reply.

17

Onstage, Nedda Fiske might play the average woman, but she did not choose to live like one. Her apartment was in the controversial 998 Fifth Avenue, a new luxury building that offered apartments to wealthy New Yorkers who no longer cared to manage an entire house—especially given the shortage of skilled domestic staff. A former governor of New York was said to live there, as well as one of the Guggenheims. The building had been created with instructions to the architect to do whatever necessary to lure the fantastically rich to the property, and there were those who resented 998 Fifth Avenue as offensively expensive.

When we arrived, I suggested to Louise that I stay behind in the car. As the groped party in the uproar that had ended in Mr. Lombardo's banishment, I wouldn't evoke any happy memories for the actress.

"No," said Louise. "But you could serve as a reminder that Mr. Lombardo doesn't deserve such prolonged grief."

At first the point seemed moot; the maid who answered the door told us that Miss Fiske was not receiving visitors.

"Oh," said Louise and looked sadly at the package she had given me. "I brought her soft-shell crabs, perhaps we could leave them. I worry they'll get cold, though . . ."

Another thing she had learned from the show: how to subtly pitch her voice so that it would carry.

The maid was expressing sincere regret when Nedda Fiske appeared. A week after Floyd Lombardo's death, she was very nearly the woman I remembered from the early days of rehearsal. She wore a lovely day dress, her hair was styled, and the rubber face was no longer slack with grief.

"I'm not at home to people," she said. "Crustaceans are a whole different story."

The ladies ate in the dining room with its formal table for eight. The maid—whose name was Tess—briskly laid the table with two place settings. Miss Fiske noted that Louise had brought an awful lot of crab; would Tess and I like some? Tess declined, saying she had wash to do if she wasn't needed. Having never had crab, I didn't know if I'd like it. But I did very much want to hear the conversation so I said yes and took my plate to the kitchen, which happened to be just a few yards of hallway away from the dining room. If I stood close enough to the swinging door, I could eat my crab—which looked far too much like the original animal for my comfort—and listen to the conversation, which began by Louise asking how Miss Fiske was.

"Terrible."

I waited for the customary but: *But I am managing. But every day is better. But I realize I am better off without him.* It did not come.

"Of course," said Louise, wading bravely into the silence. "Such a horrible way to lose someone you care for so deeply. The shock of it . . ."

"It wasn't a shock. Or it shouldn't have been. I knew Floyd was in trouble. I should never have let Warburton push me into that fight with him."

Interesting, I thought, that she blamed the producer.

"He was just trying to protect you."

"I didn't need protecting," she said sharply. "Floyd did. And if I wanted to do it, that was none of Warburton's business. He cost me the only man I ever loved."

Now the silence was pained, weighty. I could sense Louise struggling to absorb the intensity of Nedda Fiske's feelings, much less the idea that a woman could take care of a man. A willingness to listen despite her distress must have showed because Miss Fiske's voice was gentler as she said, "You don't understand, do you, Mrs. Tyler?"

"I'm trying to. But I think a woman of your gifts deserves a gentleman."

"You like how I sing?"

"I do. Very much."

"Well, when you perform, you give. A lot. Everything you feel, it all goes over the footlights and out to the audience. After a show, I don't have a drop of blood left, not a thought in my head. All I want to do is fall over."

This was true. I remembered marveling at her energy on-stage, how she employed every limb, every feature to keep people entertained. But the moment she came offstage, her face went blank with exhaustion and she barely seemed to register people around her.

"And when you give all that to people, you have to have something that is *yours*. And if other people don't understand, well, that's almost better. It's not for them to understand, it's for me. Look, I know to some people, what I felt for Floyd was crazy. I know he wasn't always a gentleman. But then I'm almost never a lady, so that was fine. I *knew* Floyd. In this business, you have a little success, you're surrounded by people who want to make a meal of you. A lot of times, they don't even ask—even the people you pay to take care of you. My very first manager, he loved me. It wasn't just business, I was a daughter to him. He always said, anyone who tried to cheat me, he'd break his neck. I don't have to tell you he ran off to Canada with my money—and my furs and some very nice shoes—do I?"

From the way Louise gasped, I knew she was sitting, gloved hand to mouth, eyes wide, torn between horror and an appalling desire to laugh.

Nedda Fiske *did* laugh, saying, "Now, for your information, Mrs. Tyler, there's something about someone stealing your shoes that makes you see the world in a different light. A man who's getting paid good money leaves you flat broke in a lousy hotel room, bill unpaid, in the dead of winter with no coat and no shoes. You're standing at the front desk in your nightgown, *barefoot*, trying to explain and nobody cares, because who listens to a woman dumb enough she gets taken that badly—that's when you decide I'm never going to be that woman again. The world takes, Mrs. Tyler. Not because it's bad, not because it's good. We're animals, it's what we do."

"I can't believe that, Miss Fiske. I don't believe you do either."

"That's because you never had your shoes stolen." I could hear the grin. "Floyd was a mooch, I knew that. But I knew how far he would go and he knew how far I would go. Most men you can't be honest with. I could be honest with Floyd. And he was a good time. Was I happy about the other women? No. But waiting for the star gets dull real fast. A man's got to keep himself amused, I understand."

Remembering Nedda Fiske's reaction to the news that Floyd Lombardo had grabbed me, I doubted she was always so sanguine about Mr. Lombardo's infidelities. On the other hand, there were couples who couldn't exist without conflict. Perhaps part of the thrill for Miss Fiske was losing Mr. Lombardo—and then getting him back.

"Have the police given you any idea who might have killed him?" Louise asked.

There was a long pause. "Sidney Warburton killed Floyd, the minute he made me give him up. I guess I did, too, because I let him."

"You were in a very difficult position."

"Floyd had already blown one show for me, I didn't need him blowing another. After the Follies, I warned him. Money or girls, you need to quit grabbing everything in sight. And when he couldn't stop, I played it Sidney's way and sent him away for a while. Teach him a lesson. I thought he could make it a few days without me—that was my mistake. I never thought they'd move so fast."

. . . *so fast.* Again, the tickle of something missed about Floyd Lombardo's death. For a moment, I went back over what I knew, stopping at the memory of Jimmy Galligan, sour and rotting in the Nag's Nose. The broken hand. Belmont. Galligan. Debts. That was where it ended, I should leave it there.

"Perhaps work would be a good distraction," said Louise.

"Maybe it would, but not in that snake pit. Too many vipers with their fangs out. The Ardens want this to be their show. I already told Mr. Harney: I can't go back and be fighting them for everything, not without friends. Say this for Warburton, he knew what he had with me. The Ardens kept at him to cut me out, but he never did because he knew I would make the show a success. Now they're both gone and I don't know who to trust."

She was plaintive, sincere. But to my ear, there was an unmistakable note of bargaining. I remembered Mr. Harney: *She wants something that is not in my power to give.* I had thought he meant the return of her lover. But it was something much less sentimental: she wanted assurances that the Ardens would not be allowed to diminish her.

"You can trust me, Miss Fiske."

Nedda Fiske observed that Louise was rather new to show business and that—no offense—she did not look skilled in the breaking of necks.

"No, but I won't steal your shoes either. The show needs you."

A silence as that was mulled. Nedda Fiske asked, "What's in the envelope?"

"Nothing you'll need if you're not coming back," said Louise.

"Well, I can tell from the shape it's not a diamond necklace."

"No, it's better than that." The rustle of paper being slid across a table. "It's a song. Mr. Hirschfeld wrote it for you."

Another long agonizing pause. Then the flap of paper as Nedda Fiske examined the contents.

"'The Things Everyone Says.' I like the title."

My heart did a hard little twist.

"If you play it, you'll see . . ."

"I can read music, Mrs. Tyler. I see. What about Mrs. Hirschfeld?"

Yes, indeed, I thought, and leaned in to hear.

"Mr. Hirschfeld wrote the song for you, that's all I can say."

Almost to herself, Nedda Fiske hummed the opening melody; it was the same sad, tentative tune Leo had wrestled with the night we danced. I could already hear her breathing warmth and strength into it.

Then she asked, "You don't worry that I killed Floyd?"

Agog, I wondered how fast I could get to Louise if Nedda Fiske attacked her. Were there weapons in a living room: Letter openers? Lamps? Throw cushions?

"I mean, who would have a better chance to steal his gun? Come to think of it, maybe I killed Warburton, too."

"It seems to me you would have killed one or the other," said Louise with astonishing calm. "But I happen to know you did not kill Mr. Lombardo. And if you didn't, you couldn't know he was dead. And I think revenge for his death would have been the only thing to compel you to kill Mr. Warburton. Who, as you say, knew your value and was your ally. In his way."

This was an excellent analysis and I pulled an appreciative face at the remains of my crab.

Then I heard the rustle of paper again. "He's a smart fellow, Mr. Hirschfeld."

"I can't tell you what I'd give to hear you sing that song."

"Well," said Nedda Fiske, "you did bring me soft-shell crabs."

I took it as a good sign that Nedda accompanied Louise to the door. Joining them, I did my best to be inconspicuous and hoped we would depart without delay. But Louise paused, looking from me to Nedda Fiske. There were amends to be made and she expected Miss Fiske to make them.

The actress turned to me. "I guess I owe you an apology. I'm sorry Mr. Lombardo grabbed you. But he was scared. When Mr. Lombardo got scared, he went wrong. I'm also sure he wasn't the first man to grab your behind and he won't be the last."

Louise glanced at me: Was I satisfied? For her sake, I thanked Miss Fiske. But to myself, I vowed that Floyd Lombardo would be the last—at least the last to grab and keep his hand.

Then Nedda Fiske said, "Careful, Mrs. Tyler, you're turning into a producer. I'll see you at the theater tomorrow."

★ ★ ★

That night as she got ready for bed, Louise announced, "I have come to the conclusion that I do not understand people in the slightest. How can a woman as talented as Nedda Fiske still cling to the memory of that blackguard?"

"People fall in love, Mrs. Tyler. You're producing a show about that very phenomenon."

"All marriages should be arranged. When people 'fall in love' nothing good comes of it."

"Oh, but didn't you fall in love with Mr. Tyler?"

I felt confident in my impertinence. Before their marriage, Louise had spent many evenings regaling me with the wonders of William Tyler. But my observation was met with distressed silence.

"Mrs. Tyler, please forgive me . . ."

"No, no," she said, looking at the hands in her lap. "But perhaps it proves my point. When things are arranged, you don't expect so much to agree. It doesn't seem so important to . . . like the same people or enjoy the same things. I can't remember the last time I saw Mother and Father talk to each other. Or even be in the same room for very long. They seem to manage."

Thinking of the morning breakfast, I said, "I can remember the last time you and Mr. Tyler were in the same room and talking. Very happily." I felt it expedient to throw in that last little lie. They had talked happily, just not the last time.

"And yet I feel William's so unhappy with me."

There are times when servants are required to manage more of their employers' lives than their clothing or train tickets, and this was one of them. As the woman who cared for Louise's clothes, certain realities were obvious and we were high past time Louise stopped keeping her secret.

"Mr. Tyler will be very happy when you give him your news. And a baby will certainly be a shared interest."

Caught out, Louise smiled. Then blinked. Then started to cry.

Crouching by her chair, I took her hands. "It's perfectly natural to worry . . ."

"I'm not *worried*," she said irritably, letting me know I had condescended. Which I had and had done before without objection from her. I reminded myself, this was a new Louise, one who went to Rector's, who brought soft-shell crabs to actresses, who had stood up to her husband and insisted on spending money she called hers.

She was still Louise Tyler, though, because she apologized. I told her she had been right to correct me.

"I *was* happy, when I first thought . . . when I realized. We were still in Europe. I spent a day just imagining all to myself. What William would say when I told him. What the baby would look like. Names, boy or girl. But that night, we went to one of those dinners, I don't even remember the house or the name. And I sat there for hours, among people I didn't know, knowing the only interesting thing that would occur the entire evening was the changing of one course to the next. Talk, talk, talk—from all these people who did absolutely nothing. I would never have thought it possible to do so little in life and yet talk so much. With so much self-importance. I thought of how many days and how many hours we had spent like this, thought how I was supposed to feel lucky, that this was now my life. But I felt like I was drowning. At one point, I felt I would leap up from the table and fling myself out a window just to get away from the monotony of smiling and swallowing and digging my nails into my palm just to keep from shrieking."

She had, I remembered now, crescent spots of red on her hands one night. I thought a glass had broken.

"The next morning, I practiced in my head, telling William. I thought how happy he'd be, but also . . . how protective. I imagined him hovering over me, my mother telling me not to do things, you—I'm sorry, Jane—you running about fetching things for me, making me sit, lie down, not move. And I just thought, *No!* No, I don't want this. I don't, I can't. Then the show began and I thought, Oh, yes, this is . . ." Her shoulders raised, a yearning gesture that suggested all the difficult words: "want," "love," "need." I remembered her face, radiant at the window as she promised Leo, "I'll be there." No one had asked her to do things she never imagined she could, then praised her success. I had worried Louise was falling a little in love with Leo. But really, she had fallen in love with herself.

I thought to say that it was almost opening night; the show would fail or succeed, and that would be the end of it. Then realized, the end of it was the very opposite of what Louise wanted. Unless Leo went to jail for killing Sidney Warburton—or I shipped him to Siberia—he wouldn't give up his patron. And his patron would not give up on him. Or herself. Baby and Broadway would have to be reconciled.

Louise said, "You're going to tell me to tell Mr. Tyler."

"If only because he will soon be able to guess. But tell him the rest of it, too. He knows you're unhappy and it makes him unhappy. Give him a chance." I thought of them, heedlessly planning dogs and ice cream and card game tournaments in the car on July Fourth. They did want the same sort of life; they had just never seen such a life before and so these two kind, deferential people who had always done what other people expected were going to have to create it for themselves.

I raised my hand. "And I do so solemnly vow never to make you sit. Or lie down. Or not move."

Just then I heard William's footstep. Louise nodded to indicate that I was dismissed. Pausing at the door, I wanted to tell her that personally, I was thrilled, that I could not wait for this tiny Tyler to enter the world. But Louise didn't need to be overwhelmed with my feelings; indeed, it was not appropriate for her to know they existed at all.

★ ★ ★

Returning to my room, I was surprised to find a letter slid under my door. Sitting on my bed, I opened the envelope to see familiar handwriting. More lectures, I thought. Masses said for my soul. Reminders of the virtues of milkmen.

> *Dear Miss Prescott,*
> *I am writing to apologize for my remarks. They were*
> *uncalled for.*

Dutiful language, I thought. The flat, correct words one offers up when an apology is required, but not felt.

> *Frankly, I don't know why I said it. It is none of my*
> *business what sort of education you pursue, Parisian*
> *or otherwise. I will only say what should be obvious*
> *by now and that is I hold you in high regard and do*
> *not like to think of you being made unhappy. Rather*
> *than say that, for some reason, I insulted you. Your*
> *response was fair comment.*
>
> *I hope you can put it down to lack of sleep on*
> *my part or the general idiocy of men. As part of my*
> *penance, I am abstaining from giving further advice.*
> *I will only say in closing that one of the many things*
> *I admire about you is your devotion to those you care*
> *for. You deserve the same—and a great deal more.*
>
> Yours,
MB

Going downstairs to the kitchen, I picked up the phone and asked to be connected to the *Herald*. When I heard Michael Behan's voice, I said, "I thought you might like to know that Nedda Fiske is returning to *Two Loves Have I*."

There was a pause; had I gotten his letter? I decided to neither confirm nor deny.

"Well, that's happy news, isn't it?" he said finally. "Although not for Miss Tempest."

"Miss Tempest has other stairs to climb."

"And no one's concerned about how Miss Fiske's lover's gun was used to kill Warburton?"

The same question had occurred to me. As she herself had said, Nedda Fiske was the most likely person to have gotten hold of Floyd's gun, and it might have suited her mood at the time to frame her lover for the murder of her nemesis—then ride to his rescue with lawyers paid for by her vast funds. But her conversation with Louise told me that Nedda Fiske's madness was strangely efficient. She loved Floyd Lombardo, because he served her needs, connecting her to a wildness she fed off. Sidney Warburton did not inspire such feelings—and he paid handsomely for the work that Floyd inspired and lived off. Even her latest collapse had been strategic, a way to force Leo's hand into giving her something the Ardens did not have in the show.

No, I did not think Nedda Fiske had shot Sidney Warburton. Other names, other sorrows, floated through my mind like the brief glimpse of images in the turning pages of a scrapbook. But those names were not for Michael Behan. Not yet.

"The show must go on, Mr. Behan. Good night."

★ ★ ★

The next day, Nedda Fiske returned to rehearsals as if absolutely nothing untoward had happened. Leo welcomed her pleasantly.

Roland Harney smiled broadly. Peanut wriggled until he was set down so he could trot over and lick her hand. The Ardens exchanged looks. Then Claude stepped forward to say, "A genuine pleasure to have you back, Miss Fiske."

Violet, I noticed, was quite still. She had been waiting, I thought, to see the reaction of the rest of the cast, hoping against hope they might take her side. When it was clear she had been abandoned, she tried to make the best of it, saying, "Well, I guess it's back to the staircase for me."

"We'll see," said Leo.

Later, Roland Harney came up to me, jowly face alight. "Please tell Mrs. Tyler that she has my undying gratitude."

"What soft-shell crabs can achieve." Soft-shell crabs and the best song in the show.

Picking up Peanut, he ambled in his strange, lolling gait toward the stairs. Watching him brought to mind someone else who did not move well. Who had been very angry. Ranting against those who had in abundance: fame, comfort, admiration, all stolen, in this man's view, from their betters.

Who, now that I thought of it, had tried to kill Sidney Warburton that very night. And possibly succeeded.

18

Roland Harney had said that on the night Sidney Warburton was killed, he had seen an individual who had good reason to want him dead. There were, I knew, a few such individuals. But only one had tried to do it in front of witnesses.

It took a few days to find him. My first searches were either too early or too late; during the day, the police were more aggressive about keeping the street around Rector's inhospitable to vagrants. Finally, I went around to the back door of the kitchen and made inquiries. Yes, said the busboy, he had seen the man. He usually turned up around four to pick through the garbage after the lunch rush. He liked the man, even if he wasn't right in the head; unlike some, he didn't leave a mess behind. And he sang a funny little song.

"Can you remember it?" I asked.

He squinted, trying to recall the exact words. "'. . . Zoltan, man of steel . . . Zoltan, what power he wields . . .' Something like that."

At four o'clock, I waited. And saw him lurching down the block, his ragged gray curls swaying. He was tilted, the wooden leg was poorly made. But he moved with speed and purpose. Unlike the night I had first seen him, he did not seem deranged. Still, I approached him with some caution, catching him just before he turned the corner into the alleyway.

Holding up the dish Mrs. Avery had consented to make me, I said, "I wonder if you would care to have lunch with me."

It took the additional offer of a dollar. He was, after all, Zoltan the Mighty and I, a nobody. But in the end he accepted.

★ ★ ★

He looked nearly a foot shorter than the muscled colossus in Mrs. Warburton's picture. The broad shoulders that had once supported a pretty girl each were now stooped and rounded. The mighty arms had gone to fat, the mustache was now just more greasy overgrowth on his face. The eagle's nose broken, large pored, and purple. The proud dark eyes, the inheritance of generations of Magyar warriors, were rheumy, resting on bruised, wrinkled pouches of flesh. Sometimes they had their old fire. Sometimes, they darted anxiously, as if he were reminding himself, *I am here now, this is where I am. Yes, I still know where I am.*

The wooden stump that had replaced his right leg lay between us on the pavement, its point worn and uneven.

"Did you really lift an elephant in the air?" I asked.

He took a bite of stew and coughed slightly, sending bits of meat and carrot into the air. "Of course."

"How big an elephant?"

He smiled. I had guessed the trick. Holding out a shaking hand, he said, "Baby. We put a bonnet on it, make the joke, Zoltan the papa. Sing the baby to sleep, rock the baby . . ."

He took another bite, chewing energetically with what teeth

he had. "Doesn't stay baby though. Better to say, Zoltan—
'Powerhouse Who Lifts Pachyderms' on the poster and be done."
He smiled. "I lifted the girls. The barbells. I fought the lion. Girls.
A lot of girls."

"I'm sure." I let him eat a while longer before asking, "How
did you hurt your leg?"

A spasm that was half laugh, half bile. "My leg, my back, my
hip, my neck . . ." He tugged at his ear. "This part, maybe, doesn't
hurt."

"But what was your last show?"

He sighed, felt around his foul clothes. "Last show for Zoltan.
Warburton says, 'Zoltan, I am bored. Audience bored. Girls,
lion . . .'" He made a wet, dismissive *brr* with his lips. "'We need
something new, something big.' I say, 'Yeah, sure—what?' He
says, 'Zoltan, you will lift train.' I think, *Train?* There's no baby
trains, you know? How we gonna make this work? He says, 'Don't
worry, I get the newspapers, the crowds, the train—you rock it a
little, we put weights inside so it tips, maybe on a little hill. It goes
up, we get expert to measure. Headlines: "Zoltan Lifts Train!"'"

"Would people believe that?"

"*Yes*, people believe. First, it's only the ones at the front who
are going to see anything. All you have to do is get them to say,
'He did it! He lifted the train!' Everybody behind them is going
to say, 'Really? You saw this?' 'Yes, I saw, absolutely.' Now they're
special because they saw this miracle. They were there, they saw
it happen."

He shoveled more stew into his mouth. "And also, you pay
people to say, 'Oh my God—did you see that?' No one wants to
say they missed it. 'Yeah, I saw it, I saw it!'"

"What happened?"

"The day comes. Big crowds. Newspapers. I am there in my
tights, mustache—everyone loves Zoltan. It was a beautiful day."

He sat lost for a moment.

"In the train, there are bank vaults to tip it. Big, heavy. And a little hill. Only the hill . . . doesn't go the right way. The track it . . ." He gestured: *goes down.* "And I say, Sidney, 'This train it better not move.' He says, 'No, no, we put blocks on the wheels, it's fine.'

"So the big moment comes. I raise my arms." The old arms in their tattered coat rose. "The camera flashes. I step to the train, I heave with all my might. Sidney says, 'Do it three times, so it looks hard.' Once, twice . . . I feel the train rock forward a little. One more time . . .

"The blocks gave way. Maybe . . . they were never there. The train moves forward. I am caught under wheel. I wake up, no more Zoltan. For months, I am ill. Every day of my life, in pain. I cannot work. I have no friends. I look for Sidney. He is nowhere. I never see him again until that night."

"I would understand if you shot him," I said quietly.

"I would never have shot Sidney Warburton. I would have taken him by the throat with my two hands and crushed him. I would have liked to see his eyes as I did that, as he realized it was me. But . . ." He shrugged. "Not to be."

I watched him as he spoke, trying to judge the truth of his statement. Even a man whose life had been so thoroughly destroyed might hesitate to give up his liberty. He would not fare well in prison as a frail, crippled old man. He might well have accosted Floyd Lombardo one night as the gambler made his way to Rector's revolving doors, gotten hold of his gun. But this was still a man with great pride in his strength—and his showmanship. Killing Warburton would have been the final act of his life. I couldn't believe he would refuse to take his bow. For a moment, I imagined him storming into the main dining room, pistol held aloft, to announce his triumph to all those happy, glittering people on whom the lights still shone. He would not have left the pistol at the scene to frame Floyd Lombardo; he would have wanted credit for his last performance.

Besides, he was a pungent character. It would have been very hard for him to slip into Rector's undetected.

I said, "The composer of Mr. Warburton's new show saw you when he was a boy and remembers you fondly. Perhaps if you stop by the theater . . ."

"What?" A weary half smile. "He's going to put me on the stage?"

"He might have a job for you."

One shoulder lifted: he would consider it. But he did not believe it.

"It's the Sidney Theater. If you don't come, you'll make me come all the way back here on my day off. You wouldn't want to do that, would you?"

He laid a grimy hand over mine, patted it, and said I was a nice girl. A very nice girl.

"Stay away from theater," he advised.

And then he got up and made his exit.

★ ★ ★

As I walked the few blocks back to the Sidney, I knew I had been given very good advice. I just couldn't follow it at the moment. Lost in thought, I passed by the *Times* building. A small crowd had gathered and people were staring upward—a contagious condition, and I looked up as well. In the windows, in big bold red letters, the paper was assembling a headline for the people below: AUSTRIA BREAKS WITH SERBIA. More posturing, I thought irritably, and hurried on.

As I rounded the corner, I saw another young lady who had failed to follow Zoltan's advice standing at the theater doors. She was pretty, no doubt also nice. But her gloved fingers were tightly interlaced, she paced a few feet right to left and back again, clearly longing to go in while terrified to do so.

"May I help you?"

Her nerves were so strained, she jumped at the sound of my voice. Hand to her breast, she collected herself. "Do you work here?"

I nodded.

"You must see a hundred girls a week who say this, but Mr. Warburton said I should come by . . ."

Now I remembered: the charming brunette at Rector's, the breathy one who had distracted Warburton just as Rodolfo was trying to make an impression.

"You must know Mr. Warburton is dead."

"I know, I know. It's terrible." The speed at which she spoke belied sincerity. "But you see—you'll think I'm making it up, but truly I'm not—he wanted to see me about an understudy role. For Miss Fiske's part. And I read in the papers that she's been absent from the show, so I thought I'd try my luck. Maybe Mr. Warburton mentioned me?"

Dear God, I wondered, were all actors so desperate and delusional? "Miss Fiske has returned."

"But she'll still need an understudy, won't she?"

Her pushiness made me blunt: "She has one. Miss Tempest. Who is also Mrs. Hirschfeld. The wife of the composer."

"Oh." All liveliness left her as she realized Violet's claim far exceeded her light acquaintance with Mr. Warburton.

Then she frowned. "*She's* the understudy? But she was there that night, Miss . . . Mrs. Hirschfeld."

"Yes, she was sitting quite close, between Mr. Warburton and her husband."

"Well, now I feel just awful."

Taking this as a gambit to hold my attention, I was about to say I was sure she would recover, when she added, "She did seem upset by our conversation. I thought she was . . . well, under the weather." Rallying, she tried again to advance her cause. "But she's quite wrong for a part played by Miss Fiske. I mean, she's a chorus girl. The part requires real skill. In fact, Mr. Warburton said that very thing . . ."

"Did he."

"Yes, he did. Mr. Hirschfeld got quite agitated about it, but Mr. Warburton said it was absurd to think of her in the part. In fact," she added defiantly, "he said she shouldn't even be in the show."

That must have been when Leo threw the glass. Whether out of loyalty to his wife, rage at Warburton's bullying, or concern for his own lost revenue should Violet record none of the songs—I could not say. Perhaps a mix of all three.

The brunette held out her hand. "Please—take my card."

My mind already on other things, I took it. Then I went through the doors, thinking she really hadn't been nice at all.

My mind was still rearranging the events of the night at Rector's as I wandered into the main theater, where Nedda Fiske stood alone onstage. The rest of the cast, most unusually, was watching from the seats. As the first notes were played, I realized she was about to sing the song Leo had written for her, "The Things Everyone Says." I turned sharply, headed to the stairs.

Then decided I might as well hear it.

Until now, all of Nedda's songs in the show had been comic. This was different, the impassioned lament of a woman in thrall to a man who does not deserve her. She seemed to confide her troubles directly to the listener, eyes wide with anxiety that she might be judged. Gradually she grew more defiant and confident in her devotion, because it was something beautiful in and of itself. Yes, you could go through life attached to those who require no deep feeling, saying only the accepted words to the acceptable people.

But safe was not true. Just as she had in her comedy, she made a mockery of our pretense to chilly virtue, even dignity, and yet, made us feel better for wanting, loving—even hopelessly. The song made . . . one . . . feel proud of every time you had let your heart rule your head and if you had never done so, well, the more fool you, you weren't fully alive. We are the honest ones, she seemed to say, the open ones. Don't let the prigs and prudes shame you into straitlaced misery. We all want love. Only the brave deserve it.

For a moment, I felt panicked: What if I had gone downstairs? What if I had missed this? It seemed a singular moment, something so raw and authentic, it would happen once in a lifetime. I was not the only one to applaud as the last piano note sounded. Mr. Harney, Mrs. St. John, even the Ardens. Overwhelmed, I looked to Leo at the piano. I thought of love and of loss. Of infatuation . . . and indifference. What it meant to be wanted, chosen. What it meant to be . . .

On instinct, I hurried to Harriet, and asked if I might look at her book. There was something I needed to check. Bewildered that I could be thinking of stage direction after what we had just witnessed, yet too emotional to object, she passed it to me.

Going to the back row, I turned to the beginning of the book. Here were Harriet's first notes. On page one, the year "1914" was writ large, suggesting that this was to be the account for Warburton's show for the year. At first, there were only a few names. Sidney Warburton, shortened to Mr. W, and the Ardens. With the arrival of the Ardens, the show's first name: *So in Love.* The entry for March 7 recorded the agreement to hire Adele St. John.

I realized the Ardens had joined the show thinking it was to be a showcase for them—as all their other shows had been: the simple story of a boy and a girl, one poor, the other rich. The stage the domain of a single name, two people content to share the spotlight—but only with each other. No factory girl, no comic relief. No rivalry. This explained their constant sniping about love triangles and things the show did not need: namely anyone but themselves. I remember Claude's words: *This is not the show we signed on for, Sidney.*

Then came Harriet's note for March 28: *Mr. Leo Hirschfeld hired to write songs. (Do contract.)*

> April 3: New role added at Mr. Hirschfeld's suggestion:
> factory girl. Mr. W says Ardens are to stay the focus.
> April 5: Auditions begin for role of factory girl.

There followed a suspiciously brief list of names, all with short, concise dismissals. *Weak voice. No stage presence. Bad fit for C. Arden.*

Then on April 15: *Violet Tempest to play factory girl. (Do contract.)*

I sat back, looking at Harriet's perfect script. Violet Hirschfeld had been the original factory girl. The role that Blanche had called "a very, very good part."

Leo had brought Violet in, created the role just for her. Had he done so out of loyalty to his wife? Instinct that audiences were eager to hear stories about people who were not rich? Or the desire to have a part of the show that was solely his?

Whatever Leo's motives, the part—and its casting—caused problems. Harriet always kept the notes neutral in tone, but it was clear that the Ardens made their displeasure known from the start. There were arguments over the number of songs Violet got. Criticism of the way she performed them. I imagined that it would take a strong performer to persevere in the face of such hostility. Violet was not a strong performer. At one point, Harriet noted that Violet had still not learned her lines. At another: Mr. Arden left rehearsal early, so that others could rehearse more.

In early June, Harriet's notes became even more terse, written almost in code. Songs for the factory girl were added by Leo.
Their removal demanded by Warburton. Rehearsals ended at
irregular hours, indicating blowups and walkouts. Then . . .

> *Mtg. W&H. Office. Funds. Is show "big enough" for further*
> *investment?*

In other words, Warburton had threatened to pull his backing
unless he got his way.

At the bottom of that entry: *H agrees to change.*

What that change was became clear on June 23: *Nedda Fiske*
to audition for factory girl.

> June 25: *Nedda Fiske to play factory girl. (Do contract.)*
> *Violet Tempest to play new role of maid.*

I turned past the days immediately preceding Warburton's
murder to the days just after. Harriet had dutifully noted Nedda
Fiske's absence and Violet's reinstatement in her old part. The
entry for yesterday, the day Miss Fiske had returned, read:

> July 27: *Nedda Fiske to resume role of factory girl. Role*
> *of maid eliminated. "One Smart Gal" eliminated. Violet*
> *Tempest to work in chorus.*

Returning to the first row, I gave the notebook back to Harriet. Then I went to Leo at the piano. Still flush with triumph, he
whispered, "So, what did you think?"

"Wonderful. Where's Violet?"

19

Violet was not in her dressing room. I hadn't expected her to be. She was in Nedda Fiske's dressing room. That, I had expected.

Although I hadn't thought she would be holding Nedda's voice tonic in one hand and a tin of Lewis' Lye in the other.

For a long moment, we stared at each other, wondering who would be the first to state the obvious.

She said, "You could just turn around, pretend you never saw me."

"I'm not very good at playing pretend," I said. "I'm not an actress."

"Me, neither." She smiled crookedly. "But people like me better when I put on a show. You know . . ."

Eerily, she let her features fall into their customary look of friendly bewilderment.

The shoulders fell back, the bosom rose, the lips parted. Then she tucked it all back somewhere inside herself and said, "At least they hate it when I don't."

"Do they?"

"You know they do." Now she squared her shoulders, raised her chin, and widened her eyes a fraction; when she clasped her hands at her waist, I recognized an impression of me. "'Yes, Mrs. Tyler.' 'Yes, Mrs. St. John.' 'No, Mr. Lombardo. Let me go, Mr. Lombardo.' I bet she never apologized to you, did she?"

Knowing she meant Nedda Fiske, I said, "She did. In her way."

"And you said, 'Yes, Miss Fiske, thank you, Miss Fiske.' The whole time, thinking . . ."

She articulated my thoughts in terms that were brutal. But not inaccurate.

"But you put on the show because otherwise you don't get paid. How would Mrs. Tyler like it if you said what I just did. If you showed her what you really felt. I'll tell you—about as much as Sidney liked it. Everything was fine as long as I was . . ." A brief transformation was achieved with a widening of the eyes and a slackness in the jaw; she really was more talented than people gave her credit for.

"I've been in this business since I was a kid. I know how it goes, I know the rules. You can't just do whatever you want to do, you have to do what the people want to see. I understand that. My father said it, Sidney said it. But to my father, I was just . . . part of the act. Until I got too big and then I wasn't. It was Sidney who told me I was special. That people would want to watch me. But I had to do something they'd come to see."

Special. I remembered that conversation with Michael Behan, wondering why it was so important to have your name known. Then feeling so empty at the thought that no one would ever know my name. That I was in no way . . . special.

"And in case you think I'm an idiot and I didn't know what 'special' meant to a man like Sidney, I did. I know he called a lot of girls 'special.' But he kept coming back to me. He gave me singing lessons, dance lessons, helped me build a new act. Because he believed in me. I never asked for things, I never made him promise. But when he did promise, when he said he'd do something and then he changed his mind—that's when I got mad."

Her voice rose and I began to hear the woman who had stomped off the stage. How petty of her, I had thought. How childish.

"One time I said to him, 'You just put people on a stage, then sell tickets. You just sell, that's all you do. You're not any great showman. We put on the show. We're the ones they come to see.'"

You're not special. Strangely, the voluptuous chorus girl and the pop-eyed producer had that terror in common—that they would go unnoticed, unrewarded, discarded, even. Warburton had no talent to win applause, but he needed power and significance. If he could not be a star, he would put them in his debt—and make them feel it every single second. He would show other men he was their better by seducing their wives, show women that their beauty and talents were nothing without his imprimatur. His bullying of Leo came out of awareness that here was a young man ready to take over, even if he, Warburton, was not ready to let go. Violet had understood that fear, I felt, and instinctively exploited it when she took up with Leo. That, I imagined, had goaded her lover into the vicious contempt I had seen.

"What did he promise you?"

"That he would take care of me," she said flatly. "That I would always have . . . a place with him."

Like Roland Harney, I thought. But the comic's arrangement with the producer had been different. He could grow old, grow fat, and still be beloved.

"But this year? He started forgetting about me," she said. "On the show before this one, I had to make him give me a number. After everything we've . . . I shouldn't have had to ask."

I wondered what she had threatened to make Warburton

agree. Violet had known the producer some time; it was likely she had quite a lot of information he would not want made public.

"I wanted to try something new. Everyone had already seen the staircase act, it was a joke in all the papers. I was tired of being a joke. But Sidney said Salome on Stairs, that's who I was, that's what I do. He gave me a terrible time in the lineup. I didn't complain. Then through the whole show, he was mean. One time he tried to hurry me through my song, making me go so fast, I almost tripped. That would have put me out of work for weeks. I couldn't believe he wanted me to do that."

Because there were new women, I thought, remembering the star who wanted Violet's time. But Violet wanted to stay in the spotlight, needed to, in fact. Without it, she had no paycheck. No living, no life. How angry Sidney Warburton must have been: a woman refusing to disappear when he told her to.

"But then there was Mr. Hirschfeld," I said.

"Yeah. He understood about me and Sidney. He had to. Sidney gave him his career, same as me."

I suspected Leo would disagree, but decided not to challenge her. "It was Mr. Hirschfeld who brought you into *Two Loves Have I*, wasn't it? He created the factory girl part for you."

"And I was *good*," she said, reverting to the point uppermost in her mind. "But the Ardens wanted to be the stars and they kept messing me up. Then Sidney says, 'We need to make a change. You can be the understudy.' I told him he couldn't do that to me. But he said he had to have a big star in the part. The Ardens weren't enough, he had to have Nedda Fiske. And that"—a violent jab at Nedda Fiske's robe hanging on a peg—"took my part. Never said sorry or nothing. Just walked in and took it like it was hers. She was never nice, treated me like nothing."

She had. Like many talented people, Nedda Fiske had no patience for those who lacked skill, but presumed space in her domain. In fact, her competitive spirit was such, she could barely be civil to the Ardens, who were undeniably talented. Them, I didn't worry about. But to Violet, she should have been kinder.

"She treated you like a chorus girl."

"Right! Like I only had the part because of Sidney. Or . . . Leo." She had trouble, I noticed, remembering Leo. Warburton loomed so large in her mind, she still wanted to believe he was her benefactor.

"When Nedda came on, I was polite. Friendly. First day, Leo says, 'This is your understudy, Miss Fiske.' You know what she did? Looked me up and down and laughed."

"That was very wrong of her."

"Fiske and Arden, they think they're better because they started different from me. They don't know who I am, they don't know what I can do. After she took my part, I asked Sidney, 'What do I do now?' And he said, 'What you always do, bend over.' I said, 'I can't keep doing that, Sidney. I have to have something else.' But he just said, 'What Sidney says . . .'"

Bizarrely, as she quoted the producer, her face began to crumple. "I didn't mean to kill him. I didn't mean to, I swear it. I just got mad, you know?"

"What happened at Rector's, Mrs. . . . ?" I was still not sure what to call her. Mrs. Hirschfeld was an absurdity. Violet presumptuous. I settled for not calling her anything.

Violet gazed down at the table, unwilling—perhaps unable—to say what had made her mad. I thought of Warburton's insults, how he had called her a bicycle. But that wouldn't have been enough. He had insulted her so many times before. Then I remembered the producer's liverish lips descending on the lovely brunette's hand.

"Mr. Warburton was going to audition another girl for the understudy, wasn't he?"

"My part!" She slammed her fist against her breastbone. "That was written for me. I couldn't believe it. I thought, Maybe I heard wrong. Maybe I didn't understand. I just wanted to talk to him. Truly, that's all I wanted. Talk to him alone and say, Why? Why are you doing this to me? First you say you don't want me around you—*says*, mind you. Believe me, he changed his mind quite a few times."

Remembering the reports of meetings at the apartment, I said, "I believe you."

But Violet was deep into her rant against her lover. "*Then* you don't want me in the show. Then when I am in the show, when I'm good and I'm working as hard as I possibly can, you give my part away. Then you try to give my songs away. Now this? I deserve better than this."

"What did he say to that?"

"Oh, I didn't say any of that. That was all in my head. I just asked if I could talk to him."

Here she went quiet, pulled at her fingers. "He said no."

That would have been the last mistake Sidney Warburton made.

"But you didn't give up."

"No, I did not give up," she cried, pleased that I understood. "I didn't. I thought of it, but then I thought, No, I am going in there, and I am going to make him see, I don't care if it's the men's toilet. Believe me, it wasn't anything new."

Believe me—it was something she liked to say. The demand of a woman used to being dismissed.

"What happened then?" I asked. "What did he say?"

"He just said, 'Oh, for Christ's sake, Violet.' 'Cause I'd followed him into the men's room. And you know, I felt embarrassed? I thought, Yeah, that was pretty dumb of me. You can't do that."

She frowned, as if trying to reassemble the pieces of something broken. "But in my head, that turned into *He can't*. He can't do that, he can't. And I just took out the gun and I . . ."

Unable to say the words, she shook her finger at the wall. "Right through the door."

I wondered, would she have been able to shoot her lover in cold blood? Would the fear in his eyes have stopped her? Then I remembered the gun. She had had it in her purse for a reason—two reasons, really—and she had had it for days. Once it was in her hands, the fantasy had started. The dream of standing up to Sidney Warburton, with the power all on her side and the terror all on his. For once, he would feel what she had felt. He thought he could make her not exist. But she would obliterate him.

"I just got mad," she whispered.

But not so mad that she had forgotten to place Floyd Lombardo's gun at the scene of the crime. Glancing at the lye, I said, "And you were mad when you stole Floyd Lombardo's gun. Because you knew he owed money to some very impatient people and maybe if he didn't have that gun, he couldn't stop them the next time they came to break something. And you knew that if Nedda didn't have Floyd, she might not be able to perform."

"In my part."

"In your part, yes. So, you had to get rid of Floyd. First by taking his gun, and then by getting him kicked out of the theater and Nedda's life."

She nodded. "If I hadn't caught him mauling you, I was going to say I saw him mauling Blanche."

Because she knew Warburton wouldn't care if Floyd Lombardo mauled her. "So, you told Mr. Warburton what Lombardo did to me."

She made a face. "I didn't have to. I told Leo I'd caught him groping you by the cloakroom. He went straight to Sidney and insisted he get rid of Lombardo. Sidney'd promised Nedda she could keep him like some kind of rabid pet. But Leo said if Lombardo stuck around, he'd send you home, which meant St. John would lose her assistant and Sidney would get an earful."

"I can't imagine that worried a man like Sidney Warburton."

"Not too much. But then Leo said he would walk. Apparently, he thinks mauling you is his prerogative."

Histrionic proofs of love; even Leo Hirschfeld could succumb to storytelling. I remembered listening at Warburton's door, how I had heard Leo say, "Well, if she goes, I go." I had thought he meant Blanche. Or Nedda. But . . . he hadn't.

Here Violet had raised another sensitive point: my connection with Leo. She said she didn't care, but from her casual insult, it still made her mad. It would make most women mad. But most women would swallow their rage as pointless and Violet was no longer most women.

"I do feel terrible for what happened." Choosing words I hoped would mean something to her, I added, "It was unfair and unkind."

She had wanted abasement and gotten it. Now she could be generous. "I wasn't brokenhearted. But I thought if Leo moved on, I could be in trouble."

"Because he was your alibi."

She nodded. "And I was his. So I went to the police, just to let him know he needed to stay in my good books."

"He would never have turned you in," I told her.

"Men and promises, doesn't always work out."

Wanting to be off this subject, I said, "So you told Leo what you saw Mr. Lombardo do to me. Mr. Lombardo who was already in trouble with Sidney Warburton—" A thought occurred to me. "Did he steal Mr. Warburton's cane or did you?"

She smiled.

"So, you got Mr. Lombardo banished from the theater, arranging it so that Miss Fiske would be publicly humiliated and feel the need to break ties. But you had to make sure he didn't come back. Either to the show or to Nedda. But I don't think . . . ?"

I trailed off, believing that tact is essential when accusing someone of murder. I still believed Jimmy Galligan had killed Lombardo for nonpayment of debts—and for seeming to be everything Jimmy Galligan wasn't: wealthy, spoiled, handsome, accepted. But Violet Tempest had far more initiative than I—or anyone—had given her credit for. The question over Lombardo's death that had nagged at me for weeks came into sharp focus: how had Owney Davis known that Floyd couldn't pay?

"I didn't have to kill him," she said. "Floyd had no gun, no home in a nice safe building. All I needed to do was call up an old chorus girl pal and say, Gosh, Nedda threw Floyd out and I think it's for good. Don't know what he's going to do, he's flat broke."

Yes, I remembered people's irritation that Violet was always on the phone. Leo telling his wife to stop gossiping with her friends, many of whom kept company with reporters. She had claimed she had nothing better to do, when in fact, she was signing Floyd Lombardo's death warrant.

"Mr. Lombardo was killed. Miss Fiske fell apart. Left the show."

"It's sad."

"But then she came back."

"She did, but you know, her mind still isn't right. That song Leo wrote her, it could put her over the edge. She could do herself a terrible harm."

So the lye was not to be just the destruction of Nedda's voice, but a suicide. As she spoke of murdering Nedda Fiske, Violet's voice was oddly detached. As if she were sincerely worried Nedda would kill herself, even as her hand settled on the lye tin. I would have accused her of acting, but she was not that talented. A part of her did not, could not accept that she intended to kill. In the same breath, she could admit to shooting Sidney Warburton, but insist that she did not mean to, that she had only shot at a closed door and something unthinkable had happened as a result.

Sidney Warburton had always turned away from Violet when she was angry; no doubt many men had—and women. How callously we had dismissed her fury as petulance, whining, the selfishness of an untalented person who demands center stage. But it was Warburton who had mattered to her. For years, she had felt that if her anger were unacceptable to him, it must be put aside, for her own survival. Disavowed. Never acknowledged, like an illegitimate child. But like children, it had grown, nonetheless. Unrecognized and unchecked. And become lethal.

Eyes on the tin, I said, "You should write plays. You're very good at pretend."

"Thank you, that's kind."

She was slipping back into pretend now. The sweet, dim, big-breasted girl who didn't quite understand the effect she had on others. Certainly, she had never meant to cause fuss. Or distress. Or death. She had just . . . gotten mad.

Lowering her voice, she said, "I'll tell you a secret, me and Leo, we're not really married. I had something in Ohio, never got around to doing the papers. I changed my name so many times, it's too hard. So, he's all yours, I won't tell."

Tell—when surely she meant to say "mind." This I realized was the request: I was to step out, not see, keep quiet. She would not tell and I would not tell.

There was a knock at the door. Detective Fullerton making himself known. I had told Louise to have him wait—and listen— outside the door.

I reached for the doorknob. "I don't think I can do that, Miss . . ."

In the agony of the moment, her name again eluded me.

"But believe me, I am sorry."

20

"New beginning!"

The Ardens, Mr. Harney, and Miss Fiske gazed wearily at Leo. After Detective Fullerton had marched Violet out of the theater, Leo had ordered everyone back to work. With only a few days to go until opening night, he argued, they couldn't afford time off. Too stunned to question him, everyone had rejoined rehearsal. When it was over, Louise had approached Leo and tentatively inquired if he wished to stay at her home; returning to his own under the circumstances would be difficult. He said, "That's very kind, Mrs. Tyler, but I'm staying here tonight. Too much to do."

"Oh, but you shouldn't be alone."

His gaze shifted to me for a moment. "Alone is good right now, Mrs. Tyler. Alone is just fine."

This morning, the cast had arrived to the news that the show had an entirely new opening number.

"We're scrapping the strings, the waltz, all that stuff," announced Leo.

"And what are we putting in its place?" inquired Blanche. "A phalanx of policemen? A gallows?"

Leo ignored her. Instead, he handed Claude a tin pail; I recognized it from the janitor's closet. Then he handed him a spoon. Louise looked inquiringly at me. I shrugged.

"What on earth," said Claude Arden.

"Bang on it," said Leo. "Once."

If one could strike a pail with sarcasm, Claude Arden did so.

"Two more times," said Leo. Nedda and Blanche glanced at each other. Had their director lost his mind?

Intrigued by Leo's intensity, Arden banged twice more.

"Bang . . . stomp your foot."

Arden had begun to see what Leo was after, because he did so in perfect rhythm, then began experimenting. Two rapid, two slow, echoed by his feet. Leo called, "Blanche, you want to join in? Maybe . . ." He looked around, spotted a broom in the wings. "That."

Blanche Arden swiftly inverted the broom, began following Claude's beats. Nedda stepped forward, adding a foot stomp and hand clap. Leo smiled, pointing to each one to keep time. Then called, "You, too, Harney!"

Mr. Harney was seated on the couch, and for a moment, he froze, apparently torn between character and the deep desire to move. Then abruptly, he fell sideways. Then sat up. Fell sideways. Sat up. All in perfect time.

"This is a ragtime show," Leo called over the clockwork clatter. "It's about syncopation. Beat. Step. Rhythm. Yes, it's a show about love, but love isn't always melody and harmony. It's elemental, what you feel here." He struck his chest. "Beat. Step. Rhythm. Forget the strings, the swooning, the pretty—that's old. This is new. The audience won't have seen anything like it before. But they're going to feel it—in here—and they're going to love it because it's true."

As if propelled by his energy, the four began to improvise, wildly, joyfully. For the first time, I saw them not as the Ardens or Nedda Fiske or Mr. Harney—but as a genuine company, even though each individual stood out as they never had before. Leo strode in and around them, fist clenched, shouting, "Yes! Good! Great!" From my seat, I leaned forward, inclining toward the dynamic, pulsing energy. I wasn't sure I didn't prefer the old pretty beginning. But having seen this, *felt* this, I knew we couldn't go back.

We ended late, but exhilarated. Leo asked Louise if she would mind very much if he took me out to dinner.

"Anywhere but Rector's," I said.

We ate in a Chinese restaurant. Leo took off his jacket and tie, then ran his fingers through his hair until it doubled its usual height. Then with a sigh, he let his head fall on the table.

"He's fine," I told a concerned waiter. "If you could bring two glasses of beer . . ."

We didn't say much until the lobster and chicken chop suey had arrived, speaking under and around the subject we both knew lay ahead. We speculated as to the number of hairs remaining on Claude's head, marveled over Nedda's performance, and made bets as to which tiny Warburton would cause the most trouble at the premiere. I suggested a change be made to Roland Harney's role. Leo considered, then said yes, he could see it.

Finally he said, "Okay, go ahead. Ask me."

"I don't have to ask you."

"Tell me then."

"Leo Hirschfeld never lies."

"So I hear."

"Except when he does."

To his credit, he said, "Except when he has a very good reason to."

"Was this a good reason?"

"Yes."

I was surprised at the intensity of his answer. Leo, who never
seemed to care very deeply about anything beyond his work, felt
very deeply about the rightness of lying about where he was when
Sidney Warburton was killed. Which meant he felt deeply about
the rightness of killing Sidney Warburton.

He said, "Remember—I wasn't the one who told the detective
where we were when Warburton was killed."

Yes, Violet had been the one to stammer out the embarrassing
"truth." "When did you know?"

"Around the time Violet found me outside Sidney's apartment, told me she'd killed him and I had to help her. You can ask
why I did, it's okay."

"Well, either you love her more than I think or hated him
more. Or—and I think this is most likely—you didn't want to take
time away from the show by dealing with the arrest of your wife."

He looked appalled. Opened his mouth to protest. Then sucked
on a lobster claw.

"Well?"

"All of it? My first thought was this is crazy, I have to get the
cops, Vi has to confess, we'll explain he was a bastard, we'll think
of something. My second thought was, why am *I* thinking of
something, she just killed a man, let her get herself out of it. It's
not like we were the love match of the century. Till death do us
part wasn't supposed to cover the murder of other people."

"But then came the third thought."

"The third thought. Which was, Right, hand her over. Walk
away. Then you can be just like old Sidney Warburton. Which I

swore from about two minutes after I met him was never going to happen. Ever. No matter how successful I was or how big a failure, I was never going to treat people like he did. Violet is . . . well, she killed a man, that's how she is."

Sensing an excuse for Miss Tempest, I said, "Two men, actually."

"Two?"

I explained how Violet had stolen Floyd Lombardo's gun, then made sure Owney Davis found out Nedda had cut him off. "And in case you're about to argue that she didn't do the actual shooting, be aware that she was about to put lye in Nedda's throat tonic."

Leo took a long drink of beer. I thought to say that had Leo not provided an alibi for his wife, she might never have had the chance to murder Nedda Fiske—and that had she been successful, he would have been an accessory to that crime. At least morally. I could tell from his silence he understood.

"Violet mentioned a father. Does she have family?"

"I don't know where they are. But sure—the Flying O'Briens." He mimicked their pose, arms up, broad grin.

Stunned, I said, "She was an acrobat?"

He nodded. "Eileen O'Brien. That was her. Till she was about twelve. Then"—he gestured around his chest—"and her father told her she was too big. Said she didn't look right, couldn't be part of the act anymore. That's when Sidney had a brilliant idea for a new act."

Revolted, I said, "He didn't make her do the stairs when she was twelve."

"No, for a while, she was the klutzy girl who dropped stuff. Girl on a swing who flies too high. When she was around sixteen, Sidney dumped the family somewhere in Kansas, brought Vi to New York, and started the *Spectaculars*. That's when she became Salome on Stairs."

"What did she do as a Flying O'Brien?"

"I never saw her, but those tumbling acts are something. They throw each other around, jump from each other's shoulders. Twist themselves in all kinds of crazy ways. Trapeze, if the theater has one."

The old song—heard anew—came to me: she flies through the air with the greatest of ease, that daring young girl on the flying trapeze.

"She was an athlete."

"I guess."

And her family had rejected her when her child's body became a woman's. No use to them, they said, but of great use to Sidney Warburton who had turned her into a joke, claiming he was making her a star. They had stopped her from jumping and flying and made her mince down a flight of stairs, merely displaying her body, when she had once walked on her hands, somersaulted, and proudly balanced atop her sister's shoulders. Eileen O'Brien had twisted herself into a new shape, one she didn't even recognize. Violet Tempest.

"How can she think she loves him?"

"You've never met some of the characters on the circuit. And you've never seen how desperate these people are, how they'll cling on to that one person that can get them work. Everything he did to her, she somehow decided wasn't that bad. Even him marrying her off to me to hide 'the baby,' she saw as taking care of her. It took her a while, but she got there. He never even realized . . ."

"Realized what?"

For a moment, he dug through his chop suey. "You remember that day when we visited Mrs. Warburton? All those little Warburtons? I looked at the second oldest, she's what, nine? And I couldn't stop thinking, You had one kid already, another one on the way. Only not with Mrs. Warburton."

He let me take that in.

"But you tell your girlfriend, 'Get rid of it.' And she does, because what Sidney says . . . Sidney's a little vague about paying for it. A little vague about where to go. It's not his problem, right? He's got other things to think about. Violet asks some girl she works with, finds a real gem. She almost bleeds out, gets an infection. When it's all over, the doctor says, 'No more worries for you, young lady.' And that bastard doesn't even realize she can't have kids. Never even asked."

In many ways, Leo Hirschfeld would be a miserable husband. He would not be attentive and he would not be faithful. And yet I felt sad that Eileen had not realized the wisdom of taking up with him.

"Will you testify for her?"

"Sure. I wouldn't cast her in a show. But testify? Sure. She should go to jail. But not the chair."

Mildly annoyed by his lack of rancor over his ex-wife's—no, never wife's—behavior, I said, "And you're not worried the detective will charge you with helping her?"

"He has no proof against me. For all he knows, Violet shot Sidney and pounced on me as her alibi."

"What if she tells him otherwise?"

"Why would she do that?" I was about to argue she could lower her own sentence by naming an accomplice when he added, "Look, my bet is Violet isn't going to spend a long time in jail. The press likes her. The men on the jury will like her. You watch, she'll say, 'I didn't know it was loaded' and none of them will wonder what she was doing with a gun in the first place. When she gets out, she'll need a friend."

"You'd be her friend?"

"Why?" He grinned. "You mind?"

"You know you were never actually married to her," I said,

exasperated. "That there's a husband out there wondering whatever happened to Eileen . . . or Violet."

"You do mind."

"Do you?"

"Not really. Saves me getting a divorce. It also saves me ever getting married again." Raising his head, he said in a lofty voice, "I'll stand by her. No matter what. She's not really such a bad girl, your honor, more . . . misunderstood."

Planting an elbow on the table, I held up the lobster cracker.

Meekly, Leo returned to his chop suey. "You, on the other hand, are a real menace."

The theaters had not yet let out by the time we left the restaurant. For Times Square, the streets were quiet. As we passed by the Sidney, I looked up at the marquee and said, "In two days, you'll know."

Leo contemplated his name, then said, "You want to go to the movies? I bet I could get the piano player to take the night off."

As it happened, I did. The piano player did not take much persuading beyond the dollar Leo gave him. And for one last night, the boy who had predicted he would be the biggest thing on Broadway played the piano for *Cruel, Cruel Love*, while I thrilled and swooned and menaced just like the shadows above us.

★ ★ ★

I cannot tell you how the final dress rehearsal went as I spent its entirety belowstairs and backstage. Leo had taken my suggestion that Mr. Harney's part be changed from father to mother. For Mrs. St. John the joy of throwing away Mr. Harney's old costumes was offset by the necessity of creating new ones. That morning, Louise and I had called her mother and persuaded her to give up some of her more "old-fashioned" looks; we would helpfully clear out her wardrobe. Mrs. Benchley was smaller than Mr. Harney, but the rough outline was the same and with extra panels, a magnificent ensemble was coming together. Mrs. St. John gave me the honor of creating Mrs. Frobisher's signature hat out of a singularly ill-judged purchase of Mrs. Benchley's. Between us, Mr. Harney and I created something so vividly awful that Mr. Harney said it should have its own credit in the program.

I sewed, pasted, pinned, and painted. I carried scenery, soothed nerves, swept sawdust, ran sheet music upstairs and down. All hierarchy and pretension fell away; there simply wasn't time for it. At one point, I crossed paths with Claude Arden and we got caught in a tight spot, as my arms were too full for him to get by. "Is this going downstairs?" he asked. I nodded. "Give it to me, I'll go."

I can't even remember what time it was I slipped into the bathroom, more for a moment to collect myself than anything else. I was not alone. One of the stalls was in use, but not for its usual purpose. The occupant was kneeling—and being violently sick. Noting the plumpness of the leg and the sensible shoes, I said, "Miss Biederman, do you need help?"

The answer was emphatic and negative. After a moment, she emerged, still looking unwell. She was flushed, her brown bubble hair clung to her cheeks. Self-consciously, she went to the sink and drank from her hand. As she dabbed at her mouth, I said, "You should go home."

"Tonight?" She smiled wanly. "Nobody goes home tonight."

"But if you're sick . . ."

"I'm fine. It passes."

It struck me that "passes" was an odd way to put it. As if she often threw up and it was of no consequence. The only way it would be of no consequence was . . .

". . . Congratulations?"

She smiled as if relieved to have someone know her secret.

"Thank you. It's very bothersome, all this . . ." She gestured to the toilet. "I know, I have been a little distant with you. But you notice things and I did not want you to notice this."

"I had no idea," I said, thinking how admirably she'd carried on.

"Please don't tell anyone. The wedding isn't until next month and it's . . . I am a little embarrassed."

Pleased to be on friendly terms again, I said, "How on earth could such a happy thing be embarrassing? But you should tell Mr. Hirschfeld if you're feeling ill. I'm sure he would . . ."

"No." She turned the faucet, began bathing her face.

"He's really not the sort of man to fuss over a few months."

In a voice that strove for lightness—and failed—she said, "I would really rather Mr. Hirschfeld not know."

Puzzled that Leo could inspire such fear in a woman who was quitting anyway, I was about to press when Harriet said in a voice choked with tears, "I'm so sorry, I did not want you to ever know."

For a moment, I remained utterly bewildered. Then I realized, not just that I had been stupid, but the depth of my stupidity. And insensitivity. Placing a chair under the door handle, I suggested we both sit down on the settee. Harriet glanced upstairs, worried.

"They can manage without us," I said.

A small smile. "Are you sure?"

"Well, at least let them try."

★ ★ ★

Hours later when Louise had taken the cast out to dinner, I walked into the main theater to find Leo standing in the middle of the empty stage, gazing out at the seats. He was in his shirtsleeves, collar open, hair at its messiest and most vibrant. I fixed the image in my mind, then made myself known.

"There you are!" He scrambled off the stage. "Everybody went on to dinner. I wanted to wait for you. And Harriet, where is she?"

"I had to send Miss Biederman home. She wasn't feeling well."

He made a brief expression of sympathy, then it was back to buoyance. "So you want to go? I know it's late, but I'm starving."

Taking my hand, he started up the aisle. I held him back. "I have a question for you."

"You have a question for me."

"Have you spoken with a lawyer? About an annulment?"

"Sure, because I've had all this time."

"You should speak with a lawyer. Soon. I'll have Mrs. Tyler recommend one."

A little fearful, he said, "I hate lawyers. Why so much concern over my marital status?"

I took a seat on the piano bench; he followed and we sat facing each other like children on a seesaw. For a moment, I wondered if I really had to say what I was about to say.

Then I said it. "I'm afraid you're going to have to talk to lawyers. And I'm afraid you will be getting married again."

"Yeah? Who's the unlucky girl?"

"Harriet Biederman."

This was not the name he had expected. "I think Harriet's spoken for."

"Think, Leo."

He did. "That? That was one time. You weren't back yet. I was married, she was engaged . . ."

"She wasn't engaged then. She just told you that so you wouldn't worry."

"Why would I worry? It was a late night, a scene wasn't working. Warburton had screamed at her. Violet had screamed at me. We went out for hash," he added as if the humble meal underscored the meaninglessness of the encounter. "Then we came back here to work and . . ."

"Was it nice?"

He half smiled. "Yeah, it was. She's nice to talk to, she knows everything about theater. It was . . ."

Breaking himself out of the reverie, he took both my hands in his. "But it was just the one time, I promise. Harriet's . . ."

Before he could dismiss the mother of his child, I said, "Sometimes that's all it takes."

All humor went out of his expression as he finally realized. "Why didn't she tell me?"

"You're married, Leo," I reminded him. "And she values your work more than anything. In her eyes, you're a great man, and you don't bother great men with petty details like a baby. You certainly don't ask them to be good men. You, however, are going to be both."

He looked doubtful. "How do you know it's what she wants? Maybe she loves the butcher."

"Of course it's what she wants, Leo. She doesn't care about the butcher, she adores you. She has since you met, but you were too busy with Miss Tempest to notice. She had some hope when it became clear you and Violet weren't blissfully happy. But then I came back. She ran out of Rector's partly because she was sick, but mostly because she saw you watching me on the dance floor, and whatever she saw, it made her unhappy. She loves you, Leo. Why shouldn't she? You happen to be rather lovable."

Swinging my hand, he said, "For two people who dance well, we have lousy timing."

I smiled, sharing his regret. "All Broadway is about to become one big Leo Hirschfeld production. You need a wife. Not just a wife, you need Harriet. And she needs to work. Don't make her give that up."

"Believe me, Harriet will have all the work she wants from me."

Then with more difficulty than I had anticipated, I added, "And your child needs you."

The thought of imminent Hirschfelds seemed to cause more apprehension than joy. But he managed, "My mother will be happy. Confused, but happy."

I suspected Mrs. Hirschfeld would not be in the least confused. "She'll like Harriet."

"Well, that's fine for my mother. But . . ." He waved a hand between us.

A year ago, Leo's way of saying he cared was to announce that he never wanted to not know me. At the time, it had seemed a thin substitute for "I love you." Now it seemed big and wide enough to encompass a whole world of feelings, from friendship to flirtation to devotion and yes, love.

"You will never not know me, Leo Hirschfeld."

"That stinks, using my own words."

"What better words?"

We left the theater. I asked him to tell Louise I had gone home. But he was on his way to Harriet's apartment, having found the address in her precisely kept records. As we went past the *Times* building, I saw the headline in the window had changed: GER-MANY DECLARES WAR ON RUSSIA. How had that happened? I wondered. How had we gone from that ill-fated car ride to this? But I had no answer and the question quickly faded.

As we turned to go in our various directions, Leo said, "Can I ask you something?"

I stopped.

"How come you never fell in love with me?"

"How do you know I didn't?"

21

There was one final, crucial decision to be made: what would Louise wear to the opening night? For days, she had been too busy to even consider the matter—at least when I asked. But when Mrs. St. John put the question to her point-blank, she said, "I thought something quiet." She looked at Blanche. "People aren't coming to see me, after all. It's your night."

"But you have paid for this night," said Mrs. St. John crisply. "And at the party afterward, you are the person intelligent people will want to meet."

Louise looked panicked. I thought to defend her inclination to dwell in the background. Then asked, "Did you have a suggestion, Mrs. St. John?"

"As it happens . . ."

She went to the dress rack where we kept the costumes and pulled out a dress I had not seen before. Its base was a simple cream gown of silk chiffon, almost Grecian in its flow. A deep neckline left the shoulders and breast barely covered, but the long sleeves trimmed in great plumes of ostrich feathers made it both dramatic and elegant. Over the right half of the dress was a metallic material Mrs. St. John called silver lamé, that looked almost like a half plate of armor; a sash of gold and green ran down the length of the skirt. It was goddess and warrior in one dress, and without thinking I breathed, "Oh, Mrs. Tyler, you must."

Louise stared, no doubt thinking this was not a dress that would permit corset or bra, any more than it would permit its wearer to hide. "I've never worn anything like that. I'm not certain I've ever *seen* anything like that."

Mrs. St. John smiled, pleased with the compliment. "You've never produced a show before either. Try it on."

Louise did. And when she presented herself to Blanche Arden and Adele St. John, they paid her the compliment of applauding.

That evening, as I arranged the sash so the slight swell at Louise's middle would neither be squeezed nor revealed, I said, "I can't wait until Mr. Tyler sees you."

Louise had been gazing at herself in the mirror, still stunned by this new self. I had arranged her hair in the closest approximation of Blanche's style I could manage.

Now her expression turned melancholy. "I'm not certain he'll come. He said he would, but he hasn't mentioned it all day. I have the awful feeling he'll find some reason to stay home."

It would not be appropriate for me to express disapproval, so I did not. If William was still uneasy about Louise's involvement in theater, this was not the night to make those feelings clear. Not if he wanted to be told he was going to be a father—something Louise had sworn to me she would do after the show.

Anxious eyes on her reflection, Louise said, "After tonight, will you please explain to me how Mr. Hirschfeld came to be"— the precise status being complex, she avoided it—"with Miss Biederman? And why you're not upset?"

That was also complex. My heart did hurt to think of losing Leo. But the truth was, I didn't want to marry Leo Hirschfeld. I wanted to dance with Leo Hirschfeld, laugh at movies with Leo Hirschfeld, run down beaches, share coconut candy, and forget myself on divans with Leo Hirschfeld. Probably, I always would. But when I thought of Harriet's life as Mrs. Hirschfeld, endless days in theaters, taking the phone calls he didn't want to take, managing actors, typing contracts, soothing nerves, prompting lines—in short, making his business hers, his life hers, I realized it would make me as unhappy as it was going to make Harriet blissful. Even the baby, I suspected, would not keep her from the theater for long; that child would be raised in the wings. For Harriet, it was her passion and the man she loved. For me, it was a man I adored, before I'd had the chance to figure out if I even had a passion.

"Yes, Mrs. Tyler. Shoulders back. Head up."

Louise complied and I stood back to judge the effect. The dress was marvelous. But there was something missing. Earrings? I fretted. A different necklace? Then I heard the chime of the clock; whatever it was, Louise would have to do without.

We left the bedroom with some trepidation: would William be waiting for his wife or no? But then I saw him standing at the bottom of the stairs. He looked absolutely splendid in white tie. For a moment, the Tylers gazed at each other.

"Oh, William," said Louise.

"You look . . . magnificent."

And with that came the final ornament the dress needed: Louise's smile.

My own dress for the opening night was far more modest, although Louise had insisted I have "something nice." It was a dusky pink silk with a silver velvet sash and silver thread through the bodice and a fashionably hobbled skirt and short sleeves. I had not wanted to think much about my appearance; I wasn't at all sure I would be attending the party at Churchill's afterward and no one would be looking at me anyway. Yet at the last minute, I had done up my hair in a Psyche knot, tying it back with a swath of rose satin. Tilting my head in the mirror, I thought I did look rather . . . fetchingly forlorn. Mr. Harney had made me promise him a dance and who knew? Perhaps Rodolfo worked at Churchill's on Tuesdays.

As we went through Times Square, I noticed the streets were more crowded than usual. At first I thought it was simply the pretheater crush. But people did not seem to be moving; instead they were gathering by the *Times* building. Glancing out the window, I saw a new headline in red letters: FIRST SHOTS. We rolled past before I could see more.

If the crowd outside the theater were any indication of future success, Louise's investment would be returned severalfold. Louise and William were startled to be greeted with cheers as they left the Ghost and made their way through the front doors.

As I made my way through the crowd to the stage door, I heard people calling out the names Arden and Fiske as if conjuring them would make them appear. I thought of how many people I would never see again after this night: the Ardens, Nedda Fiske, Roland Harney, Harriet . . . possibly Leo. I hadn't seen him at all today and couldn't envision a moment when I would see him this evening. Which perhaps was for the best.

Then to my surprise, I heard my name and turned to see Michael Behan. Who asked, "What are you doing out here on your own? I thought you'd be with the maestro."

"He's busy at the moment, and don't be rude."

"Well, he'll like the dress."

It took me a moment to understand his assumption—and decide whether or not I wished to correct it.

I said, "It's not actually important whether he likes the dress or no."

He frowned. "He's free of the clutches of Miss Tempest—who I now hear is Mrs. Bigamist Somebody or Other—what's stopping him?"

"A very nice girl he'll be marrying in a month or so."

"A very nice girl . . . who isn't you."

"Who is not me."

"I stand ready with that punch in the nose."

I laughed. "Not on my account, but thank you. Anyway, I can deliver my own punch in the nose if need be."

"I have no doubt."

I opened the stage door. "I don't suppose you want to see the show? After everything you've heard about it . . ."

"Isn't it a packed house?"

"You can share my spot in standing room. One condition."

"It's the biggest show in town since Moses and the Red Sea."

"Exactly."

Louise had of course offered me a seat but I had told her I preferred standing room. Seeing the show with an audience for the first time was going to be nerve-racking and I didn't relish the thought of absorbing the full weight of someone else's anxiety by sitting next to them. In standing room, I would have the freedom to step back, even away if need be. Leaning on the cushioned barrier, I pointed out various wealthy and famous people in the crowd—including Detective Fullerton, whose success in arresting the Killer Chorus Girl had only increased his own celebrity. I may have gestured too ostentatiously at that gentleman, because he made his way over. He wore white tie very well and I told him so.

"Miss Jane Prescott."

"Detective Fullerton. This is Michael Behan of the *Herald*. I don't suppose you'd like to tell him the true inside story of how you caught Sidney Warburton's killer."

"I would like to." The little eyes glittered. "But it seems to me that is your story to tell."

"Yes, it seems to me as well," said Behan, notebook at the ready. "Miss Prescott?"

Startled to be the focus of attention, I stammered. The Nag's Nose, the brunette, Harriet's notebook, the growing sense of the rage behind Violet's vagueness—not to mention what I had learned in clearing the rest of the cast. None of it was the sort of thing Mrs. William Tyler's maid should be telling the papers. Mrs. William Tyler's maid should not be in the papers.

Of course, there was no law that said I must continue being Mrs. William Tyler's maid.

Lightly, knowing the answer, I said, "Are you offering me a position, Detective?"

"You might be another Isabella Goodwin," he said, referring to the city's first female detective, promoted just two years ago after solving a bank robbery sixty male detectives failed to.

"That lady is exceptional."

"Do not decide . . . so quickly . . . that you are not," said the detective. Inclining his head, he made his way to his seat. Behan and I settled on the low wall; nudging me with his elbow, he whispered, "Exceptional."

"Stop it."

"Ah, you're pleased. You going to give me the story?"

"Not in a million years. Sh, they've rung the bell."

The audience was certainly ready to be enchanted—or appalled. They would be happy either way, I thought. A hum of excitement greeted the dimming of the house lights. I felt both intrigue and apprehension as the actors took their places without fanfare, Claude with his pail, Blanche with her broom, Nedda still and thoughtful, and Mr. Harney dignified and dressed to the nines on the divan. I sensed turned heads at Claude's first beat, amused smiles as Blanche tapped the broom on the floor, but then growing interest as Leo's opening continued. The energy began to flow from the stage into the audience and back again, creating an electric connection that grew stronger and stronger with the ever increasing tempo.

Then as one, the performers ceased all movement, all sound. Claude announced, *"Two Loves Have I."*

And was answered with the first rousing ovation of the night.

Having seen the show in parts so many times, I found myself listening to the audience. Leo had described to me the coughs and dead air that mean failure to connect. No deadness here, the air was alive and humming. Around me, I sensed shoulders bobbing, feet tapping. Whenever the music signaled that the Ardens were about to take flight, there was an all but audible intake of breath in anticipation, followed by the wondering silence of people caught up in the spell of perfect movement. The chuckles that welcomed Roland Harney—and the cheers for Peanut—grew into shouts of laughter and applause as he exited. Nedda Fiske captured the audience's heart the moment she appeared. The silence that followed "The Things Everyone Says" was stunned; it took a few moments for people to gather themselves enough to roar their approval. When the curtain came down, there were actual screams of happiness as the audience realized they had been the very first to see something the city would be talking about for months.

It would be impossible to say who got the larger ovation at the curtain call. Possibly it was Leo, who was pulled onstage by Nedda Fiske and Blanche Arden. Spreading his arms, he seemed to dive more than bow in acknowledgment of the applause, then he waved for everyone to be quiet.

He said, "A few weeks ago, the theater world lost a giant. A man who gave many of us our careers . . ."

The Ardens and Roland Harney nodded.

"Sidney Warburton put me here today. This is his theater. It will always be his theater. And it wouldn't be right if we didn't honor him tonight."

Leo nodded to the orchestra. What followed is now an anthem of show business, a raucous, defiant love song to the thrill and madness of performing, the joyful delusion that people will pay attention, that a few minutes of the world's eyes on you is worth any sacrifice. It was, when I considered the man who had inspired it, a complete falsehood. And yet my heart took it as eternal truth and I found myself grinning and tearful because it was all just . . . so good.

When I had collected myself, I turned to Michael Behan, who seemed amused by my reaction.

"That's a love story?" he said.

"*Yes,*" I said, dabbing at my eyes.

"I did like the dog. The dog is talented. Don't suppose you could get me an interview with him?"

I promised an interview with both dog and owner. As I did, I saw Mrs. Hirschfeld fighting against the crowds swarming out of the theater to reach her son. Behind her was a gray-haired gentleman with an elegant mustache and a gentle smile. His light eyes wandered the theater, at times fixing on something beyond sight. Mrs. Hirschfeld, I noticed, kept one hand on his arm at all times. That would be Leo's father, who could never keep straight the names of his children.

Then I felt a tug on my skirts and looked down to see Simon Warburton.

"Where's Papa?" he asked.

Stalling, I introduced Simon to Michael Behan, who, hearing the name Warburton, grasped the situation.

"Simon, I write for a newspaper. Your father's a very important man, isn't he? Everyone knows who he is."

Simon nodded.

"Tell me something they don't know. What do *you* like best about him?"

Simon twisted as he thought. Finally he offered, "He's funny."

"He's funny. Thank you, Simon."

I held out my hand. "Come, let's find your family."

If Mrs. Warburton had noticed her brood was one short, she gave no sign of it. She was having her photograph taken with Leo. Harriet stood patiently to the side. Seeing me, she raised her eyes heavenward. I smiled in sympathy; as the owner of the theater, Mrs. Warburton would be in Harriet's life for some time. But as I drew close, she murmured, "Mrs. Warburton is considering a move to Chicago. I think Chicago is a very wonderful city, don't you?"

"Ideal," I agreed.

She squeezed my hand. "Please, do tell her so."

Then in a light maternal tone, she added, "And you should say hello to Leo. He has been looking for you all day."

Simon was returned to his family. Leo shook many more hands. Harriet tactfully cleared the crowd, then removed the Warburtons to Churchill's. I waited until Leo had no more hands to shake, then offered my congratulations.

"I think 'triumph' is the word they use."

Leo had had a lot of praise poured on his head; he was drenched in goodwill and sweat, and almost breathless from thank-yous. His hair reached toward the ceiling. He took my compliment with a wide smile, then noticed Michael Behan. As a matter of course, he held out his hand. "Leo Hirschfeld."

"Michael Behan of the *Herald*."

". . . Critic?"

"No, no. Merely documenting the . . . someone called it, 'theatrical event of the century.' I don't know that she was entirely sober though."

"Fine with me," Leo said with a grin. "Well, come along to Churchill's and keep documenting. Jane, you're coming, right?"

At this point, Behan said he wanted to talk to ecstatic audience members before they got into cars or passed out; could he meet us in the lobby? We said he could. Leo watched as he left. Then tugging at his suit, he said, "I would hug you, but I'm disgusting. Harriet has another one of these waiting at the restaurant. But—"

He spread his arms, leaned in. I spread mine, touched his hands; for a moment our foreheads rested.

"Congratulations, Leo Hirschfeld."

"Thank you, Jane Prescott."

As we headed up the aisle of the now empty theater, he said, "So, tomorrow, I want to try . . ."

"I won't be here tomorrow, Leo."

"What?" He pulled up short.

"I am never setting foot in a theater again unless I have a ticket. You and Mrs. Tyler can make whatever business arrangements you need without me."

"But when am I going to see you?"

He was, I thought, impossibly greedy. Pressing his hand, I said, "You will see me, Leo. Next week, next month, next year. When we're . . . ninety years old, you'll see me. I promise."

"All right."

Feeling that was well settled, I let go of his hand and walked toward the doors to the lobby.

Then Leo called after me, "Thank you, by the way. For answering my question."

There had been so many questions over the past month, I had no idea what he meant. I was about to ask him to explain when I became aware of shouting outside. The audience, I thought, excited by the sight of departing Ardens or Peanut. But this was not the happy, excited hubbub I had heard when I arrived at the theater. This noise twisted my stomach, raised the hair on the back of my neck. I hurried to the doors and pushed through to see Michael Behan staring up the block.

"It's started."

Either Leo said "What?" or I did, but the three of us slowly made our way up Forty-Fifth Street to the heart of Times Square. Ahead, I could see a wall of people, more running past us to join them. The enchanted crowds that had just left the theater were gone, either slipping away in cars or absorbed into the throng. I felt Leo looking anxiously for Harriet and assured him that William and Louise would have taken her to Churchill's.

Mr. Behan stopped one fellow and asked him what had happened. With a strange giddiness, he answered, "Germany's declared war on France, England's declared war on Germany . . ." Thrilled to the point of speechlessness, he ran up the block.

It is a strange force that draws you toward catastrophe. I knew perfectly well we should turn around; we were due at Churchill's, people would be worried. Why move toward the thousands of people who had gathered to see the paper bulletins posted in the windows of the *Times*, screaming the final declarations of war in bold red letters? Turn back, go inside, to the lively, joyous party, music and dance and champagne and celebration. It made sense for Michael Behan; he was a reporter. Yet Leo and I followed, somehow wanting to face the truth of how this night would be remembered.

It shouldn't have been a surprise, I told myself. For days, the *Times* had posted those red-lettered bulletins in its windows, announcing each escalation of hostilities: AUSTRIA CHOOSES WAR, RUSSIAN AND GERMAN RELATIONS SEVERED, FRANCE REFUSES PEACE. There had been talk of bringing Charlotte and her husband home, but it had been mild fretting, easily quieted by Charlotte's airy telegrams: it would all be over soon. And it had seemed so far away.

At first we stood at the outskirts of the crowd, but as more people joined, we were pulled deeper into the crush. Surrounded by people so caught up in great events, they were heedless of those around them, I grew nervous. Then I felt the weight of Michael Behan's arm around my back, the grip of his hand on my arm, and felt steadied.

Hearing two men arguing in German, Behan asked Leo if he had family in Europe.

"My parents get letters from Lemberg, wherever that is." His tone was light, but his eyes stayed on the mass of people around us; he was a man who absorbed mood and energy by osmosis, and his expression told me he also felt the danger. "You?"

"Quite a few. But they've got their own war."

Around us was the rumble of conversation, discussion, debate as to how long it would last, what the kaiser really wanted, if Serbia could hold out, and what it all meant for Hungary. Then voices began to join, become melodic as a group of men started singing in German. Immediately other voices rose with "La Marseillaise." One cannot sing and stand still, apparently, because people began to march through the crowds, pulling others with them until groups began forming in large numbers, each singing their song with bellicose pride. At one point, the French and German crowds veered too close; men splintered off, fists raised, and the crowd as a whole surged around the battle. I was buffeted as some were drawn closer and others sought to flee.

"Let's . . . ," I said.

"Yes," said Leo.

We shouldered our way out of the crowd, which had grown much larger in the brief time we had been part of it. Once free, we stood under the marquee of the Sidney. The theater was now dark and lifeless. The street deserted. Irrational, I looked up, hoping to see the twenty-foot electric kitten with its ball of yarn. But we were in the wrong place and I couldn't find it.

"Well," said Leo. "Shall we go on to the party?"

Behan looked back at the crowd. "I should stay."

To be pleasant and—I suspect—wanting more publicity, Leo said, "Come on, it's a bunch of tired, old eagles bickering over their share of the guts. It's over there, not here."

"Still. I'll give a good write-up to the show, though."

"Of course you will, it's a great show."

Behan looked at me. "Enjoy the festivities."

Somehow I didn't think I would. What I truly wanted was to go home, shed my party gown, curl up in bed, and pull the covers over my head.

But everyone was waiting for Leo. And Leo was waiting for me.

"Good night, Mr. Behan."

22

The next morning, a howl of joy announced the fact that Louise had finally told William he was to be a father. This was followed by a hasty gathering of the staff to share the momentous news, before the parents-to-be tore off in the Ghost to tell her father. Later in the day, they traveled to Long Island to see the ladies of the family, William's mother and sisters, as well as Louise's mother, Mrs. Benchley, who had just arrived at the Oyster Bay house. As it was a family occasion and only overnight, Louise said I could stay in the city. I thanked her; the future arrival meant there was a great deal of work to do.

When I had assessed Louise's fall and winter wardrobe for what might be carried over from last season and could be let out, wondered whether Mrs. St. John could be enlisted to make maternity dresses any more attractive, and learned of the existence of nursing corsets, I made an idle tour of the house until I found a sunny little room that had been vaguely designated Louise's office. Would it be the office? I wondered. Or the nursery? Would

Louise's grand fling with the theater be a once-in-a-lifetime experience before she retired into motherhood? Or would Mrs. Tyler's grandchild be raised in backstages and dressing rooms? I could not imagine it, but then so many things had happened in the past month that I could not have imagined.

That afternoon, I called the number Anna had given me and left a message. An hour later, Ethel told me I had a call. Five minutes later, I had plans for dinner.

We ate at her uncle's restaurant; from the delighted reactions of the waiters and kitchen staff, I had the feeling it had been some time since Anna had visited. This time, we talked easily about our old subjects: her aunts, my uncle, her brothers. The older one was out of jail, both were still looking for work. As we talked, I realized in some small part how the flood of her life had continued without me, how much I did not know, how alone I had left her. I was about to ask what she made of the war—whatever she thought, it would not be what I read in the papers—when she said, "I see the chorus girl wife was arrested for murder."

Startled that she would pay attention to the shooting of a theatrical producer—and admit it—I said, "Yes, she was."

"And?"

"And he's getting married again. To someone else. I suggested he should."

Initially Anna's jaw dropped, but she regained her customary sangfroid as I explained. When I was done, I sat back and waited to hear I had behaved splendidly.

Anna said, "That sounds nice for you."

"Nice for *me*?"

"Of course. He likes you, you like him. But you don't trust him. So, you arranged things so you don't have to concern yourself with a man you don't trust. Now he's some other woman's problem."

"They arranged themselves," I said. "I just suggested they make it legal. Anyway, I don't see that I did Harriet Biederman such a bad turn. Leo Hirschfeld is about to be a wealthy man, not to mention the father of her child. If the marriage is not a success, she will have recourse. Which she would not have had with the butcher."

Anna nodded in approval of my pragmatism. "So, no regrets."

"No, I do have regrets. I regret that I was not a better friend." She looked at me questioningly. "A good friend doesn't disappear."

I could see that she was considering whether or not to take my apology seriously. A wave of the hand would consign us to a false friendship; goodwill, pleasantries—but no truth. No risk.

Finally, she said, "You were happy. Dancing. Laughing. Doing . . . Lord knows what!" She mimicked a scandalized aunt. "I was jealous."

"Jealous?" Of all the things for Anna to be.

"Yes. I thought, why can she do those things and I cannot? Well, no, at first I thought, she is frivolous and shallow, maybe once she was halfway intelligent, but now, with this boy . . . this songwriter . . . she's just like everybody else."

"I hope there was a second thought."

"There was, that was rude, too. And the third one and the fourth. Only with the fifth thought, maybe sixth, I thought, What is that like?"

"Don't tell me you've never gone dancing," I said.

"Of course I've gone dancing. And then, my brain starts and it all seems so pointless. As if I'm lying to myself."

"Tell your brain to mind its own business and not be so censorious."

"I can't because my brain is right. It is stupid—worse than stupid, it's criminal—to dance when the world is about to end."

She was not exaggerating; her tone and expression told me she was sincere in her choice of words. Unnerved, I said, "That seems to me the exact right time to dance. And the world isn't ending."

"Yes, it is. It has to and there will be a much better one afterward. But to get there will be hard."

Taking a drink of water as if that would stave off apocalypse, I said, "I think it will be like the Balkan messes. They'll . . ." I did not actually know all that much about the Balkan messes. ". . . shove some borders here and there and everyone will go home."

"The homes won't be there anymore. Not the same ones. And many people won't come back."

For as long as I had known her, Anna had worked for a new world—not just a better law or more people voting. A completely different society where not only would I not work for the Tylers, families like the Tylers would not exist. She wanted that future with all her heart, brain, and sinew. If she had believed in prayer, she would have been on her knees for hours. And now she saw it coming, and she did not rejoice.

I thought to say something cheerful, as if I could dispel her dark mood by giving her an opportunity to think me dear, but naïve. In the past, it had been my way of reminding her there was affection in the world as well as conflict. Now it seemed insulting—to both of us.

I waited until we had left the restaurant to say, "It seems the police have given up hope of ever finding the other people involved in the Lexington Avenue bombing."

Anna was noncommittal. But her silence felt not disinterested. I went on. "I suppose Mr. Murphy was their only specific suspect. And he seems to have vanished."

"Yes."

"I hope he's safe, wherever he is."

"Let's say he's far out of reach of American law enforcement."

Canada, I thought. Or Mexico. Or perhaps even Europe. I

had the feeling Anna knew exactly where he had been sent and that she had helped him get there in some way.

"It must be a hard thing, to leave your home knowing you might never come back."

"Home—what kind of home brutalizes its children this way?"

Anna had always been cynical about America, but in the past, it had been a raucous, energized disdain, the exasperated mother of a ne'er-do-well son who could nonetheless anticipate the day when he finally grew up. Now I heard no such hope—just bitterness and contempt.

"Tell me about Ludlow," I said.

There was a long pause. Eyes fixed ahead, Anna said, "I had nightmares about those children. Trapped underneath, choking in the smoke. The more they screamed for help, the less air they had and the more they suffocated. No one heard them. Or they didn't care. I couldn't get it out of my mind, what I would do if I were there, how I would comfort them about dying in a world that didn't care. I couldn't think how I would do it. I kept imagining them crying because they knew they were about to die. And what could I say? I wondered if the women hoped the children would die before they did so they wouldn't be alone at the end."

"Anna . . ."

My hand hovered at her shoulder; she twisted slightly, rejecting it. "Everyone knew: we had to do something. In the past, people had not wanted to listen, but here it was, the proof of what happens when you place your faith in the Rockefellers of this world. But as always, there were some who said, 'We must be better than them, we must not provoke. We must bring people to our side.' So we gathered outside the Standard Oil building to mourn. 'We will mourn in silence,' they said. 'Let us everyone see our silent mourning.' Some wore black armbands. So correct, so dignified. But even that was 'provocative.' The police arrested people just for standing outside a building. People were annoyed we were blocking their way. Stores complained. We accomplished nothing.

"That's when I decided, silence is what they count on. They murder children and know that the police will arrest anyone who even talks of shooting back. So, you can't just talk."

Hands in her pockets, she met my eye. She had made her confession. Immediately, I thought to say, *Well, yes, I understand, of course, but . . . the timing was wrong, the bomb went off early, and aren't you relieved, a little, that it did? Yes, Rockefeller, but who knows who might have been in the house with him, the secretary, the maid, one of his children. It didn't work, you see that, that way doesn't work . . .*

But looking at my friend, I understood that we saw different things. People destroyed, we both saw that. But not all the deaths were of equal importance. To Anna, some of the deaths mattered enormously, some not at all. Some were even cause for rejoicing. Still, I could not question the genuine grief that had driven her to that point. And perhaps she thought I also placed more value on some lives than others.

"Canada is cold," I heard myself say.

She laughed, and there were tears in the laughter. "Well . . . I would miss some things," she said.

"I would. Very much."

The words "too much" were in my head, but that would be asking for a promise she couldn't give. In her uncle's restaurant, they began to turn off the lights. It was time to go home. I realized I did not know where she was headed; I still didn't know where she lived. Anna was smiling, she had recognized the same thing. Briefly, she glanced down the street and I sensed she was probably headed in the other direction.

Then she asked, "You're going to the train?"

I said I was.

"I'll walk with you."

* * *

The following afternoon, William and Louise returned to the city in high spirits. I smiled to hear the Tylers laughing as they came in the door, regaling each other with the more memorable pieces of advice Mrs. Benchley had to offer on the subject of child-rearing; figs it seemed were of the utmost importance. Then I heard Louise say, "Oh, Ethel, would you find Jane for me and tell her we want to see her in the parlor?"

I descended with caution. If it were bad news, Louise would have sounded anxious, and she had sounded anything but. Still, I sensed change. And happy people are often . . . unimaginative. So caught up in the contemplation of their own perfect present and future, they are poor predictors of what will make others joyful or miserable. Had Mrs. Benchley's maid, the Matchless Maude, gone to her gin-soaked reward? Had Louise, anticipating maternal seclusion, suggested me as a replacement? She wouldn't, I thought, grip tightening on the banister. She couldn't . . .

They stood before the fireplace, swinging to face me as I came in. William said, "Jane, Mrs. Tyler and I have been talking . . ."

I braced myself.

"And we think you ought to go back to school."

The switch from dread to education was so unexpected, I could only repeat the word. "School?"

Louise said, "You're so intelligent. If Emily can go to Vassar, certainly you could attend something like the Female Normal . . ."

"They call it Hunter now, dearest. Or perhaps Grace Institute. They have business courses now, secretarial."

Business? Institute? Bewildered, I said, "But I'm . . . happy here."

"And you'll stay here," Louise said, taking my hand. "You could take night classes."

William broke in. "We would give you some evenings off if you need them. Will you think about it? We'd pay of course, if there are fees. I should have said that up front."

"We don't want to lose you, Jane. But we don't want to hold you back. We want you to be happy."

I had been very proud of not crying over Leo Hirschfeld. But William and Louise's kindness left me helpless. Blinking tears, I said, "I am happy. Very happy."

Louise passed me her handkerchief, even as I insisted, "I *am*."

This made us all laugh. William said, "You'll think about it?"

I was about to explain that nothing in my background qualified me for higher education. But they had been so kind, I simply said, "Yes. I will think about it."

Epilogue

After more than one attempt at conviction, Mrs. Florence Carman was found not guilty of murdering Lulu Bailey. There wasn't much question as to whether she had fired the gun. There also wasn't much question as to whether her husband had been a philandering cad. Feeling sorry for Mrs. Carman, the jury let her go. She died in 1939.

Violet Tempest was not as fortunate. She was a mistress, not a wife, and it was not lost on the men of the jury that she had tried to frame her husband for the crime she committed. She was sentenced to twenty-five years in jail, but released after ten. I suspect Leo used his influence, but I have never asked him and he has never said. At any rate, someone bankrolled her tour of the country as the Killer Chorus Girl, which she always ended with "I was too drunk to know the difference—or was I?" and a big wink. In later years, the wink was accompanied by a stumble, the provocative last line slurred. She fell down a flight of stairs in New

Orleans in 1928 and did not survive her injuries. A sad end, I thought, for the last of the Flying O'Briens.

Leo and Harriet married quietly out of town and soon thereafter, she gave birth to twin boys. Their arrival was kept out of the papers until it could be announced at a more decorous time. As twins, said Leo, they were small, so who would notice? It was not until they were forty years old and fathers themselves that Leo bothered to tell them their birthdays were in July rather than December.

It was a very happy marriage. Leo was often faithful, and when he was not, he was careful. Except once. But that is a difficult story and I will not tell it now.

After lunch, we took a walk through Times Square. As we passed by the statue of George Cohan, Leo said, "I remember Warburton telling me with *Two Loves Have I* that I needed a patriotic number. Flags. I said, 'I don't do flags, I'm not Cohan.' He said, 'No, you're not.' But if I'd known they gave you a statue . . ."

"They tried to give you a theater," I reminded him. Years ago, there was a proposal to rename the Sidney Theater as the Hirschfeld. Leo declined. If they were going to call it anything, he said, better to call it the Biederman. Without his wife, it was unlikely the world would have any interest in naming anything after him. Of Harriet's many friends and associates, there were several still alive to support the change, and since the name Sidney Warburton was no longer considered important in theater history—even Rector's closed after the war—Harriet got her theater.

"The Things Everyone Says" may have been the first hit Leo wrote for Nedda Fiske, but it was by no means the last. The two continued a contentious and highly successful partnership over decades. As he told the *Times* when she died in 1973, Nedda was never not brilliant and never not infuriating. "I was always either falling at her feet or wanting to wring her neck." *Two Loves Have I* saw the triumphant rebirth of Eugenia Hollyhock, who starred in several Hirschfeld shows before settling into the long-running hit *Mother, May I?*

But Leo's first show was the last time audiences saw the Darling Dancing Ardens perform together. Throughout the run, they were flawless, the partnership of dreams, floating in perfect harmony. Night after night, they clasped hands as they bowed to worshipping audiences, Claude always gallantly stepping back to present his beautiful wife. But at some point, they both decided that enough was enough. I do not know whether Blanche's decision to do a film precipitated the parting or if Claude saw what the height of fame and success was . . . and that it didn't hold a candle to Ruth. At any rate, they both headed west, but to different futures.

To my surprise and delight, Adele St. John also headed west, although not without snide references to sand, snakes, and insect life, the scale of which she imagined bordered on the cataclysmic. The week of their departure, they had lunch with Louise, followed by a walk through the park. As we passed by the Bethesda Fountain, Mrs. St. John smiled up at the bold winged angel, and said to me with sudden energy, "Did you know that was created by a woman? A brilliant artist by the name of Emma Stebbins. Look at the way she's striding. That powerful front leg and the way the dress flows back as she moves forward. Sleeves pushed up, the wings flaring upward. She's not some placid, sorrowful guardian. No hobble, no hoops. She's a woman going somewhere."

I never did get the chance to dance with Rodolfo again, as he, too, left New York for California. No one can say for certain whether he is in *My Official Wife* or no. But as Rudolph Valentino he became the most famous man in the world.

As Leo and I took our leave of Mr. Cohan, I saw the names

of his biggest songs carved into the base of the statue. Briefly, the strains of "Over There" came to mind; my heart became heavy. Then Leo suggested we get a cab. I was looking especially pretty today, he said, did I know that? Not wanting to cast a pall on the day, I said that I did, as a matter of fact.

The cab stopped first at his building. Getting out, he said, "Dinner tomorrow?" I said of course. Then headed on a few blocks to my apartment.

Coming home, I was greeted by my favorite photograph, which stands on the hallway table, so that when I return, I can smile hello to the person in the picture, as if he had welcomed me back.

They are a handsome couple, these two. They are outside, and I can't now remember whether it was a baseball game or a political event; at any rate, the gentleman regards the camera with wary good humor as if he wants to ask that his picture not be taken, but knows it's pointless. The lady is smiling, amused by the gentleman's irritation. It's hardly the first time they've been photographed. His hand is on her back, she leans into him. I can date the image from the clothes. The '20s had crashed to their terrible end. Waists had returned. Hats were wider. But the gentleman had long ago traded in his derby for a fedora. At his wife's urging. It was often said that having once been a lady's maid, she understood the value of a good hat.

Acknowledgments

I always enjoy research, but this book let me do a deep dive into the history of Broadway in the 1910s, making it my most joyful experience to date. It brought me back to a place I spent a lot of time as a kid, the New York Public Library for the Performing Arts, Dorothy and Lewis B. Cullman Center.

I had an unforgettable day touring the Belasco Theater, one of the few Broadway theaters that date from the late Gilded Age. You don't just get to walk around a working theater and I am forever indebted to Gretchen Michelfeld for making it happen. Huge gratitude also to Jill Cordle and Brian Aman, my fantastic, informative guide. With the theaters dark, I'm thinking of all of you. What a day it will be when you are all back on Broadway.

The vision of what a musical was at this time as well as the importance of Rector's to the theater community comes from *Shall We Dance?*, Douglas Thompson's excellent biography of Vernon and Irene Castle. I also consulted *Better Foot Forward: The History of American Musical Theatre* by Ethan Mordden and A *Pictorial*

History of the American Theatre: 1860–1976 by Daniel Blum, enlarged and revised by John Willis. For the history of anarchists in New York at this time and the Lexington Avenue explosion, I am indebted to Thai Jones's excellent book *More Powerful Than Dynamite.*

As always, Mike Wallace's *Greater Gotham* was my bible.

I also thank the wonderful team at Minotaur, who handle my books with such skill and care—even during a pandemic. My editor, Catherine Richards, puts up with my "But what about that moment on page 183, did that work?" queries. I also thank her excellent assistant, Nettie Finn. Eternal appreciation to my agent, Victoria Skurnick. Thank you to Kayla Janas and Allison Ziegler, David Rotstein for the gorgeous cover, production manager Cathy Turiano, and production editor Chrisinda Lynch. Last but never least, copyeditor Justine Gardner and proofreader Laura Dragonette.

I would like to thank Karen Odden for reading an early draft of this novel. Gratitude also goes to Sharon Collins and Pearl Hanig for their kind and generous support of this series.

This may sound odd, but any writer will understand. I thank the characters. They're their own people who were kind enough to wander into my head and share their stories. They've been good company through some pretty lousy times and I am very grateful to them.

Finally, wholeheartedly, I thank the readers.